Cake and Courtship

A tale of love, regret and the occasional nerve tonic

Mark Brownlow

Lost Opinions e.U.

Cake and Courtship
© 2017 Mark Brownlow
All rights reserved

Print Edition

ISBN: 978-3-903230-00-2 (ebook)
ISBN: 978-3-903230-01-9 (print)

Author: Mark Brownlow
Cover design: Aimee Coveney of Bookollective
Editing: Sarah Pesce, Lopt & Cropt Editing Services
Formatting: Polgarus Studio

Publisher: Lost Opinions e.U.
Paschinggasse 8/28
1170 Vienna
Austria

For more Austenesque creations, see:

Web: lostopinions.com
Twitter: @markbrownlow
Facebook: facebook.com/lostopinions/

For Renate

An unpaid debt

A letter awaited my late return from London.

"Is it from a relative?" They only ever wanted money or sympathy, and I had little of either to spare.

Mrs Bennet shook her head. "No, husband, it is not."

I took the missive from her outstretched hand, held it to a candle, then turned it over like the final card at the whist table. "From John Barton. Goodness." My fingertip rubbed at a scuffed and ragged edge. "This has been on quite a journey."

My first inclination was to leave it for the morning sunlight, but there are few powers stronger than curiosity and few pleasures greater than the breaking of a seal. John's penmanship was crisp and strong, each sentence ending with a flourish of ink.

"What does it say? Does he talk of his father?"

"He does." I folded away the letter, holding it in hands clasped behind my back.

"Oh, do not tease me so, Mr Bennet!"

I cleared my throat. "Well, my dear, it seems Henry is back from the Caribbean and now enjoys the rather colder embrace of the Austrian Empire."

"Has he no plans to return home?"

"Apparently not. The two Bartons spent the last year in Vienna, no doubt indulging Henry's love of music. He has swapped the sun for sonatas."

"John must be a young man by now. Is he well? Is he *married?*"

"Those are questions, my dear, you may ask him yourself." My smile did little for her look of confusion. "He intends to visit us next month."

~ ~ ~

The following morning, I tried not to think of the cost while presenting the girls with their gifts from the capital's bookstores. A new collection of moral essays drew a rare sigh of contentment from Mary. Lydia and Kitty were less enthused at their books on etiquette for young ladies.

"For you, Jane," I said, handing her a thin volume. "You should find these preferable to those indifferent verses that suitor once gave you. Brecknell himself assured me of their quality. He has never let me down, so I must trust his judgement on this. You know *my* thoughts on poetry." My eldest daughter's gentle kiss brought warmth to my cheek. "And for you, Lizzy, tales of Moscow and St Petersburg. If a mind as sharp as yours cannot travel to the great cities of Russia, then these great cities will have to come to you. Or at least to our library."

"But the expense, Papa. You should not be so generous," said Lizzy.

"Books are the one luxury I deem a necessity. If my purchases lead us into poverty, then at least we will be well-read paupers. Now, run along all of you and allow your father some peace to enjoy his own gift to himself." I patted the smooth surface of Scopoli's *Hortus Blattae*.

I soon left the library for my study, so Kitty and Lydia could return their gifts to a bookshelf unobserved. Once inside, my eyes were drawn to John's letter. It lay on the desk, untouched since last night.

"Papa?" Lizzy stood in the doorway to the hall, brow a little more furrowed than usual.

"Lizzy, dear. You are not happy with your present?"

"Quite content and very grateful. More so than Lydia and Kitty, certainly."

"Ah, yes. I do not expect them to read their new books, but the threat of having to do so may at least encourage more moderate behaviour."

"Is all well, Papa? There was a quietness about you earlier in the library."

"I could not be better, child…just a little distracted." I picked up the letter, then waved it at her. "You remember the Bartons, of course?"

Lizzy slipped into the room. "You have news? Is this what distracts you?"

I dropped the letter on the desk, sending glistening motes of dust into the air. "John has written from Vienna." Her expression prompted my best impression of a gallic shrug. "You may well ask why they remain overseas, even now. It seems time will not diminish the memory that keeps Henry away from us and England. But it does not keep his son away. In fact, he may already be in Gloucestershire; the letter took uncommonly long to reach us."

"John is returning to England?"

"Temporarily."

"Will he visit us?"

"I believe so."

"How wonderful, but—"

"That is not what troubles me, although the thought of a young man in the house makes me a trifle uneasy. You girls will descend on him like crows on a battlefield corpse."

"I wonder if he has forgiven Jane and me for all our teasing."

"I daresay he will not hold it against you since he bore a whole summer of it with commendable fortitude. He could not have been much more than twelve the last time we saw him here with his father…and his mother. All so content together." I turned away from Lizzy to dab at my eyes with a handkerchief. "This dust gets everywhere; I must have a word with Mrs Bennet."

"It is all the books."

"You think so? Anyway, John may be much changed, and not just with age; travel leaves its mark on a man. But it is the reason for his journey that worries me. He does not reveal it, which has sent my imagination down unpleasant paths."

"Perhaps it is simply for his education or a matter of personal interest."

"You may be right." I glanced at Henry's box, perched on a high shelf. "His father was…is…a fine man, the very best of men. However, estate management was never a strength of his, and years of travelling cannot have been easy for the family finances. I fear John may be here out of necessity, to raise funds."

"From us?"

"Possibly. When young men visit older acquaintances, it is

usually in search of a loan or a wife. Of course, if it *is* funds he needs, he may be in England to sell land." I took a deep breath. "And where land departs, name and rank are sure to follow."

"You read too much into a simple visit, Papa. Besides, the Barton finances are surely none of our concern."

"*Everything* about the Bartons is our concern…my concern." Lizzy took a step back as my gaze wandered again to the box and its contents.

"Papa?"

I did not respond immediately, but my daughter was wise enough to keep silent.

"Forgive my sharpness, Lizzy. With regard to the Barton family, there are memories. And debts. Debts of honour. John's letter reminds me of them."

"You speak of your time in the army?"

"Among other things. But, yes, those days in particular." Lizzy knew me well enough not to pry further. "Suffice to say there is no debt greater than the one I owe Henry Barton and, by extension, his family. There is little I would not do for him or his son." My eyes closed as the memories of a slick forest floor threatened to overwhelm me.

The soft touch of Lizzy's hand on my arm brought me back to Longbourn. "Likely I worry for nought. Let us wait for John's next communication. Perhaps he misses English rhubarb. Or simply wants to play hide and seek with you and Jane again." My smile was almost genuine.

"Hide and seek? That would be most improper at our age. Shall Jane and I still call him John? Or will he be the very serious *Mr* Barton?"

"For me, he will always be John, however gentlemanly and refined he may now be."

"I wonder if a man so well-travelled can even enjoy our quiet English manor?"

"Quiet? My dear Lizzy, he is a gentleman and likely unmarried. His arrival is certain to cause considerable agitation among your sisters and mother. Quiet it will most certainly *not* be. There will be even more silliness than usual, and I shall have no peace at all."

Lizzy took my hand in hers. "Then, Papa, you must lock yourself away in the study and leave John to us."

I looked down into those dark eyes of hers and, with my free hand, pushed back the stray curl that always infuriated Mrs Bennet. "That would be very cruel to John, to sacrifice his peace for mine."

Once she left, I picked up the letter again, twisting it round and round in my fingers, echoes of the past clamouring for the attention I was unwilling to give.

A new arrival

The cut of the wind across the open carriage banished all further thoughts of the Bartons as I travelled into Meryton to meet with Jackson. The new guns in Blackman's demanded our attention and his blustery enthusiasm left no space for introspection. I had almost forgotten John's letter by the time we retired to the Flighted Duck for a little refreshment.

An observer might have described my demeanour as 'sprightly' when I left the inn. It was hard to feel anything but optimism with a stomach full of tart and gingerbread. Then I saw Sir William. Unfortunately, and despite my best efforts to hide behind the convenient frame of my cake-filled companion, *he* also saw *me*. And so our newly-knighted neighbour came bounding across the old square, seemingly determined to engage me in conversation.

"There is news, Mr Bennet. Great news! Netherfield Park is to be let to a single gentleman with a *significant* income." The words came between great gasps of air, his arms flapping and cheeks puffing like a blacksmith's bellows. "His name is Mr Bingley. A capital name, is it not?"

"It is indeed." I suspected it would appear somewhat less so if its owner were not both rich and unattached.

"The name speaks of fine manners and good breeding, no?" I did not respond. Sir William always took a rather generous view of grammar, so some of his question marks were little more than vivacious full stops. "I should be happy to welcome him to our little part of Hertfordshire," he added.

"You will not be alone in doing so. Once this Bingley's presence and income are widely known, the mothers of Meryton will descend like cats, spitting and mewling as they jostle for a chance to pounce. I almost pity him."

"No doubt Mrs Bennet will be glad of the news, too. Who knows how many other young gentlemen may accompany him? Perhaps there will be enough for each of your daughters." All that was missing to complete his joy was a tail to wag.

"The good Lord has been kind enough to send us one bachelor in Mr Bingley," I replied. "Let us not be greedy and ask for five." A few pleasantries later and it was into the carriage and back to Longbourn before the approaching rain spoiled both road and view.

There would be no escape from talk of balls and bachelors, not with *two* new arrivals to anticipate.

~ ~ ~

At home, Mrs Bennet was nowhere to be seen.

"She is in bed, Papa, resting after taking her nerve tonic. It is a new concoction, prescribed by Mr Jones on the recommendation of a physician who once attended the Prince Regent." Lizzy's face suggested she did not believe the claim.

"I presume it came in a very garish, expensive bottle, then?"

She ignored my cynicism. "Did Mr Jackson purchase his gun?"

"Of course not. He never buys a new gun, but we enjoy the pretence that he might do so one day."

"And is there news from town? Idle talk may be the tonic Mama requires most."

"None of any import."

They would find out about Mr Bingley soon enough without my intervention. Besides, a gentleman should never appear better informed of such matters than his spouse or daughters, lest they think he has an interest. I passed the evening with a glass of port and the rare self-satisfaction of a husband in possession of precious gossip before his wife.

~ ~ ~

The rain departed overnight, leaving a cloudless morning and sufficient light to spend the time in my study labelling the last of the summer's catch.

I always enjoyed bringing order to the chaos of creation, particularly when every beetle and butterfly held memories of warm evenings in my flower-filled gardens. Each year, while the girls sought daisies and dandelions, I set traps for the winged and unwary. That summer my nets had caught *sixteen* Silver-washed Fritillaries, almost as many as Stanhope found, and double the catch of Fielding. These delightful creatures had become decidedly rare in our neighbourhood, though I could not understand why.

It was a scene that never ceased to give me pleasure: my old oak desk, set beneath the bay window to catch the sun through to the afternoon. On one side, the box of recent finds and the relaxing chamber. On the other side, the pins, labels, tweezers, and display trays, the latter all dark polished oak and bright brass fittings.

With a smile and a sigh, I held up the first beetle to the window. A fine specimen, wing cases of dark green that revealed a ring of argent in a stray sunbeam. I was at peace with the world in that moment but, regrettably, the world refused to reciprocate. A brief knock provided insufficient warning as the door crashed open, the draught sending pins and labels scattering like the bugs they were intended for.

"Papa! Papa!"

My practised look of fatherly despair had no effect on Lydia. She was too busy bobbing up and down to notice, apron strings hanging loosely to the side, hands clasped to stop them shaking.

"You must come, Papa—there is such news!"

"Indeed? Has Napoleon surrendered? Are we to have a new parliament?"

Lydia stopped bobbing and frowned. "No, Papa, proper news! We are all so merry at the thought. Imagine!" She turned and ran out, leaving a trail of giggles to follow her by. I returned the scattered items to the desk, replaced the stopper on the ink, and then said a silent goodbye to my insect companions.

Mrs Bennet had finally learned of our prospective neighbour at Netherfield. The information had the girls flustered and fretful as if a wasp was in the room. Even Jane and Lizzy were barely able to contain themselves.

"You must visit him when he arrives, Mr Bennet," said my wife. "And before anyone else. We must show him the girls as soon as possible. He will be sure to fall in love with one of them."

"Show him?" I said. "Are they artefacts to be handed around a drawing room?"

"You know very well what I mean, husband."

Inevitably, the only topic of conversation for the rest of the day was the pending appearance of two young men, though most of the speculation concerned Mr Bingley. A possible bachelor passing through on his way abroad was merely a distraction. An actual bachelor living nearby was an *opportunity.*

~ ~ ~

Sunday morning offered the chance to reflect on the benevolence of the Lord for sending Mr Bingley. At least this was the general opinion whispered behind church pews as Mr Toke held forth on the evils of gluttony and other sins. His warnings might have enjoyed a better response had the pulpit not creaked so under his weight. Toke's sermons were the Russian winters of ecclesiastical discourse—rather unpleasant, far too long, and likely to darken the spirits of all who survived them.

Still, the walk back to Longbourn was pleasing enough. The oranges and russets of the turning foliage delighted the eye. There was certainly more to marvel at in nature than in the cold walls of Toke's church.

"Well, Lizzy, we must enjoy such family walks while we can. If your mother gets her way, one of you will be firmly settled in Netherfield within the month. Perhaps it will be you?"

"If Mr Bingley only has an eye for beauty, then I fear dear Jane will take precedence." This brought a brief blush to the face of my eldest. "But if he is also wise and intelligent, then…" She paused, laughing. It was a sound that still warmed my heart after twenty years. "Then I believe dear Jane will also be his first choice."

"Oh, Lizzy, really," said Jane, smiling—a sight that had warmed my heart for even longer than Lizzy's laughter.

"If he does not choose you, Jane, then he has neither taste nor worth," replied her sister.

"No worth?" came a familiar voice from behind. "He has over four thousand a year!" My dear wife, ever practical in her thinking.

"So you see, Papa, you shall not be rid of me quite so soon." Lizzy linked her arm in mine.

"I would not wish to lose you." I gave her hand a pat. "Those two, on the other hand…"

Kitty and Lydia had run on ahead, eager to put the confinement of church behind them. It was then that Mary, with her usual grasp of good conversation, decided to give the discussion a theological turn. "I am not sure Mr Toke was clear on the importance of patience in our faith. His quoting from Romans was misleading."

"There is little need for him to explain the role of patience, Mary. His sermons are an exercise in that virtue for his entire congregation." I paused to take in the colours of a fine birch, all white bark and golden leaves. "They are not designed to educate or enlighten, otherwise he would pay more attention to their content. No, he is testing our patience and our faith. We are ever under examination. Though, if we are fortunate, he may offer us respite and feel the need to call upon his relatives in Chichester."

"I would not consider his absence a boon," said Mary. "Mr

Spigott is a fine gentleman, but he does not have Mr Toke's way with words."

"One of many excellent characteristics possessed by the curate. Where Mr Toke teaches us patience, Mr Spigott condescends to teach us absolutely nothing. His humility is most praiseworthy."

"You should not tease Mary so, Papa," said Lizzy. "Besides, I have heard you talk of one pleasing feature of our good vicar—his fine larder."

"Indeed, he does run a most excellent dinner table. If he fed our souls as well as he feeds our stomachs, we would all be assured of a warm welcome in heaven."

A past revealed

As September drew to a close, all the talk at home continued to concern itself with Mr Bingley and John Barton. Unfortunately for our much-anticipated neighbour and much-travelled friend, their true selves could not hope to live up to the romantic expectations of five girls.

According to my daughters, both gentlemen would be tall, excessively handsome, good riders, and better dancers. Adventurous. Educated. And well-mannered. Most importantly, their words would light fires in the hearts of all young women without attracting the disapproval of their mothers. The girls agreed on all these points. There was, however, some debate as to the most appropriate colour for their horses. Of course, Mr Bingley had two advantages over John: he was a guaranteed bachelor and his immense wealth would make matriarchal approbation somewhat easier. I half hoped to find Netherfield's tenant a wretched creature with a morbid fear of animals and the manners of a bear, just to see the look on everyone's faces.

Poor weather offered no respite from the autumnal tedium, no opportunity for long walks or rides to escape Longbourn and girlish chatter. Such was the rain the heavens chose to bless us with again that Sir William suggested we might soon be hunting with fishing rods. He once declared angling a worthy test of patience, a presumption that ended all interest I had in the sport. I had Toke's sermons for that.

A second letter from John brought both relief and trepidation. I valued little in life more than peace (and, possibly, cake), and knew he would likely bring neither. Yet I found myself surprisingly intrigued at the promise of a reunion. The first letter had cast a shaft of sunlight on darkened corners left undisturbed for many a year. Memories stirred. Few of them good, still fewer truly welcome. But I did have warm recollections of sun-filled days in Gloucestershire, and was curious to see whether John retained the good nature of the boy I once knew so well. And if I could help him in some way, then perhaps I might discharge my debt to his family. John's closing sentence left me somewhat uneasy, though.

"Lizzy." She looked up from her book. I held up the letter to her from the other end of the library. "News from John. He writes from his Rudford estate and expects to visit in some ten days' time."

"This *is* good news." She placed her book to one side, a pressed flower serving to mark the page. "And does he remove your fears for his family's welfare...and ours?"

"He does. More or less. He has completed his estate business and seems in good spirits. The message is most amiable, suggesting his character remains as pleasant as I remember it to be. And it appears he is, as yet, unmarried, though that is a thought we should keep to ourselves for now. Let us not raise any false hopes, especially given his final words. Listen to this, Lizzy: *I also beg leave to seek your advice on a personal matter… concerning a lady.*"

Lizzy seemed to struggle to contain a smile. "And this disturbs you, Papa?"

"It does, though it rather depends on what he means. I hope he does not wish to discuss such matters as her suitability, or how he might set about winning her affection."

Lizzy lifted a hand to cover her laughter. "Be at ease, Papa. I do not think he would look to *you* for advice on such topics."

"My dear girl, I am always happy to play the victim for your teasing but here it is entirely misplaced. Such things may not interest me *now*, but I'll have you know I was once thought of as a great master of the rituals of courtship. Henry Barton certainly thought so. One or two young men owe their success as suitors as much to my guidance as to their lands and titles. Imagine, Lizzy: I once even believed in romance *and* the persuasive power of poetry. Still, I daresay all men have the right to be fools for at least part of their lives."

"Only a part?"

"Well, when I consider many of my acquaintances, you may be right."

"With such a talent for courtship, Papa, I wonder you took so long to marry yourself."

I turned my head so she would not see my face. A careful smile and the scent of lavender flitted at the edge of my memory, kept out by a wall of regret. "As you get older, Lizzy, you will discover that life does not bow easily to the wishes of even the most romantic of souls. Quite the opposite. Life must be mastered with pragmatism and sense, which explains why so few people succeed at it."

"Did you help Mr Barton court *his* wife?"

"Not directly. My ideals had long since shattered on the anvil of disappointment by the time Henry met Sophia, though I, too, was tempted to seek her affection. This was before I was introduced to your mother, of course. His love was true, and I left the field clear for him. Sophia chose wisely when she married Henry and I envied their joy. It survived the wilting of passion that does for so many arrangements."

"It sounds like John should better talk with his father, then."

"Let us not get ahead of ourselves, Lizzy. Men may talk of a lady without intending to wed her, whatever Mrs Bennet might believe. But if he does have an eye to marry, John's father will not speak with him on such matters. Not because he fears the idea of female companionship and affection, but because he mourns the loss of both so deeply. Besides, by the time they exchanged letters on the subject, the lady in question would no doubt be wearing someone else's ring."

Lizzy stood and moved to the window. "*For where thou art, there is the world itself, / With every several pleasure in the world, / And where thou art not, desolation.*"

"Suffolk, no? In *Henry the Sixth*?"

"Part Two."

"Yet Suffolk could still find joy that Queen Margaret lived. Henry has not even that consolation. But hush, girl, John's letter and your questions make me sentimental and that will not do at all, for I have business to attend to in town."

"Business?"

"Of a sort. A lecture from Mr Criswick."

~ ~ ~

Having missed the previous meeting through my London trip, the prospect of visiting the Meryton Natural History Society again was a joyous one. Unfortunately, the anticipated pleasure only lasted some five minutes into Criswick's description of his Jamaican travels. His talk proved as long and dull as the sea journey that took him to that storied island. We all feigned excessive enthusiasm, though, in the hope it might encourage him to return to Kingston as soon as possible. All except Jackson, of course, who fell asleep just as Mr Criswick's ship left Liverpool and woke in time to move to the inn, where we had a room for the meeting of the committee, upstairs and away from the square, assuring us of a little quiet. Mr Tincton never charged us for the space we occupied, knowing how the committee's prodigious appetite for both food and drink would fill his inn's coffers equally well.

With the business of the Society completed, we turned to the prospects for this year's shooting. The warmth of a brisk fire and the timely arrival of port and cake meant few of us were in any rush to return home.

"I do so love the smell of cinnamon," said Jackson, nose deep in his third slice of Mrs Tincton's baked delights. I merely mumbled an acknowledgement.

"You seem out of sorts, Bennet," he continued, with a keenness of eye he normally reserved for spotting pheasants. "Not hungry? All the more for us, then."

On another day, I might have kept the reason for my wistful disposition hidden, but the port loosened my tongue. "A letter arrived recently from the son of a friend. You will forgive me for leaving out the particulars, but he asked for advice."

Stanhope brushed crumbs from his waistcoat. "Ah, boy not keen on his filial duties?"

"No, no, it was just, well, he thought I might have some advice on 'personal matters.' I rather fear he might even seek my guidance on…" I gave a little cough. "Courting."

Stanhope's pristine moustache rose as his mouth fell open. Eventually, he found his voice. "I am all for love, Bennet, but *that* is surely a matter for ladies. I am surprised at the suggestion."

"Quite," added Elliston. "A gentleman's mind is suited to weightier matters, like dogs, horse breeding, or wine. I will pick you out a good pointer any day of the week, but a suitable wife…" He raised his hands in surrender.

"It is a shame, though, that we leave such matters to the other sex."

All heads swivelled as one to see the source of such a contrary opinion (excepting Jackson, who had dozed off again).

One of the unspoken rules of our society was that committee members had to wear spectacles. They gave us an intellectual air we did not all deserve. Fielding was cleaning his pair with a napkin. "My wife offers her opinion on *my* business with some regularity. Perhaps we should return the favour?"

"We could," said Stanhope. "But why would we want to? There are ladies enough to handle these things without our intervention. Does your friend's son not trust his mother in these matters?"

I closed my eyes briefly and, for a moment, saw Henry cupping John's small hand delicately, as one might hold a butterfly, shoulders heavy and dark rings under his eyes to match the absence of light within them. It had been hard to see a friend suffer such a loss.

The words of explanation hung in my throat, the silence that followed mercifully broken by Jackson's timely resumption of consciousness. His eyes focused slowly on the empty plate before him. "Any more cake?"

"It is of no consequence," I mumbled. "No doubt he means to talk about some other matter. Now, let us see about feeding Jackson. Pass over that tray, Elliston, if you would."

Life always has more cake. It is one of its few redeeming features.

~ ~ ~

"Jackson was right," said Fielding as we sat alone a little later. Used plates, dirty glasses, and a last forlorn slice of cake were all that remained of our colleagues.

"Right about what?"

"You *are* out of sorts. I cannot imagine you so alarmed by the possibility of a conversation on courtship."

"Truth is, well, it is not just the conversation that bothers me." The chair creaked as I shifted position.

"No?"

"The young man in question—John—will visit. That something I welcome in principle, yet I worry it might remind me of certain events. Events that are perhaps better left in the past. Added to which, I really do doubt my suitability as a source of advice on matters of the heart, if that is what he seeks from me."

"Ah." Fielding steepled his fingers and pursed his lips. After a minute of silence, he exhaled deeply. "You once had a talent with the ladies, though. You cannot deny it."

I failed to hide a smile. "I did, as I reminded Lizzy only today. But a talent employed most successfully by everyone *except* myself. The one time I might have enjoyed the fruits of my abilities…" I gripped my glass, the smile fading. "Forgive me, Fielding. Pay me no attention. All I have from my youthful adventures in love and war are regrets, disappointments, and a handful of unpleasant memories. And perhaps a little wisdom."

"That is as may be, but do you want to help this young man?"

"In principle, yes. I owe it to his father. Besides, all he perhaps wishes for is a mere hint or two to set him on the right road. Even I can manage that."

"Then I do not understand why you are so disturbed."

"You will not stop, will you, Fielding? It was ever so with you, poking around into our souls. Then let me lay bare my faults to you so you may leave me in peace." I leant forward and held his gaze. "It is my selfishness. I am very comfortable as I am now. My friend's son may bring reminders of who I once was, who I might have become. But do not worry, I will not shirk my obligations and my concerns will pass."

"Very well. I have no wish to lure you into melancholy with my questions. I say only that not all memories need be kept locked away. Not after so long. But I shall hold back my curiosity and give in, instead, to greed." Fielding reached down and held up the last of the cake.

"If only our pasts were as easily disposed of," I said.

Bachelors abroad

"He is here!" Such were the words that greeted me at the breakfast table.

I settled into my chair and began contemplating the day's most important decision—eggs or ham. There was no cake.

"Who is 'here,' my dear?" I was rather pleased with the rhyme, though only Lizzy and Jane smiled.

"Mr Bingley! He is at Netherfield. Cook heard from the boy who brought the tea and coffee this morning, and she told Hill, and Hill, of course, told me. Such a good housekeeper!" All roads led to Mrs Bennet.

I chose the eggs.

"Mama, shall we walk to Netherfield this morning? I can wear my new bonnet. Perhaps we will meet Mr Bingley, and he will fall in love with me."

"Don't be so silly, Lydia, we cannot meet Mr Bingley until your father has visited." Forks and mouths ceased movement and six sets of eyes settled in my direction.

I took a sip of coffee. "Are you all practising for a sitting? It would make a lively painting."

The sound of breakfast recommenced, though the ting of metal on crockery seemed a little louder than usual down the other end of the table.

"Is there something the matter, my dear? Shall I send out for Mr Jones to see to you?"

"Oh, Mr Bennet!"

I thought it best to change the subject, hoping a second bachelor might distract them from the first. "I have received another letter from John Barton. Has Lizzy told you?"

Mrs Bennet snorted, and her glass thumped against the wooden table.

"I hope he is well and not missing his father too much," said Jane.

"Does he say if he is married?" asked Lydia. There must have been a reason why there was so great a difference between our first and last girls; the former selfless and sensible, the latter selfish and silly. Perhaps the children were fated to reflect the state of their parents' marriage at the time of their birth. If so, it was fortunate we stopped at five.

"It is of no consequence if he is married or not, Lydia." After a brief pause, my wife continued: "Pray tell, though, husband… did his second letter mention if he was attached?"

I exchanged glances with Lizzy, then opened the newspaper sharply and let the snap suffice as an answer.

Mrs Bennet shook her head and sighed deeply. "I often think of his father. Such a tragedy, girls, to lose his wife so. How Henry suffered at the end."

"That he did." I peered over my spectacles. "I am sure there are few men who could be more affected by such a loss. Indeed,

I know of some who might even welcome it." Lizzy gave me a pointed look.

"A distraught widower—how romantic." Kitty sighed.

"Show some respect, please, Kitty." I was a little louder than intended, so softened my voice and my attitude. "You will all discover everything about John soon enough, for he is to stay Saturday night on his way to London on estate business." I could not have given the girls a better present.

"Oh, Papa," said Lydia. "A gentleman in the house. I feel sure he is single and come to court us. We shall make such a merry party."

"Perhaps we should ask Mr Bingley to join him for dinner, dear?" I said.

"Oh, Mr Bennet. If you will not visit, how can we ask him to dinner? You vex my nerves so!"

~ ~ ~

My wife spent the rest of the day feigning indifference to my disregard for neighbourly duties. She busied herself the way people do when angry with another in the household, tackling the embroidery with such fury I thought the outcome might rival Bayeux by the time the light faded. But she could not stay upset for long, not with the prospect of a Bingley nearby and a possible bachelor soon to stay, however briefly. She sent the girls on missions with all the skill of a seasoned spymaster, seeking news from servants, tradesmen, neighbours, and friends, not to mention Mrs Phillips, the spider at the centre of the town's web of intrigue. Whenever a new fly landed near Meryton, the vibrations soon reached *her* parlour and out she scuttled, armed with invitations, coffee, and cake.

I marvelled at the ladies' capacity for gathering intelligence where an eligible bachelor was concerned. "Consider, husband," said Mrs Bennet, her hands shaking in what I presumed was excitement. "Mr Bingley possesses a chaise and four."

"I cannot see how *that* is of great importance," said Mary.

"My dear child, it is of overwhelming importance," I said. "For a man's worth is defined as much by the number of horses attached to his carriage as the number of titles attached to his name."

"But what of his character?"

"Goodness, Mary, you have much to learn." I removed my spectacles and waved them to emphasise my point. "Kind or cruel is of little consequence, provided a man can present a good figure in a book of accounts *and* on the assembly floor."

"You cannot believe that, Papa?" said Jane.

"I should have practised dancing more as a young man, instead of foolishly improving myself with education. Latin cannot compete with a Cotillion or an expensive carriage. *Sic vita hominum est.* Ask your mother." All heads turned to Mrs Bennet.

My wife looked up. "A chaise and four. Imagine…"

~ ~ ~

The reluctance to visit Mr Bingley did not sit well with Mrs Bennet. As the days darkened, so did her disposition.

She began making grim prophecies concerning my lack of enthusiasm. It seemed only a matter of time before Beelzebub himself would descend on Longbourn to punish me for my sedition. I hoped for his sake he was already married.

John's imminent visit meant Mr Bingley would have to wait.

The idea of male company in the evening was certainly a grand one. The girls, too, let the prospect of John's arrival distract them from the ongoing mystery of Netherfield. Whenever I emerged from my study, they would be rushing past, fretting about colours and curls. All except Lizzy.

"Do you not have some great decisions to make concerning the correct choice of bonnet for our esteemed guest?" I asked as she lounged like a satisfied cat on a sofa, book in hand.

She shook her head. "I believe friendship and affection—even love—come from matching characters, not matching ribbons."

"Well said, my dear. There is hope for this family yet. Before his correspondence ceased, Henry always spoke well of his son. We shall judge John for ourselves, though. I place little store in a father's opinion; he can hardly be objective. And while many men are excellent judges of good wine, few can recognise good character. There is too little of it around for them to practice on."

"Will he come directly to Longbourn?"

"No, I shall meet his coach in Meryton. I have not seen him since he was a young boy and doubt ruffling his hair and offering a dried apple from the stores will now be an appropriate greeting. We shall eat in town and find the privacy your sisters will deny us here at home."

"You should not keep Kitty and Lydia from the pleasure of his company for too long, Papa. They will be most grieved otherwise."

"We will see. If against expectations he turns out to be an unpleasant sort of fellow, I shall introduce him to them as soon as possible."

~ ~ ~

Meryton was full of people scurrying about their business as if someone had poked an ant hill with a large stick. Or rather with a regimental sword, as I learned we were soon to enjoy the presence of the militia.

I did not know who seemed more excited at the prospect— the ladies or the tradesmen. Mr Weintraub looked particularly pleased, his face flushing the colour of one of his better Spanish reds as he took delivery of more crates from the London warehouses. The tailors and vintners appeared to forget that amounts billed and amounts paid rarely tallied where the military were concerned.

There were, then, more than the usual number of waggons in the square, and much coarse language as boys with wheelbarrows clattered into each other like drunken bullocks. Into this chaos rode a coach to London, horses flecked with sweat and steaming in the autumn chill.

The door opened, and a young man climbed down slowly to stand before me for the first time in over ten years.

Inevitably, his face had lost the softness of childhood, but his dark eyes still hinted at a playful intelligence. I could not say if he was handsome, for that is the domain of wives and daughters. He certainly had his father's looks, and those attracted many an admiring glance back in the day. His fine blue coat had frayed edges, revealing more than any letter or credit note ever could.

We gave each other deep, serious bows, like actors on a Shakespearean stage, and so the ice of conversation was shattered with a gesture. "You remembered," he said, then returned my nod with a smile of sincerity rarely seen among superior society.

"You are much changed from when we last met, John." I lifted my hand to indicate how he stood a full inch taller than myself. "They must feed you well in Austria. Or is it the mountain air? I am no longer willing to carry you on my back while the girls try to bring us down with swords and axes."

"And you, sir, are not changed at all." It was a lie, of course, but an honest one.

"Are you hungry? The Flighted Duck does a fine mutton stew and I would grant you a little respite before we return to Longbourn—you will find no peace there."

He nodded. "Famished and most grateful for mutton stew, fine or otherwise."

We walked the short distance to the inn, careful to avoid the sticky traps left by nervous horses and oxen. Inside echoed to the shouts and laughter of cart drivers snatching a quick ale before their return journey and tradesmen spending the profits of their militia dealings, both real and imagined. Even so, a quick reminder to Mr Tincton of where the Society intended to hold its forthcoming meetings ensured he found us a small room and privacy. John tackled the stew and wine with the enthusiasm of the long-distance traveller, so I let him finish eating before troubling him with conversation.

"How is your father?"

"He was no worse than usual when I left Vienna and sends his regards. He very much hopes you might visit one day." No doubt Mrs Bennet would have enjoyed the fine Viennese pastries, but I could never have inflicted her on the Austrians— they were our allies, after all. Nor could we have afforded it.

"Perhaps he might come to Longbourn? He must return to England sometime."

John paused before replying. "He never speaks of returning. It is too early. I think it will always be too early."

The room seemed to darken a little; I was not sure it was a passing cloud.

"And you, John? If I recall your father's earlier letters correctly, you have become quite the artist."

The corners of his mouth twitched upwards. "It is true that I paint and sculpt a little."

"We all paint, John. Some of us even sculpt. It does not make us artists."

"You will forgive my modesty; self-doubt is a condition of my calling. To be an artist is to doubt. It is what drives us to improve, since we are never satisfied. My work hangs in the homes of many of our Austrian acquaintances, so my head tells me I am truly a painter and sculptor. But my heart sees the palaces in Vienna, rich in reminders of my own artistic inadequacies. The world calls me an artist; I merely claim to paint. And sculpt a little." He rose from his seat and then walked over to the window to view the scene below.

"There is one thing I am most curious about," I ventured, with the care of a man stepping into a puddle whose depth he does not know. "You wrote of a lady."

He turned and stood quietly for a while, staring at his hands, rubbing one palm with his fingertips. Then he looked up, his eyes unreadable.

"I was in Bath." He hesitated before continuing. "It will be common knowledge soon enough, so I may as well tell you.

Selling a piece of the estate to settle some bills." I looked away briefly to hide my embarrassment for him. "I will not speak ill of my father, but if he continues to spend as he does, Rudford will soon be nothing but a house and a wine cellar."

"Knowing Henry's eye for good wine, that would not be such a bad thing. Do not be harsh on your father, John. He misses the guidance and temperance of a good woman, for which he bears *no* blame. You were speaking of Bath, though. The purchaser was a lady? How extraordinary."

"No, no. After concluding our exchange, the purchaser and I took tea on Milsom Street." He smiled, seemingly enthused by a memory. "Then I was hit by a musket ball."

"You jest, surely? If not, Bath has changed a great deal since I was last there."

His smile widened. "Papa told me once how he felt when he got his leg wound. The unexpected blow. So it was that day when I first saw her. I have enough intelligence to know the folly of my immediate affection, but I can no more stop my feelings than Papa could stop that musket ball. There is always a battle within me. The free spirit of the artist against the dutiful, sensible heir to a small estate. But in matters of love, the artist seems to have the upper hand."

"I see." I shook my head slowly. "John, may I suggest you avoid using the musket metaphor should the occasion ever arise. Women like to be compared with flowers, even summer days, but undoubtedly not muskets. That much I know."

He simply shrugged. "I could not be introduced. Papa has neglected all connections beyond yours and my cause is hopeless anyway. I am heir to little of consequence, and she is, so I learned from my buyer, Miss Anne Hayter, the only child of the late Archibald Hayter, owner of Highcross and half the wine trade with Portugal. She has wealth and position, while I have little of either in comparison. I hoped you might have some advice."

"Me?" I took a step back. "I am a man with five *unmarried* daughters, a man who prefers the company of books to ball gowns. You will get no sense out of me on such matters. None at all."

"But Papa said…" John's brow grew deep furrows. "Have you not been in love?"

"John!" I shot him a sharp look. "You must know such a question cannot be answered and should not even be asked. I will put it down to tiredness and your foreign upbringing."

"My apologies." His shoulders crumpled before me. "I was too presumptuous. It is just that I have nobody to speak to on such matters."

"No, I know, and I am sorry for it." I took a deep breath before rubbing my face with one hand. "You are right. I *have* been in love. And learnt little but the futility of being so. You should move on. The feeling will pass." I drank deeply from a glass of wine to stop my face betraying the lie in my words.

"Should I speak with Mrs Bennet?"

"Goodness, no. The fuss would be unbearable." Besides, I knew she would likely seek to shift his attention to one of our daughters. I might have approved of such a match, but not after John had confided in me so.

"My apologies again, Mr Bennet. I shall not mention the subject in future."

"My dear boy, you may mention it as often as you like. Just

do not expect much guidance from me." He looked miserable. "Perhaps you may find a way. And, if not, you can console yourself that many an artist has drawn inspiration from a broken heart—it is practically a requirement of genius." He did not smile or speak. "I will give it some thought, too. But do not have high expectations. Virgil once claimed that love conquers all, but he never had to face the rules of English society."

We drank the last of the wine in the silence of small talk. Even while he spoke, John's fingers were rarely still, always rubbing at some surface or tracing patterns across the table top. "Your fingers seem in need of a brush or a chisel. We must find you other distractions. Come, let us depart to Longbourn. We may not solve your problem, but I know Jane and Elizabeth will lift your spirits. They are most eager to see you."

"And I them, and also to make the acquaintance of your younger daughters. They were very small when I last saw them. If they are half as delightful as your eldest, they will be fine companions for the evening."

"Ah. Let us talk about that on the way."

With a strange sort of friendship renewed, we took to my carriage and left a teeming Meryton behind us.

~ ~ ~

John's reception at Longbourn was, as expected, warm. Jane and Lizzy greeted him like the proverbial long-lost brother, which to them he was. And though he did not arrive on a horse and lacked the self-confidence of a man backed by a successful estate, Kitty and Lydia, and even Mary, were all smiles. "How darkly handsome he has become," confided Mrs Bennet.

We slipped easily into the informality of previous days as we gathered for a light supper in the late evening, just a few cold meats and tarts.

The days of travel seemed to tug gently on John's eyelids through the evening, but he did his best to satisfy the good-natured curiosity of the girls.

"Do tell us about Florence, Mr Barton—is it as beautiful as they say?" Kitty, in particular, was eager to engage his attention.

"Bella Firenze?" he replied.

"Bella Firenze," repeated Kitty. "How romantic—a ball in Florence."

I pinched the bridge of my nose. "Let us strike a deal, Kitty. You shall not speak again this evening, and I will not bring up the topic of your education. That way we may disguise both your ignorance and my failings."

John coughed politely. "I should have loved to visit Florence, Miss Catherine, but the war has cut us off from so many pleasures—Paris, Venice, Rome…"

"Then tell us about Vienna." Inevitably, it was Jane who sought to move the conversation to safer ground.

"Oh, please, yes," added Kitty. "I am sure it must be very pretty."

"It is a grand city, though the French were very unkind to it."

"And they have forced poor Archduchess to marry Napoleon," said Mrs Bennet. "Though at least she is to be married."

"Perhaps I can show you how grand." John had a parcel with him, all string and brown paper, which he now opened. "I should have given this to you earlier when there was still sunlight. It is a small token of the friendship between our families."

He held out a painting.

"You are most kind," said Mrs Bennet as she took it carefully, then passed it to Lizzy.

As she placed it near enough to her candle to see, Lizzy's hand flew to her mouth.

"It does not bear comparison with the great court painters, but you can at least gain an impression of the Schönbrunn gardens. I painted them in the mornings, when the sun catches the arches of the Gloriette. Father sleeps late, but I have always favoured sunrise. It seems to offer fresh hope that today will be special. A foolish hope, perhaps."

I was curious. "Well, Lizzy? Has John talent?"

"It is wonderful," she said, finally raising her head to look at John. "It is just as I imagined from all the books. More beautiful even."

"Well, John," I said. "You have already convinced the harshest critic of the family. Perhaps you will now believe the world when it says you are an artist. We should keep you here at Longbourn and have you paint all the girls." After the squeals had died down, I gave him a look of apology.

"What a fine idea, husband. I am sure Kitty would like to sit for John, would you not Kitty?"

The darkness hid Kitty's probable embarrassment but offered no protection from Lydia's giggles.

"Do you attend many balls in Vienna, John?" asked Jane.

"Some. And…" Here he dropped his voice to almost a whisper and checked to see if any servants were nearby. "I have even seen a waltz!"

His admission brought forth gasps from all around.

"I have always said the Austrians are not to be trusted, have I not, husband? Such shocking behaviour. I hope Napoleon truly was very cruel to them."

"Well, they say the waltz was a particular favourite of his, and he gave instructions that his officers all learn how to dance it." I could not be sure, but I thought John winked at Lizzy.

Mrs Bennet placed her hand on her heart. "It is not to be borne. Imagine if he should ever reach England. He would have us all waltzing and goodness knows what. It would be most—"

"Vexing, Mama, we know, but I think we may attend the next ball safely for now," said Lizzy.

"And I will be sure to inform you if I spy any Frenchmen in Meryton," I added. "I have my doubts about our wine merchant. He says tea does not agree with him, a sure sign of French perfidy."

Lydia had more important issues to discuss. "But what of the fashions? How do they wear their sleeves in Vienna? What of their bonnets?"

John's mouth hung open like an embarrassed trout, his awkwardness broken by the girls bursting into laughter.

"Did you see the Emperor?"

"I did, Mrs Bennet, but not to speak to. And a good thing, too, for I would not know how to address him. When he enters a room, the list of his titles takes a full five minutes to announce."

"Though I think Napoleon is doing his best to ease *that* particular burden." Laughter travelled around the table, skipping those who did not understand my meaning, then we slipped into a short, but contented, silence.

"Why have you returned, John, after all this time?" Lizzy's

tone was serious. "We have missed you."

I could not read John's face in the shadows. "My father has enjoyed the diversions of a foreign home, as far as possible from Gloucestershire but with a steady supply of port. And *tea*." He looked pointedly at Mrs Bennet. "But diversion has its price, and our estate needs a guiding hand. Our steward has done his best largely unsupervised, but I am here to take a firmer grip. It offers me little pleasure—I am no businessman, but an only child has little choice in this matter. And, of course, it does give me an excuse to visit old friends." He raised his glass to us.

"Well said. It is a shame your father did not return with you," said Lizzy.

"He is not inclined to travel to destinations that remind him of…of the past." In the quiet that followed, all we could hear was Mrs Bennet's jaw worrying a piece of cold beef.

"What is a waltz?" Shrieks of glee at Mary's question chased away the memories.

After a few hours of his company, I began to see more of the man that had emerged from the child. John laughed with the girls, but not as readily, or as long, as during those happy days in Gloucestershire. He certainly dressed like a gentleman, but with a studied disregard for any final touch that would distinguish him from his peers. His mind often seemed lost to weightier matters, though whether these were his father's finances, his love of art, or his love of something—or someone—else, I could not say. The enthusiasm of Lydia and Kitty at least suggested Mrs Bennet's assessment of his changed appearance was a correct one.

He reminded me a little of Lizzy in his manner. He was a great observer. But, unlike Lizzy, he kept whatever he might have learned to himself and was kind to everyone, even those undeserving of his praise. In that, he was much like Jane. He would have a made a fine son-in-law had his affections not lain elsewhere.

The foolishness of men

While my study and library were both adequate sanctuaries, neither had a door thick enough to keep curious ears at bay. True privacy at Longbourn was only possible in the exposed, open spaces of nature.

The two of us would have made a fine scene in one of the novels the girls were fond of, wind tugging at the tails of our coats and catching at John's hair as he walked, hat in hand, his shoulders weighed down by matters of the heart and hearth.

I had followed those paths many times after church, most often with Lizzy and Jane. They would take delight in everything new I could point out—the scrapings where a badger had made its burrow, now long abandoned, or the beech mast the pigs so enjoyed in autumn. The nuts littered the ground that day, cracking as two pairs of boots marched across the edge of the woodland, sending pigeons into the sky as we passed.

It was a pleasure to walk with young John. He had a painter's appreciation for the world around him and there were no dainty young girls to wait for.

"Forgive me for broaching the matter, John, but are you

serious about this Miss Hayter? You spoke most earnestly of her yesterday, but it seems you barely know her. I was a young man once and fancied myself in love several times." I broke off a twig to twist as I spoke. "I did not know which one was true until much later." A pair of azure eyes swept across my memory before I could push them back into the darkness.

John was silent for a while as we continued toward the bottom stream, patches of gold and shadow guiding our way alongside the trees.

Finally, he stopped, turning to face me directly. "Can anything be certain where love is concerned?" It was not a question I felt able to answer. "As I learnt to paint, I learnt to see how the light changes across a church façade, how a cat moves as it crosses a narrow ledge." He looked down. "To pick out the shapes and shades that beech nuts make, strewn across a forest floor." Then a smile creased his face, bringing a glow to his cheeks that the wind alone could not account for. "I have watched her. The way she moves. The way she pulls aside an errant curl. The way she drinks her tea. The way she talks. And listens. Even once, I met her eyes—she held my gaze a moment too long. It was enough."

His voice trailed away at the memory, his eyes focused far beyond the border of Longbourn. "I know her intimately as only a painter can know a person. She holds my heart, though she does not realise it." He laughed, hiding his face behind his hat. "You must think me a fool."

"Not at all." At least, no more than *I* had been in the same city so many years ago. Perhaps even in the same teashop. "Who can say when an affection is foolish? Or when foolish affection makes a man a fool? You would not be the first to fall for fine eyes. Nor will you be the last."

"Perhaps I am a fool. Perhaps if I spoke to her I would soon discover my folly. But to have the chance…"

"And there really is no common acquaintance that might allow an introduction? You cannot be so lacking in connections? There was family?"

"Only distant cousins in Yorkshire. Business folk. I would not even know where to write. Much was lost after Mama…when we left England."

"What of your father's army days, then? Connections of acquaintance may fade with time, but bonds of friendship and duty do not."

"There *was* his commanding officer. A General Tilney. I visited him at his home; it is not far from us. All understanding he may have had faded once he knew of my financial situation. It seems a gentleman may drink, gamble, and fight with impudence, but to sell land is a sin against society that cannot be forgiven."

"I served with General Tilney, too. Do not be too quick to judge him. War can make a man harsh, or take away his softness. I believe he, too, knows what it is to lose a wife. Have sympathy with him, but expect little in return. He carries his own burdens. But what about Bath's balls and assemblies? Simply spend time there and build your own connections? You are not so shy."

John merely grimaced. "I frequented one or two dances in the hope of seeing her again in the short time available to me, but to no avail. It seems she keeps herself apart. Perhaps I could have made more effort, but I have been away so long I am practically a foreigner in this land. It is hard for me to play the game when I am not familiar with the rules. Besides, Bath is…expensive… and I must return to the estate and ensure our future finances do not require the loss of any more acreage. That is why I would welcome advice from any quarter. My father once said I might trust you as if you were his brother. Yesterday you claimed no special insight on such matters, but Papa often told me of your—"

"Your father exaggerated." I turned away and continued our walk. We passed a bank of ruby ivy, stretched across an old stone wall put up by my grandfather. I used to walk across its top as a young boy, never concerned about losing my balance.

"I bet there is a good view there." John pulled himself up and began to follow in my childhood footsteps. A stick helped him balance; it swayed from side to side like a sword anticipating an attack. I walked beside him, like my father once did before me, hands half raised as if expecting him to fall. Ghosts of the past were everywhere.

I stopped to sigh. "Like you in Gloucestershire, we are quite isolated in this part of Hertfordshire, but I *will* give the matter thought, John. Your welfare is important to me, of that you may be certain." In my mind, I saw again the blade descending toward me, the steel sharp with death's deadly promise, heard again the scrape and thud as it hit the ground, turned by a sword. By Henry's sword. "Perhaps there is something we might do, so you may discover if your painter's eye is an accurate one."

For the first time during his visit, hope seemed to settle her wings in John's expression. "You are the only person in all England I can trust with such matters, Mr Bennet."

"Then maybe you *are* a fool after all, John." A smile took the edge off my comment. "And you only saw her once, you say? She must have made quite an impression."

"Yes. Well, I say once." He jumped down to stand beside me, cheeks flushed. "You may think me mad if I tell you…" I kept silent. It was always the best way to encourage people to speak. "I passed the Hayters' townhouse later that night. I was told they rarely stayed there, but that night, well—"

"Let me guess. You stood in the shadows and watched the windows, hoping for a glimpse of her? And worried you might be taken for a rogue if observed? Do not look at me like that. I am no witch. You think you are the only one? Rare is the young man who has never done such a thing."

"Have you?"

"We are not talking about me. Do continue."

"It was only the light of a single candle, but enough to know it was her…"

"And…?"

"The Emperor has a menagerie in Vienna, open for public viewing. It is quite a sight with bears, lions, and all manner of exotic creatures. I wish I had my paintings to show you. There is an eagle there, too, magnificent in its beauty. But the way it sits and holds its head…it wants to fly. Miss Hayter, too."

"And you saw all that through a moonlit window?" I clapped him on the back. "You have better eyes than I do."

That signalled a suitable end to our excursion, so we traced our steps back to the house.

~ ~ ~

"John leaves shortly, so make your farewells. Who knows when we may see him again." His bags and my carriage were both ready.

"But he cannot leave. He has not painted us yet," said Lydia.

"Mr Barton, will you not stay and paint me?" Kitty twisted a strand of hair and twirled on the spot.

"This is not some village fair," I said. "John has far better things to do than paint two silly girls."

"It might be rather fun to have our portraits done by an accomplished artist, though," said Lizzy.

"*Et tu*, Lizzy? It seems a father has nothing to say anymore. John may defend himself alone from this female onslaught. I will merely bid him goodbye so I can retire to the library for some sensible conversation."

"But there is nobody in the library, Papa," said Jane.

"Precisely. I shall be able to talk with myself."

"Do not concern yourself, sir; I am quite at ease with the wishes of your daughters. I have no time to paint now, but, if you allow me to return another day, I will paint you all. And Miss Catherine Bennet shall be first."

His statement was met with rapturous joy, though Lydia was a little less effusive. No doubt she envied Kitty's position.

"You are welcome at any time, John," I said. "But take care, you will soon receive such praise as is normally reserved for officers and bonnets. It is the highest form of admiration possible from my daughters."

His departure left me strangely discontent, though I could not grasp why. My study became a cage and I a wolf, pacing up and down in dissatisfaction, in need of distraction. It was time to visit Mr Bingley.

Mr Bingley

I did not announce my intention to the girls or Mrs Bennet when leaving to call on our esteemed neighbour. Instead, I claimed to be viewing another gun with Jackson. Guns are to ladies as bonnets are to gentlemen: a mystery that neither has any wish to investigate further.

Netherfield was a magnificent sight, embraced by enough woods and copses to keep a shooting man in high spirits and game pies for months. It was as if every aspect was planned to remind the visitor of his own inconsequence, from the scale and majesty of the entrance to the detailed statuettes that graced the façade. A cheeky gargoyle grimaced at my approach. I grimaced back.

Mr Bingley greeted me with a broad smile and an honest face, one whose features I expected to hear much about in future. He seemed young enough to enjoy the strength of youth but old enough to know not to waste it.

"You find me quite alone, Mr Bennet, though I intend to travel to London to fetch my sisters and others to join me here. If we can find room for everyone." Unless he planned to invite the entire court of St James, I felt Netherfield would cope. Its outbuildings alone were bigger than Longbourn.

He was not shy in revealing his father was in trade, a family history I could not condemn. I had too many daughters to concern myself with the source of a gentleman's wealth and property. To find an amiable fellow with such agreeable manners and charming conversation was almost a disappointment, for his delightful character would ensure much silliness at home. I fought the urge to make my visit to Netherfield a longer one. There would surely be many gentlemen intent on calling, and I had no wish to keep their wives and daughters waiting.

Unfortunately, this kindness to others came at a price: I did not see Mr Bingley's library. My father always told me to judge a man by the company he keeps, but I prefer to measure a man's worth by the books he keeps for company. Religious volumes, for example, speak of strong morals or hypocrisy, while travel books indicate an open mind. Books on gardens or geology suggest a man of sound, steadfast character, while volumes on natural history are, of course, the possessions of a country gentleman. Should said gentleman own Wilde's "Butterflies of the Southern Counties," then he belongs to the truest of all Englishmen.

Which only leaves poetry.

Mr Pratt had often insisted on reading from a book of sonnets every evening outside our tents in Virginia. As if we did not suffer enough from the skirmishing! All those verses on flowers, foliage, and the folly of youthful desire did prove useful, though, when we ran out of dry firewood.

Needless to say, the report of my visit lifted the impending threat of the Apocalypse, returning me to the bosom of Mrs Bennet's favourable opinion. Indeed, you would have thought I had already arranged an engagement, such was the joy brought about by my news. For a brief moment, they all considered me a good husband and father.

~ ~ ~

It was now no longer a question of *whether* he would marry one of the girls, but *when*. At breakfast the following morning, conversation soon sought to clarify which one it would be, with Jane the early favourite. The dogs had Bingley's scent and Mrs Bennet was the master of foxhounds.

"Let us hope you inform Mr Bingley of your choice in a timely manner. It would be unfortunate if he got down on bended knee in front of the wrong girl." My daughters ignored me until they decided to turn speculation about my future son-in-law into hard fact.

It was Lydia who broached the subject. "Is he very handsome, Papa?"

"His face is not unpleasant."

"Yes, but is he *handsome*?" she urged, fists clenched.

"Jane," I said. "Be a dear and pass the butter." She smiled as she did so, doubling the pleasure of my morning roll.

Lydia's fists beat a staccato on the table as she looked imploringly at her mother, who was thrashing a boiled egg into submission with a spoon.

Pausing in her dismemberment of that oval delight, my wife sought to reassure my youngest. "Of course Mr Bingley is very handsome, Lydia. Not that it matters with *his* income."

"Money does indeed disguise many a disfigurement, girls," I said. "Sorry looks may be of no consequence in a marriage, though a poor character may demand a price that twenty thousand a year cannot pay."

The clatter of cutlery and glass continued while six minds fought a private battle between curiosity and compliance with a father's wish for peace. Curiosity won, as it nearly always did.

"Papa, you must allow us some insight into Mr Bingley. The privilege of your sex allows you to visit him; we merely exercise the privilege of ours to ask questions of his character."

"I do not deny you the right to ask, Lizzy; *I* am merely disinclined to answer." I emphasised the point by lifting the paper to block my view of the table and, more importantly, the table's view of me. "Besides, I am not used to describing young men. They are rarely sighted at Longbourn, so what I know of them comes mostly from books. My vocabulary would not do him justice."

"Then we must take another approach, Papa," said Lizzy. "You might simply compare him to other young men of our acquaintance. To John Barton, for example."

"Interesting." I lowered my paper. "Let me think. Well, let's see. Yes, Mr Bingley's eyes are decidedly bluer." I raised the paper again. My statement produced nothing but groans from the table.

"Papa," said Jane. "John's eyes are chestnut."

"Precisely," I said from behind my protective printed wall. "And Mr Bingley's are blue, so they are indisputably bluer."

"Is he taller or shorter than Mr Barton?" said Kitty.

"He is," I said.

"What about his hair?" said Lydia.

"He certainly had some." I peered over the paper. "Does that help?" It seemed not, based on the girls' expressions.

"You might at least say how he was dressed, Papa?" Lydia would not let up.

As I was old and married, fashion was now as mysterious to me as the supposed movement of the heavens. I resolved to give Lydia's question more attention at my next meeting with Mr Bingley. "I am pleased to say he was definitely wearing clothes."

Kitty and Lydia giggled. I turned down the paper enough to see even Mary raise a half smile. Mrs Bennet was still savaging her egg, which refused to give up its gold and ivory without a struggle.

"Is he a kind man, Papa?" A question only Jane would ask.

I folded away the paper and wiped all evidence of the buttered roll from my mouth. "I believe he is, Jane, I believe he is."

"It does not matter if he is kind," mumbled Mrs Bennet through a victorious mouthful of yolk. "When he has—"

"Four thousand a year," chorused the girls before erupting into laughter. They knew their mother well.

~ ~ ~

Despite the good humour in the house, I felt an urgent desire for a little solitude. All the talk of Mr Bingley had caused me to think of John and his plight.

When a man wishes to withdraw from company, he must have somewhere to withdraw to. Somewhere with nothing of interest to those whose company he attempts to avoid.

My high-walled castle was the library and its keep the

armchair, commissioned by my grandfather and worn down by three generations of Bennets into the most comfortable piece of furniture imaginable. I always fell into it like a tired caterpillar, emerging later as a butterfly ready to tackle family, finances, and the whims of life with renewed energy.

Others travelled to Kathmandu or Cape Town in search of knowledge or enlightenment. I needed only to open a book to broaden *my* horizons. The smell of the sea and foreign shores bore no comparison to that of the printed page.

These tomes were better guardians of my sanctuary than any Cerberus. Only Lizzy and Jane would brave them, and their company I usually did not mind.

On that day, however, I picked at my books like a spinster's cat picks at a tray of titbits, finding satisfaction nowhere and ending the morning perched on the armchair, drumming out an inconsolable rhythm on the arm. Not for the first time, as the worn patch beneath my fingers proved.

I stood, then moved to the window to lean against the glass, hoping the cold on my forehead might bring some clarity. In the summer, the girls chased each other around the court, but now leaves took their place, twisting and turning in the autumn wind. I thought of John at the window in Meryton.

It would have been easy, then, to wander down roads of memories long left untraveled. Back to the same Bath that had shattered my young friend with the shock of love. I caught another hint of lavender in the air.

"No," I said to myself. "It is no longer who I am."

To remember lavender would be to remember everything. Fresh loaves at Curran's. The rough bark of the great oak in

Crescent Fields and her delight at the sight of a sparrow or squirrel. Her smile. Her touch, fleeting, yet full of promise.

In that moment, I pitied John. Perhaps he would stand in his own library in some thirty years' time and try to forget the day he considered a pair of fine eyes in Bath.

Learning the rituals

I was forewarned of Mr Bingley's return visit, but not by my sighting of his black horse (considered a perfectly acceptable colour by the girls). No, I was alerted by the flurry of activity that suddenly struck the household. Aprons abandoned, cheeks pinched, and curls pulled and patted dutifully into place, then pulled and patted again.

"Papa, you will introduce us?" Kitty had the same pleading in her eyes I recalled from picnics when one slice of cake remained. Cake you could divide and share; Mr Bingley you could not.

If that young man had had sharp enough eyes, he would have seen six noses pressed flat against the window that looked down the path leading to Longbourn. Their curiosity could not have been greater if all the circuses of England had assembled in the garden.

I received him in the library, in the hope this might encourage a reciprocal meeting place at Netherfield some time in the future.

"It is so good to see you again, Mr Bennet!" As propriety demanded, I did *not* introduce him to the girls, whose beauty he dutifully praised during his visit. But I positioned him near the window, so they could all glimpse his coat.

"A marvellous collection of books!" His head shifted from side to side, seemingly unable to settle on any one bookcase.

"Do you have any particular interests, Mr Bingley? I admit to a little pride over my travel books and those on entomology. There is little so diverting, or diverse, as insects."

His red face suggested he might not be attending the next meeting of the Meryton Natural History Society. It did not matter that he had no liking for insects. After all, most young men are more interested in painted ladies than red admirals, though it would have been unfair to condemn Mr Bingley so. I sensed a little nervousness as he continued to survey the room.

"Every book I read reminds me of how much I do not know."

"Your interests lie outside the library, then? Do you enjoy shooting?"

We found ourselves on safer ground, for Mr Bingley shared my love of the country. Mrs Bennet was right, as she so often is in matters of matrimony; he would make a perfect son-in-law, even without his four thousand pounds a year. His only failing was a propensity to speak in exclamation marks. The enthusiasm was overwhelming. I feared we would drown in an excess of punctuation if he ever shared a room with Sir William.

"When we first met, Mr Bingley, you mentioned your family was in trade?" He nodded and, for a moment, his smile seemed a little tighter. "And you are from the northern counties?"

"From Yorkshire."

"I apologise for asking, but I have a gentleman friend with distant family in that very county. Business folk. The Bartons. I wondered if perhaps you knew of them?"

"Can't say I do, Mr Bennet, but I am not well informed of our business interests. There are too many numbers in business, you know. Which is not to say I can't use numbers, but there are rather a lot of them."

"My friend has been out of the country for many years and lost touch with them in the chaos of travel. I hoped I might be able to get him an address."

The light returned to Mr Bingley's smile. "Perhaps I might make enquiries, Mr Bennet?"

"Would you?"

"It would give me great pleasure to do so! I shall attend to the correspondence as soon as I return to Netherfield."

Before he left, I remembered my obligation to Lydia. There was the blue coat, of course, and some kind of breeches. That would not satisfy their curiosity, but I could hardly ask him for an inventory of his attire. He wore his neckcloth with an endearing touch of carelessness that spoke to a lack of arrogance and pride. That was as much fashion as I could reliably describe. It would have to do.

I never gave much thought to the neckcloth, but was once told London gentlemen could spend hours ensuring the correct shape and style. A city where dinner guests start their preparations before the cook was not for me.

The journey back to Mr Bingley's horse took us past the drawing room where I knew the girls were waiting. A little cruelty would exact revenge for disturbing my breakfasts with their never-ending questions. As we passed the closed door, I paused outside. "And, of course, you must meet my daughters,

Mr Bingley." The door moved at my touch, hopefully startling the occupants within. "Perhaps you might come to dinner tomorrow?" I said, before moving on.

After we bid each other farewell, I turned back toward the house quickly enough to catch the rush of movement behind the window. I put up the collar of my coat, blew briskly on my hands and thought of the welcoming warmth of the study as Mr Bingley disappeared around the thorn hedge. Then, with a final glance behind, I set off to follow him.

A gaggle of girls denied an introduction could be a fearsome sight. It was best to leave them to cool down while there was still enough light to walk the grounds easily.

～ ～ ～

Mr Bingley was unable to come to dinner as planned, indisposed by some urgent matter of business at Netherfield.

Mrs Bennet's look of sorrow at the news reminded me of Toke's after someone ate the last slice of his apple tart. The general disappointment soon dissipated, though, since there was an assembly to look forward to the following night.

Meryton assemblies lasted mere hours but always entertained us for many days. First, there was anticipation. Then participation. And, finally, the breakfast table revelations, where the pie was cold and tasteless, but the gossip warm and invigorating.

As we sat around the candlelight in the early evening, my reading to the girls fell on ears already lost to the prospect of the fiddler's bow and a gentleman's offer to dance.

"You will introduce us to Mr Bingley as early as polite, dear husband? So that he may have enough time to admire Jane."

I put down Blundell's *A Journey on Horseback*, knowing it could not hope to compete with a bachelor on a stallion. Or even one on foot.

"Is not one look enough, Mrs Bennet? Do you doubt Jane's charms?" The object of my flattery smiled.

"Mr Bennet, you know that Jane is by far the most handsome girl in Meryton. But we must be careful." She leant forward and lowered her voice—quite why I did not know, as there was no servant present. "Lady Lucas has a most devious nature. She will hope to engage Mr Bingley in conversation so her Charlotte can present herself in a better light. If he were only to see her at a distance, he would pass by without so much as a word. She cannot hope to charm him with her looks, but she may appear more favourably in conversation."

"Mama!" said Lizzy, ever protective of her friend.

Mrs Bennet sat with the knowing contentment of a monk. "It is the truth of it, Lizzy, as you well know."

I picked up Blundell's book again and began thumbing through the pages. "An introduction will be impossible, my dear because I will not be there."

"Not be there! How can that be? You must come with us, Mr Bennet—we shall be lost without you." Mrs Bennet collapsed in her chair, all semblance of monastic tranquillity gone.

"The assembly rooms are not large, so you are unlikely to get lost. No, you must rely on others for an introduction. The Lucases, perhaps?"

"The Lucases…of course," said Mrs Bennet. "Such a fine family. There is never a bad word to be said about them. I am sure they will oblige." My wife's opinions were always as changeable as the Hertfordshire winds.

~ ~ ~

The next evening, I should have been in bed but was too engrossed in Bracegirdle's *Travels in Africa* to make the short journey upstairs. When navigating the ivory and gold coasts, exploring dark rivers and darker forests, it is all too easy to forget to put on a night shift. A sputtering candle dragged me back to England.

I allowed myself the luxury of one more encounter with pirates and parrots when the shrill cries of both suddenly seemed all too real. The family had returned from the assembly, the general clamour suggested an evening rich in gossip. Curiosity chipped away at my normal disdain for such entertainments and led me to wonder whether I should have gone to Meryton with them. It was helped in its task by my promise to John, a promise given fresh urgency by a new letter:

> *I am resigned to the toil of estate affairs but hold hope of visiting again before any return to Vienna. I look forward to our continuing correspondence and any advice you might have on the situation we discussed on our walk at Longbourn.*

Though not yet ready to throw myself wholeheartedly into his business, I decided to learn more of the rituals of the assembly dance, particularly the one that continues when the music stops. There is nothing permanent except change, as Heraclitus might have said. My skills that John seemed so determined to rely on were honed in another decade. Society changes slowly, but it does change; I could not be sure my understanding of the nuances of courtship was still as sound as Henry Barton and others seemed to believe. As such, I resolved to learn what I could from those currently engaged in that activity.

I could already imagine how the actual assembly had proceeded. Within moments, Kitty and Lydia, for example, would have found the liveliest young men in the room and forced them to twirl and pirouette in their wake. Mrs Bennet would have floated through the crowd like a dandelion seed on the breeze, armed herself with a glass of punch, then fallen into the company of other mothers eager to discuss matrimonial ambitions. And Lizzy? Well, she would have crossed the assembly room slowly, taking in the assembled gentlefolk like a doctor examines his patients, reviewing all that is right and wrong in them—with particular attention to the wrong. It is an admirable quality in a doctor, less admirable in a young lady. Even those with Lizzy's extraordinary intelligence should perhaps enjoy the innocence of youth a little longer, leaving the world-weary comments to their fathers.

Like shot birds, Mrs Bennet and the girls thumped down into sofas and chairs to sit motionless as they gathered strength for the traditional post-assembly review. Kitty announced their return to life with a giggle, no doubt remembering a touch of a gentleman's hand on the dance floor. Then she and Lydia fetched cold meats, bread, and wine to provide stronger fare than the titbits of gossip now to be shared. The kitchen table, room bereft of cooks and servants, played host to this feast.

"Mary danced with Mr Toke," whispered Lizzy as I tore off a lump of bread.

"I am sorry to have missed that spectacle," I whispered back. "Toke dances like an overburdened merchant ship, unable to turn easily and always on the verge of capsizing. It is a most diverting sight. Still, Mary seems to have survived the ordeal well enough. You enjoyed the dance, Mary?" I said, raising my voice.

"It was tolerable, Papa."

"You seem happy, Jane," I noted. "Perhaps you have taken too much wine?"

Jane turned her face away. I could not see in the dim candlelight, but I was sure she blushed.

"Too much wine? Such nonsense," said Mrs Bennet. She laid her hand on Jane's arm. "Of course she is happy, for Mr Bingley would not leave her side all evening."

Jane shook her head. "Not *all* evening, Mama."

Her mother did not allow anything as trivial as the truth to contain her excitement. "Perhaps he did stand up with some other girls, but his eye was always on Jane. And well it might be, for the others were all *very* plain."

"So tell me, how did you all divine Mr Bingley's attachment? What did our friend do to inspire such a diagnosis? What makes him so worthy of admiration?" Curiosity crept across Lizzy's face at my questions.

No satisfactory answer was to come, since Mrs Bennet and our two youngest took my words as a cue to rattle off a series of compliments on Mr Bingley's cheekbones, chest, legs, and other favourable features. The girls regarded him as perfect, a declaration that revealed their lack of experience with men. Even Achilles had his heel, though I daresay Mrs Bennet would have forgiven him this blemish given the likely size of his olive plantations.

"He impresses with his conversation," said Jane.

"At last," I said. "An advantage not explained by his physique alone. And what passes for good conversation between young people these days?"

"He is—" began my wife.

"Attentive," said Jane.

"He complimented me on my gown," said Kitty.

"He is modest," said Lizzy. "He has his pride, but only that which is due to him through his position and character. And he does not consider himself above others, whatever his station in life might encourage him to think. Unlike others."

"Others?" I said.

"I was thinking of one of Mr Bingley's companions—Mr Darcy."

The shriek from my wife had me half looking for parrots again. "Do not talk of that man, Lizzy. What arrogance! I do not believe he smiled once the whole evening. They say he owns half of Derbyshire and ten thousand a year. But what is Derbyshire to us? It is practically Scotland, no doubt full of pipes and puddles."

"He certainly seems better suited to northern moors than Meryton dances." As she spoke, Lizzy's kneaded a piece of bread between her fingers until it was flat and flaky, the crumbs tumbling down on to her plate.

"It seems he has earned your disapproval," I said.

"It is of no consequence, Papa. He merely described me as tolerable, yet not handsome enough to tempt him."

"Did he indeed? Then he has certainly earned *my* disapproval." I took my daughter's hands in mine and squeezed them gently. "How often we find superior men wanting in essential human qualities. My dear Lizzy, he is a man of poor taste and poorer character. Do not give him a moment's thought. Let us return to the qualities of Mr Bingley. Modest you say?"

"Not quite so much as John, but I do not think many men are."

Modesty coupled with an acceptable degree of pride. Compliments. Attention. Little seemed to have changed from my day. And John certainly had most of those qualities in good measure.

"And he danced with Jane." Mrs Bennet clasped her head between her palms. "Twice!"

I looked at Lizzy for help, but found none.

"Twice!" repeated my wife, nodding at me furiously.

"This is a good thing?" I ventured.

"Good? Why, it is practically a proposal!" Mrs Bennet rubbed Jane's arm.

Whether I had never known this or merely forgotten was neither here nor there; the news sent my mind off to travel through the dances of my youth and discover whether I gave false hopes to any ladies by asking them to join me for a second quadrille. "To think of all the effort we men put into poems and perambulations, late-night trysts, and duels with fellow suitors. All it seems we need do is stand up twice with our beloved."

"But we are forgetting Mr Bingley's most attractive quality," said Mrs Bennet. She stared at each one of us, apparently bemused at our lack of response. "He is excessively rich!"

And therein lay John's biggest problem.

~ ~ ~

"You are fond of Mr Bingley, Jane?" I put the question outside the following day, as she and Lizzy cut strands of wild vine, its crimson foliage and blackened fruits the perfect decoration for autumnal dinners.

Jane stood and fought against the wind to brush strands of golden hair from her eyes. "He is most amiable," she said, which was as much affection as she would ever admit to in the presence of her father.

"Mind you, *you* have nothing bad to say about any man. So perhaps I should have asked if you are fonder of Mr Bingley than of other young gentleman with acceptable manners."

I did not expect a reply and Jane did not disappoint.

"You take a curious interest in Mr Bingley?" said Lizzy, as the two girls continued to snip and tease tendrils off the garden wall.

"May a father not enjoy simple conversation with his daughters without arousing suspicion?"

"He may. Though I believe, Papa, you would be equally curious were I to enquire about your fondness for a particular beetle among the many that catch your interest."

"Unlike any beetle of my acquaintance, Mr Bingley seems universally admired. I simply wonder what distinguishes him from others. He has money to be sure, but I know that would not influence your or Jane's judgement. Last night you spoke of modesty, attention, and the provision of compliments, but such qualities are not unique to our friend from Netherfield."

After dropping a sprig of leaves and berries into a wicker basket, Lizzy did the same with her knife before arching her back with a groan echoed by the distant caw of a crow.

"Papa," she said. "I do not believe there is a recipe for a good man or a prescription for genuine affection. If there were, there would be more of both. You cannot bake a man of worth."

"That all sounds like something I would say."

"Well, I *am* your daughter."

"Do not allow last night to turn you cynical, Lizzy. Men say silly things all the time. Place no weight on Mr Darcy's unworthy comment."

"Papa, if you are truly interested in matters of character and courtship, perhaps you might read more poetry—"

"To the devil with you, Jane, for such a suggestion! I would rather pursue a life of ignorance as far as Mr Bingley's talents go."

Any further enquiries were blocked by the arrival of the Lucas family, firing off greetings, exultations, and small children in all directions like Mongolian horse archers. Their visit was also perfectly timed to delay my departure to Meryton and a Society meeting.

Sir William's presence had one saving grace. He brought me a bottle from his recent trip to London, more specifically from those parts of the city home to purveyors of fine spices, wines, and other essentials demanded by the court gentry. His knight's table could never limit itself to the products of Hertfordshire husbandry alone, though I suspected much of what he bought was no different than our own humble county's offerings; it simply came in more expensive paper, boxes, and bottles.

A thick cloth bag tied with coarse string enclosed the gift, which was small enough to cup in my hands.

"A little something, Bennet, to warm you up on a cold

winter's night, eh?" Another question mark lost in a forest of grammar.

"Thank you, Sir William, you are very kind. As always." I began to tear at the string.

"Careful there, Bennet." He paused to look around the study, as if the packet was contraband and the tell-tale lights of the watch approached. "This is not your usual beverage."

I pulled back the cloth to reveal a small brown bottle, neatly stoppered with a cork and embossed with the word *Madmaidens* in a raised circle. "Madmaidens?"

He nodded, leaning back in his chair and tapping his nose as if explanation enough.

"I fear you have me at a disadvantage. It is not a drink I am familiar with."

"Ah." Sir William twirled the ends of his moustache. "Keep it safe, keep it hidden—not for the ladies, what? It will warm you from the inside out. There is no drink rarer."

"I see." I dropped my voice slightly in the hope of adding the solemnity Sir William seemed to expect.

The ladies then called us back into the drawing room to settle a dispute on court protocol, a subject dear to Sir William's heart. The Madmaidens would have to wait for another day.

All in a good cause

After seeing Sir William and family depart for Lucas Lodge, I hurried to Meryton for the Society meeting. Another lecture from Mr Criswick led to a relieved retreat to the Flighted Duck afterwards.

Our senses dulled by the inn's warmth and its proprietor's port, we settled into a gentle reverie broken only by the dying cries of a burning log and a brief, but robust, debate about the preferred width of a slice of sponge cake.

Although John's fate still troubled me like a burr in a boot, I was unwilling to revisit it with my companions, unsure as I was of their interest. Then Elliston ended the pleasant silence: "Any news of your young friend, Bennet?" It seemed my previous words *had* encouraged small shoots of curiosity that now sought the light.

"He visited us at Longbourn." Elliston pulled himself upright in his chair and I could sense some anticipation in the room. "My 'fears' were proven correct, for he believes himself in love. A glance across a tearoom in Bath was all it took."

Loud laughter filled the room, though none came from

Fielding. "How interesting," he said, all the while looking at me.

"He has yet to even speak with the lady in question. I could give him little advice, of course." This was met with murmurs of approval. "To be quite honest with you, gentlemen, I am not sure I can offer him anything useful at all, much as I would like to."

The murmurer-in-chief was Stanhope: "My wife says men are entirely unsuited to courtship. That we have no understanding of the human heart. That we should stick to port and pheasants."

"A wise woman, Mrs Stanhope," said Jackson.

"And yet our sex builds carriages, cannons, and the intricate mechanisms in clocks." Fielding pointed at the mantelpiece above the fireplace. "Surely such minds can master the arts of courtship? Especially minds that were once more than competent in that particular field of endeavour."

"Clocks and carriages obey laws of regularity. They are predictable." Stanhope pointed his own finger towards the floor and moved it from side to side like a pendulum. "Tick tock, tick tock." That was true enough, though anyone seeing Stanhope driving his chaise and four might have argued the point about predictability. "Ladies, however…"

Fielding was not to be deterred. "Why should Bennet not try and offer this young man some help? Why might *we* not do so? It would make an engaging distraction. It would certainly be time better spent than listening to Criswick describe the geology of the Jamaican coastline. Be a good fellow, Bennet, and tell us more about your friend's son. Perhaps we can manage courtship by committee."

The others shuffled in their seats, but paid attention as I

spoke. "There is little I can add, Fielding. He saw a lady in Bath, one of wealth and distinction, and he fell in what may be love." I shrugged.

"Is he a decent fellow? Does he shoot, drink, play cards?" Jackson got straight to the point.

"I am sure he does, but we are not trying to get him into a club."

Jackson waved away my objection. "A good name and income should solve everything."

"Alas."

"Then your young friend should set his aim a little lower, Bennet."

Jackson meant no insult and his words reflected my own rational opinion, yet they lit a small spark of indignation that grew brighter, stinging me into unprepared action. "Do we give in so easily? Surely we can all remember what it was like to be in love?"

In the silence that followed I could see expressions travel back into the past. Some of my colleagues may even have been thinking of their wives. As for myself, there was a dutiful glimpse of Miss Gardiner, the future Mrs Bennet, all cherry-red gown and amber eyes, a vision quickly replaced by the flash of another lady's smile.

Fielding's words after our last meeting rose unbidden: *not all memories need be kept locked away.* I gave the smile its owner's name, a name normally saved for days darkened by too much port and self-pity.

Abigail.

"John deserves better of us. He does not seek to capture a

lady's heart with a fashionable coat, a fast phaeton, or a charmed tongue. He does not impress with a title or an income sheet. Nor does he have the good fortune that so many possess of appearing better than he is. But what he *is*, is a man of intelligence and kindness. Any of us would be proud to call him a son." My voice faltered a little toward the end.

The speech was somewhat uncharacteristic for me and our little group, but as Shakespeare wrote in Macbeth: *I am in blood / Stepp'd in so far that, should I wade no more, / Returning were as tedious as go o'er.*

I waded out a little further.

"He hides himself in a self-effacing shroud of fog and rain. He is Yorkshire, with all that county's honesty and character. And I feel an obligation to bring him together with Somerset."

I did not know where my words came from and suspected I might regret them later. But then Abigail's smile returned in my memory; this time I could not help returning it.

"Why Somerset? And I thought your friend was from Gloucestershire?" Stanhope was a slave to logic.

"I was being *metaphorical*." It was lucky I stopped myself before reciting poetry, the last refuge of the romantically unhinged.

A blustery rattle on the windows marked a change in weather.

"You care for this boy?" Jackson's question was almost a statement.

"I do. His father and I served together. You know the friendships forged in combat." They all nodded.

"Beetles and butterflies. Those are my interests." Jackson held up the much-discussed slice of sponge cake. "But cake and courtship? Well, they are as good a topic as any. Why not, eh?"

"Why not indeed?" Fielding stood and raised his glass. "To cake and courtship." As the echoes of the toast died away, he leant over to grip me on the shoulder. "We will see what we can do."

A name revealed

Over the next few days, prompted by the emotion of the Society meeting, John's position pulled at my mind like an unfinished book. As did his words: *I know her intimately as only a painter can know a person. She holds my heart.*

Lost in thought in the library, my fingers found their way into the slashes in my footstool, the true Ottoman allegedly once sat upon by the Turkish general Merzifonlu Kara Mustafa Pasha over a hundred years ago.

I remembered the day I made those slashes—the work of a young boy, armed with a kitchen knife, storming the unoccupied library as a heroic dragoon. How I laid waste to the enemies of England with sword and sabre! My mother, ears finely-tuned to the sound of ripping fabric, then caused the rapid retreat of the brave soldier and ensured the footstool's survival. The reward for my battlefield endeavours? Neither medals, nor glory, but a pinched ear, sore bottom, and a cold bath.

I never knew why they left the cloth ripped. Perhaps it was meant to remind me of the penalties of avoiding your responsibilities. Perhaps it was to remind my parents.

This faithful companion sat by my side, bearing the burden of my feet without and the collected volumes of Flaubert's *Lepidoptery* within. It still gave off the age-old scent of my father's tobacco, and brought back his last words to me, whispered from the pillows of his deathbed. "Give me a grandson." Alas, I had no son to guide through the travails of life, but perhaps I could do something for John.

~ ~ ~

If I was going to wallow in the past, then it was best done with a friend. Fielding welcomed my surprise visit and immediately enquired about John's situation. No letter meant no fresh news to offer. Not that I expected to hear of any. He was home on his estate, friendless and isolated from society.

No child dragoon had invaded Fielding's home, so we sat with our weary feet propped up on undamaged footstools, wine in our hands and replete with the potted fowl and sugared puddings of Mrs Fielding's excellent cook. Thick cloud outside dulled the room, but the fire added enough light for our needs and punctuated our conversation with the crackle and spit of burning wood.

"I am grateful for everyone's interest, though one man's romantic travails are not a topic I would normally associate with the pleasures of our little society."

Fielding settled himself further into his armchair. "I believe all men have a romantic heart." He glanced at his desk, where, cloaked in the half-darkness, I knew there was a small portrait of his wife. "But it is society that bids us keep it locked away. There is no place for romance on the battlefields of business, politics, or the Peninsular. So we reject it as the dominion of ladies and dedicate ourselves to those pursuits society has deemed to be male. Like drinking." We raised our glasses. "And killing birds."

"And each other," I added, glancing over to where Fielding's old sword hung on the wall. I emptied my glass.

He nodded. "But left to our own devices, spared the company of other men, and surrounded by beauty, we would rediscover our hearts I think. Perhaps it is this hidden yearning that drives our committee to attend to your friend's plight?"

"You may be right, Fielding, though the only hidden yearning Jackson likely possesses is for another slice of tart and a warm bed."

"You are wrong about Jackson, Bennet. It is not hidden; it is there for all to see. Besides, a man who has witnessed combat first-hand may be entitled to rejoice in the simple pleasures of baking and sleep."

"Indeed, a sentiment I might share." We were quiet for a while, both lost in thought and memory.

It was the sounds and smells that always stayed with me. The cries that pierced the miasma of confusion that descended in conflict. Shouted names you did not know, not even your own. The retorts of the enemy muskets. The irrevocable fear that threatened to consume you as you struggled to make order of chaos, clinging to your sword like a raft in a sea of men and trees. Clinging to life. Some men never recover, others are fortunate to escape with nothing but memories to remind them of the fighting.

The creak of Fielding's chair pulled me back to the present as he turned to face away from me briefly. "Perhaps one of us also regrets his own choices and would see another man joined with the lady he truly loves, to have the pleasure once denied him."

"Perhaps," I said, without moving, and Abigail's smile appeared again at the edges of my memory. "Anyway, this may all be moot. For all our interest, I fail to see quite how we can be of help. Not unless one of us is familiar with the Hayter family of Highcross." Though I had already written to John asking if I might reveal Miss Hayter's name to my close friends, he had not yet replied. A brief wave of guilt washed over me.

"The Hayters of Highcross, near Bath?"

"You know them?" The spark of pleasure I got from the hope surprised me.

"Everyone knows them."

"Everyone? Except for me it seems."

"Well, when I say 'know'…not directly. And certainly not personally. The name is on all the crates outside Weintraub's. Did you never notice? A daughter of that family will have a queue of suitors lined up along the Royal Crescent, all carrying coin, land, and titles."

I squeezed out a smile. "Perhaps she will fall in love with him. And he is still a gentleman with an estate, albeit a small one."

Fielding looked at me like a schoolmaster eyes a boy who has just misquoted Ovid. "Even if that were to occur, her family would surely not allow an inappropriate match."

I found a fingernail to pick at. "Fielding, it was *you* who suggested we make an effort on John's behalf, even though I laid out similar reasons for pessimism. Why, if there is no hope?"

"I did not know the lady's name. If I had, I might have held my tongue." He poured us more wine, the clink of bottle on glass betraying the tremble of old age in his hands. "Though the world is changing, my friend. We have a regent. There are streets in London lit by burning gas. Who is to say what is possible?"

"Then perhaps we must throw caution to the winds and simply urge John to recite Byron to the lady and Wordsworth to the mother."

"We have not yet fallen so low. Let us instead turn our minds to more pleasant thoughts. Now, tell me, is your Jane still as pretty as I recall from summer?"

"If Mrs Bennet is to be believed, we may expect a visit from a jealous Aphrodite at any moment. But there are no Greek heroes likely to save us from a Goddess's wrath. Except perhaps the good Mr Bingley."

~ ~ ~

Fielding's good humour left me feeling quite amiable all through the next day, right up until the moment Mr Bingley's sisters called.

I was quick to invent business that called me away from the Netherfield harpies. They were too ready to expose the ignorance and simplicity of others without the underlying respect that separates teasing from insult.

"Oh, Mr Bennet, how droll to suggest you might have business to conduct, as if a gentleman like yourself has work to attend to. Drink tea with us and leave 'business' to your lessers," said the unmarried one, confirming my opinion of her and hastening my departure.

Their appearance proved that Mrs Bennet's Bingley campaign continued, with dinners, dances, and games seemingly the main weapons of war.

~ ~ ~

"They have gone, Papa. It is quite safe to return." Lizzy found me outside in the stables, where I had spent a pleasant hour in conversation with a favourite mare of few words.

"Excellent. And were they as impeccably imperious as ever?"

"They were. You and I share the same opinion of them, I believe, though Jane assures me they are quite companionable."

"That reflects Jane's character, not theirs." Lizzy turned to go back to the house. "Tell me, Lizzy, before you go. Do the walls of Netherfield hold firm? Or will the siege be over before winter?"

"Papa?"

"Jane and Mr Bingley." Lizzy was the only member of the family I could talk to sensibly on the matter. "I have been watching and learning, my dear. The skirmish of the sexes continues at dances and cards. And there you women may call on a range of strategies and tactics far beyond the wit of my unfortunate sex. Hearts may be won and lost during a Cotillion. How fares Mr Bingley in the game of love?"

"Mr Bingley is a fine gentleman and behaves as such. He has become very attached to Jane. Regrettably, not all his party share his affable nature."

"And since we are on the subject, what plans does your mother have regarding our friend at Netherfield?" Lizzy looked confused. "When I last visited the pigs, Froggat told me Mrs Bennet expressed much interest in his predictions for the weather. He could not say why. Something is afoot."

"Mama has said nothing to me."

"She would be wise not to place much stock in Froggat's advice." His promises of a dry day had been the ruin of many a bonnet. The weather-beaten face and economy of words gave a false impression of country wisdom. "Your mother would do better to speak with the pigs."

~ ~ ~

A letter greeted me on my return indoors. Not, to my disappointment, from John, but from a cousin, Mr William Collins. He wished to arrive on some kind of diplomatic mission and end a feud that had existed between our fathers. His sentiments were admirable, so a person less cynical might have greeted the overtures with joy and gratitude. After all, as the heir to Longbourn, his goodwill was likely vital for the future security of the girls. However, the letter seemed designed to communicate his good fortune and character more than his wish to visit. People quick to describe their qualities rarely possess them, but at least I could not accuse him of excessive modesty.

A visit would mean yet another bachelor beneath the eaves of my house, though I doubted this one would be welcomed quite as well as John or the amiable Mr Bingley. Mrs Bennet still blamed Mr Collins for standing higher in the line of inheritance for my estate than her own daughters. The terms of the entail were hardly his fault, though.

My cousin was not blessed with the same kind of happy home I enjoyed as a child. An accident of birth denied his father wealth and security, leading him down a path to misanthropy. From what I understood, he would constantly berate the young Mr Collins, happy to announce his son's failures and poor prospects to any passing soul.

Those prospects had since improved, thanks to *my* failure to bear a son. I hoped Mr Collins had blossomed in the absence of his late father, even if his letter suggested otherwise.

A promise

After lying empty for so long, the list of bachelors now seemed to grow daily. It began with Barton, Bingley, and Collins and found its temporary end in a whole troupe of officers. Or "OFFICERS!" to give them their formal title, according to Lydia and Kitty.

We were all in Meryton—the girls to see the arriving soldiers and me to see my daughters came to no harm from them. The men marched in from the north road and through the square, buttons and buckles gleaming in the autumn sun, turning heads with the clip of boots on cobbles, turning hearts with the purpose in their stride.

We were next to the vintners, whose crates and barrels helped the local children see over the heads of their elders. Everyone had stopped for the spectacle, the men casting nervous looks at their wives and daughters, the wives and daughters casting admiring glances at the soldiers.

The officers carried swords of bright steel, as pristine as if they had never been used. I suspected they had not. The jackets carried no dust, the fabric bright as fresh blood.

"I do love their red uniforms," said Kitty.

"Yes," I said. "The colour will serve the soldiers well should they ever need to surprise the enemy in a field full of poppies."

The colonel certainly knew how to put on a show. No doubt they started nearby so the journey to town would not ruin clean boots and uniforms.

As they marched, the officers stared straight ahead and fought to keep the knowing smirks from their faces. All except one, a tall fellow with a scar down the right side of his face. His smirk was there for all to see.

Even Mary could not help but show an interest. "Why are they here, Papa?"

"To eat, drink, dance, play cards, and find wives."

"How jolly," said Lydia, standing on tiptoe to get a better view, or more likely to give a better one of herself.

"I was being…never mind. They are here to maintain the peace, Mary. A peace we have enjoyed without their help for many a year. The last riot in Meryton was in 1798, when Mr Tincton's father announced ale was half price."

"Perhaps our spies have unearthed Napoleon's secret plans for Meryton," said Lizzy.

"Goodness, do you think so, Lizzy?" Kitty's eyes widened at the thought. "I shall improve my French, just in case…Bonjour officier. Mais, merci, j'apprécierais certainement la prochaine danse. J'aime votre chapeau. Aimez-vous mon bonnet?"

Lizzy and I shook our heads in mutual resignation. "Still," I said. "The townsfolk can now sleep easier in their beds. At least those without daughters."

There would be no avoiding dinners with at least some of the officers, accompanied by stories of daring and bravery in the face of the enemy, even if that was likely a few dozen drunk mill workers in Lancashire.

"They will provide plenty of distraction for you girls, relieving me of that responsibility. I may pursue my own interests in peace. And if that is the only peace they manage to maintain, I will be most grateful."

~ ~ ~

The constant talk of officers through the week soon sapped my willpower, but the company of the Society brought some relief. We were all once officers, so had no need to talk of them.

It was Fielding who, again, broached the subject that seemed to edge closer to our hearts with each passing meeting. "So, gentlemen, have any of us given any thought to Bennet's young friend and how he might capture the lady?"

I was still surprised at the interest John's story had stirred among my fellow committee members. None had ever struck me as romantically-minded.

"A net, ether and a killing jar," muttered Jackson. He opened one eye to scan his bemused audience. "Best way with beetles. Best way."

"Let us apply military principles to the problem." Mugs, plates, and cutlery clattered as Fielding swept them to one side, then folded over the cloth to expose a piece of bare table, pitted and scarred like a northern landscape.

"This is our young gentleman." He placed a decanter in the centre of the exposed area. "And this glass is the lady in question. Our task is to bring the two together. How?"

Silence.

As I feared, the assembled gentlemen had little to say. Most had stumbled into marriage by accident or arrangement.

"Does this lady have strong feelings about parsnips?" Elliston looked at me hopefully. "Or artichokes?" He, at least, had wooed his way to a wedding through a shared interest in vegetable growing.

Poetry was mentioned, of course, demonstrating once again man's inability to separate myth from reality. I began to understand why the ladies always left us out of their marital plans. Without their help, we would soon become a nation of bachelors.

Fielding tapped the 'Hayter' glass to get attention. "We are perhaps putting the cart before the horse, gentlemen. Mr Barton has spent the best part of his life abroad. He has no connections beyond our esteemed Mr Bennet, and only a small estate to his name. His character, we are assured, is most praiseworthy. His chances, poor at best. But if there is to be a sliver of hope in our story, then our two protagonists must at least meet." He looked up at me and I nodded—a letter from John had arrived that morning. "Does anyone know a Miss Anne Hayter of the Highcross estate, near Bath?"

Jackson opened both eyes this time. "The wine traders?"

"That is the family," I said.

Jackson nodded, then rubbed his chins. "I believe I can help."

~ ~ ~

Jackson promised intelligence on the Hayters within a few days, a merry thought I passed on to John by letter, taking the opportunity to reassure him of our earnest wish that he visit again. The girls wanted their portraits and I had no objection to male company at home, whatever memories such company might call forth. Since I was at my desk, I also wrote to Mr Collins, welcoming him to Longbourn. The sentiments he had expressed were honourable ones and so deserved an equivalent response from me. I only needed to break the joyous news to Mrs Bennet. The thought left me a little cold, a brief shudder sending my gaze across the room to a pocket-sized bottle sitting innocently on a shelf.

...warm you from the inside out.

It seemed an appropriate time to fortify myself with a small glass of courage.

~ ~ ~

It was late the next morning before my vision cleared and I was able to walk properly again. Mrs Bennet placed the Madmaidens under lock and key in our medicine cabinet, and I developed a new respect for Sir William's stomach. But I still did not have the strength to talk with my wife about Mr Collins.

Introducing Mr Murden

The camaraderie and jesting of the militia now guarding Meryton from threats unknown woke a better kind of memory in me than the smell of burning poetry or crimson trails of blood along a forest floor.

"Are you looking forward to today's company, Papa?" said Jane. We were shortly to entertain the Colonel and three of his officers: Mr Denny, Mr Carter, and—on his first visit to us—Mr Murden, the man with the scar I saw the day the regiment arrived.

"I enjoy their conversation. Though, like a good port, it is best consumed in small doses, with periods of abstinence to ensure a full appreciation of the flavour."

"I think they are very brave to choose army life."

"You confuse the militia with the regulars, my dear. Militia lives are not difficult—most of the orders they give are to tailors and wine merchants. The only army they must face is one of admirers, not Frenchmen; the only danger to their comfort is an impatient creditor."

~ ~ ~

At tea, none of the three junior officers paid much attention to Jane, just as fishermen ignore a trout that has already been caught. But the younger girls in particular allowed red jackets to bring a blush to their faces. Much was spoken, little was said. Though sometimes words were unnecessary, replaced by a shy glance or a timely turn of the head.

"Any news, Colonel Forster, on when you may be obliged to leave Meryton?" I said.

"Nothing official as yet, Mr Bennet, but they do not like us to stay in one town for long, just in case we become too friendly with the locals."

"I fear we have already failed in our duty on that account. Be merciful, sir, for friendship is inevitable in such company as this." Mr Murden swept his hand around the table, taking in all the girls and even Mrs Bennet.

"Then *we* must promise not to riot or otherwise cause trouble," said Lizzy. "So your loyalties are not tested."

"And I shall hold you to that promise, Miss Elizabeth. I would hate to have to lay hands on you." Mr Murden's eyes fell briefly to Lizzy's chest.

She lifted her jaw slightly as she leant forward over the table. "A sentiment I cannot disagree with." Mr Murden smiled and scratched his scar.

"I should so love to see you fight," said Lydia. "You might all be frightfully injured and we could nurse you back to health here at Longbourn."

"Let us hope that does not happen, for all our sakes," I said.

Mr Murden turned to Lydia. "Six months in Portugal is quite enough fighting for me. Now I merely wish to battle with Denny for the last of this splendid cake." He was a man of indefatigable charm and wit, and thus worthy of immediate suspicion.

Men with experience of the regular army sometimes carry a burden greater than mine. They are scarred by more than a few poor memories. Some are vicious, turned sour by battle. Others are excessively gentle or withdrawn, as if to compensate for the horrors they have seen or caused. Some are eager to experience all that life offers, knowing how it can be lost so easily. I saw a scar on Mr Murden's face, but was unsure if one lay underneath.

"Do tell us more about Portugal. Did you see the French?" Lydia's cup trembled in her hands.

"Too much of the French, and not enough of their wine." Mr Murden nudged Mr Denny as laughter coursed through the room, only broken by Lydia's shriek as spots of hot tea fell on her dress. One of us, though, did not join in the merriment.

"Our new acquaintance is quite the wit, is he not, Lizzy?" I did not like to see her downcast.

"He is."

"But?" said Mr Murden.

"I meant no offence. It is just I find little humour in war."

Mr Murden nodded, his hand wandering toward his scar again. "Nor should you. But a smile is often the companion of hope. And hope is always the weapon of choice for the reluctant soldier. It keeps him as safe as any sword or musket."

"And were you a reluctant soldier, Mr Murden?" said Lizzy.

"At times. It would reflect badly on me were it otherwise."

"Well spoken, Mr Murden," said Colonel Forster. "The

enthusiastic ones are the worst, rushing to their deaths at the first glint of the enemy's steel. You can measure the ease of victory by how many of them remain at the end. There are no enthusiastic old soldiers."

"You are right, sir, but I fear we may scare the ladies with such talk. Let us leave war behind and charge into more pleasant conversation. Your hairpins, Mrs Bennet. They remind me of those worn by a Baroness of my acquaintance. Are they a family heirloom?"

And so, at a stroke, Mr Murden won the battle for Mrs Bennet's approval.

~ ~ ~

Later, sitting alone with Lizzy in the library, I sought her opinion on our new acquaintance.

"I cannot say I have formed one. His character eludes me and I begin to doubt my understanding. Perhaps men are not as simple as I have often held them to be." She looked up from her book, frowning.

"Men are simpletons?"

"Simple, not simpletons. Well, not all of them. And not *you*, Papa." She came over to place a kiss on my forehead. "Not you."

"My dearest Lizzy. I could spend every hour of my day talking with you."

"No more today, Papa, for I must attend to Mama. We shall renew our analysis of Mr Murden's elusive character tomorrow."

"Or another day," I said, glancing at a note that had arrived in the morning. "Tomorrow I meet Mr Jackson in Meryton. He has news for me."

"News? Of what nature?"

"If I knew, it would not be news now, would it? Besides, are not fathers allowed *some* secrets from their daughters?"

A path to Miss Hayter?

As a boy, I would walk along the stream that led to Meryton, down to where two old willows arched across the water, their branches a leafy curtain that promised hidden wonders beyond. Stones littered the banks there, dark and flat. I would flip them over, never knowing what lay below: a disappointing canvas of mud or something bright and squirming to delight a young naturalist.

I felt a little of that boyhood anticipation on my way to meet with Jackson, the early hour dictated by his imminent departure on a short trip out of town.

A change in weather had thrown a white cloak over the hedgerows that lined the road and stolen the colour from the landscape beyond, shrouding the hills in a dull fog that whispered warnings of the coming winter. There were few people about, the townsfolk likely reluctant to face the early frost until the sun had dulled its bite.

After leaving the carriage, I kept my hands buried in my coat as I hurried to the Flighted Duck in search of my friend and something warming. And cake, perhaps—I was meeting Jackson, after all.

The inn was almost empty, but the smell of stale ale spoke of last night's patrons and the aroma of fresh stew spoke of visitors to come. I found my friend in an alcove half hidden by an oak column. Wisps of steam rose from the mug in front of him.

"This is quite the place for a secret assignation. If we are discovered, Jackson, our reputations may never recover." My friend snorted, then poured me some spiced wine. I sat, cupping the drink, letting the warmth seep through into my fingers. "So, tell all. What of the Hayters?"

He took a sip of wine, staring at me over the lip of his mug. "We are *friends*, are we not?"

"Must you even ask?"

He gave a little cough of apology. "There is a man I buy brandy from. Brandy that has not always passed through…all the proper channels."

"But it has passed through—or, rather, across—one channel in particular?" He nodded slowly. "Ah." I put a finger to my lips to reassure him of my silence, though he could not doubt my loyalty to an old comrade would exceed that to the exchequer.

"Fellow is in the wine business. Knows everyone. Has dealings with the Highcross people, too. Told me something of the family." He paused again to drink more deeply. "The widow's a bit of a handful. Something of a beast, it is said."

"A beast? Now there is a word used by men to cover a variety of sins. Perhaps she is truly a medusa. Or perhaps she merely has the temerity to express an opinion. Most likely she is simply adept at identifying unwelcome suitors for her daughter; a man spurned needs someone to blame for his own failure."

"If you say so, Bennet. Seems she is unlikely to give up her independence. The daughter has some of the mother's spirit. Shares her time between Bath and London."

"London for the season?"

"London for the books."

"Books?" The word pulled me up in my chair.

"Excessively fond of reading apparently. Spends November in London. Likely enough she is there now. Purchases books like Stanhope buys casks at a wine merchant. Then back to Bath with them. Before the roads become impossible. Reads her way through the winter."

"How unusual. Still, that is one thing in John's favour. There are two places in this blessed country where strangers may certainly converse without connection: one is a ballroom, the other a bookstore." It was my turn to taste the wine, hot and sweet.

"Bookstore seems more likely. My fellow says she is a rare visitor to any assemblies. Or to the Pump Room. She has the grace and conversation for both. But not the preference. Cannot say I like the sound of that."

"On the contrary, my dear friend, the more I learn of Miss Hayter, the more *I* warm to her. No doubt she has her reasons."

Keen to write to John without delay, I soon made my excuses after thanking Jackson for his trouble. "Two things, dear friend, before I leave. That brandy?"

Jackson's mouth curled up towards his ears. "I shall bring a bottle to the next meeting."

I nodded my thanks and turned to go.

"You said two things."

"Ah, yes." I leant down to rest my hands on the table. "Just out of curiosity, did your man say what Miss Hayter looked like?"

"I asked him that very question. Thought you might want to know."

"And?"

"He said he could not properly say if she was a beauty. But if he had the words to do justice to her smile, he would sell poetry, not port."

A welcome illness

My spirits rarely settled while autumn and winter tussled for supremacy. This seasonal unease was not helped by watching Lydia and Kitty's constant squabbles over ribbons, gloves, and other such trinkets of fashion. It was all a matter of principle, rather than need, like England and France fighting over a small and barren island. I found myself swinging like a pendulum between rich contentment and pernicious dissatisfaction.

The Society meeting provided welcome distraction, with Jackson proudly passing on his knowledge of Miss Hayter to the others.

"Will it help, do you think?" said Fielding.

"It is certainly more than we knew before. I imagine John will now abandon all thrift, rush to London, and waste many a day walking the streets outside the bookstores and circulating libraries." My comment provoked plenty of laughter, though my own was constrained. After all, I had once walked up and down Milsom Street in Bath some fifty times in the hope of just such an accidental meeting. My only reward had been a sixpence from a passing admiral, who assumed I suffered from some kind of mental affliction. He was not far wrong.

My friends, though, convinced themselves we had marked the trail to Miss Hayter and so played our role in forging a likely engagement. They forgot she was not a bird waiting to be flushed from some copse, shot and carried home in triumph. But I embraced their enthusiasm and the reassurance of their comradeship.

Fielding and I were, as almost always, the last to leave. He caught my arm as I made to go. "You know your friend still has little chance of success? We have discussed this."

"Of course. I would not even give his chances the privilege of being little, *but* it is still a hope. Who am I to take even that away from him? Life may do it for me soon enough. Until then, let this hope keep him warm in the chill of London."

"By all accounts from Jackson, she is a woman of intelligence. Even if they can become acquainted, he will have to earn her affection. And that of her family. Few of us have such luck, as you know." His eyes never left mine as he spoke.

"Fielding, you may pick at my scars all day long, but I will not talk about those times."

"I worry for my friend, for the hurt he still carries. That is all. I am unsure if your interest in Mr Barton is for his sake or for yours."

I began to lift myself off the seat.

He placed a hand on me again, the back still mottled from when he pulled me from a burning farmhouse. "I am sorry, I did not wish to pry. It is not my right."

I sank back in my chair and was silent for a few moments. "On the contrary, you have earned the right to speak to me as you will. Perhaps my interest in John Barton is for his sake *and* mine." His grip tightened on my arm. In the distance, I could hear Tincton scolding some kitchen maid. "Most days, it is all buried; I am taking your advice, allowing only happier memories to surface. We fought together, Fielding. Our survival is blessing enough for a lifetime. So I *am* at peace and grateful. But some days—"

"You wonder what might have been?"

"I wonder how different my life might be in a marriage built on more than just convenience."

~ ~ ~

A letter from John the next day contained little news of note, though my own news of Miss Hayter's love of books and London bookstores had naturally met with enthusiasm. His work at the estate was done, but he had no wish to attempt the arduous trip back to Vienna until the spring. As predicted, he wanted to spend the rest of November in London, though he claimed this was to "attend galleries and improve my mind and painting." He would have no time for art; London was full of bookstores and long streets. I resolved to write to our relations in the capital to see whether they might have some local knowledge that would aid my lovelorn friend.

I was musing on John's words, when Mrs Bennet flew into my study.

"Oh, Mr Bennet. It is as I hoped. Jane is grievously ill."

I stared at her a while, trying to reconcile her words with her excitement. "I know our five daughters can be considered burdensome at times, but should we really find pleasure at the prospect of losing one to a fever? Explain yourself, my dear."

"She fell ill while visiting Netherfield and now must stay until her health returns. I will not approve of a journey home until she is quite recovered."

"And when will that be?"

"I have not decided yet."

Before I could reply, Lizzy joined us, face flushed. "Mama? Papa? There is news of Jane? She is ill?"

"Quite ill, Lizzy, far too ill to think of coming home," said her mother.

Lizzy held a hand to her mouth, then began to untie her apron. "I must go immediately—"

"You may do what you like, dear Lizzy, but do not fret. My concern would be great, too, were your sister very unwell. However, I suspect the severity of her affliction is a political judgement and not a medical one. It suits your mother for Jane to stay longer at Netherfield. There she will remain until Mr Bingley falls sick, too…with love."

"Mama?"

My wife's self-satisfied look was enough to answer Lizzy's question.

"I cannot help but feel your mother has arranged all this herself. It is a shame government policy is to *defeat* Napoleon rather than *marry* him. If the latter, Mrs Bennet would assure us of victory."

~ ~ ~

Lizzy soon left to visit Jane and no doubt enliven the Netherfield conversation at the expense of ours.

I could not help but chuckle at the prospect of her bundled together with Mr Darcy and Bingley's sisters, with no polite means of escape for any of them. The skirmish of words would be worthy of a gladiatorial arena. Perhaps Mr Bingley would ask his cook to prepare baked dormice and a lark's tongue or two to accompany breakfast.

Lizzy was joined for one day by Mrs Bennet and the younger girls. They returned in the early evening, happy to leave Jane in the tender care of her sister and her future husband.

My wife's mood was both triumphant and distressed. Jane remained close to Mr Bingley, but also to Mr Darcy, who had attracted a special kind of opprobrium from Mrs Bennet ever sine he had slighted Lizzy at the Meryton dance.

"I was perfectly civil to the man," she said, removing her bonnet.

"Ah, the poor fellow. And Mr Darcy did not return this civility?" I knew the answer, but also that my dear wife would enjoy giving it.

"He did not! He spent most of the time with his back turned to us. It was most rude. I wish him the very worst for a wife, one who talks constantly and has no wit about her at all."

"Do not be too harsh, my dear. I would not wish such a fate on any other man."

Kitty now spoke up. "Mr Bingley is to hold a ball, Papa!"

"Is he? How wonderful."

This was naturally all that Kitty and Lydia could then care and talk about. The promise of dancing and young gentlemen left no room for concern for their sister's health.

"You are full of such nonsense," I said. "I would fear for your futures, but I daresay every parent finds fault in youth. Fathers in Rome likely sat with their wine, declaring that heads full of centurions and chariots would never amount to anything. Mind you, we all know what became of the Roman Empire."

"How can talk of balls be nonsense? You do say some strange things, Mr Bennet," said my wife.

"And are we to be invited to this great occasion?" It was the hope of a condemned man that there might be some unexpected reprieve.

"Of course we are." My wife tightened the hangman's noose. "Mr Bingley will want to dance with Jane and he cannot do so unless we are all invited."

"And who else is to join us at this occasion of joy?"

"The Lucases will be there. I am sure Lady Lucas has not yet given up hope for her Charlotte. She cannot see how plain she is. It would take a miracle for her to marry before one of our girls. All the local families. And the regiment of course. Oh Lydia, Kitty, there will be so many officers! You must look your best, for they will all want to dance with you! And I do hope we will see Mr Murden."

"You should take care, my dear. With so many officers, there may be one who takes a fancy to *you*. I should not like to have to duel for your honour."

My wife then handed over a note for me from Lizzy.

I read it quickly, smiling as I did so.

"Does she write of Mr Bingley?" said Mrs Bennet.

"Not of Mr Bingley, but from Mr Bingley." Our kind neighbour had made his promised enquiries and discovered the details of John's relatives in Yorkshire. I resolved to pass them on in my next letter. Jane's admirer seemed set to continually erode my natural reluctance to think well of a man. Yet much as I admired Mrs Bennet's Machiavellian navigation of the marital path, I feared Jane's hopes might eventually founder on the jagged rocks of his sisters' disapproval.

~ ~ ~

The next days were a burden without Lizzy and Jane. But they finally returned, bringing with them good sense and better conversation. It was safe to attend breakfast again. Jane looked most recovered, though I wondered whether the bloom in her cheeks was more to do with fond memories of a certain gentleman than with Mr Jones's medications.

I found Lizzy in the afternoon, tucked up in her favourite armchair in the library. She was deep in a book, her fingers playing with her hair just as she always did when a child.

"Did you have no time for books at Netherfield, Lizzy? I hear it has a grand library."

"I had the time, Papa, but not always the inclination." Her lips narrowed. "Miss Bingley professed a love of books, but she held them in such high regard that she dared not open them. Reading might also have distracted her from attempting to win the affections of Mr Darcy."

"And is she succeeding in that endeavour?"

"That depends on whether you ask Miss Bingley or Mr Darcy." She marked her place and closed the book. "She still has hope, but he can barely disguise his disgust."

"A man of taste, then, after all?" Her laughter at my quip brightened the room. "It is good to have you back, Lizzy." I rested my hand on her shoulder and felt the warmth of her cheek. "I worried you might suffer so. Your mother speaks very ill of Netherfield society and I would hate to have you even half as vexed as she is."

"Half as vexed as Mama would be very vexed indeed!"

"But do not let me disturb your reading. By the way, I have not yet told the others, but my cousin Mr Collins arrives tomorrow. If I am any judge of character, you may end up wishing for the company of Miss Bingley and Mr Darcy before the visit is over."

"If that is the case, then Mr Collins must be quite horrifying."

An unwelcome guest

My jesting with Lizzy proved more accurate than I believed possible.

Within minutes of his arrival, Mr Collins described himself as a tool of God. I could well believe it. The good Lord had clearly sent him to test our fortitude.

He had the distinction of being both fat and thin at the same time. Long, spindly legs supported a broad chest and a broader stomach, his eyes small, his head nodding continually in approval of almost everything, but particularly of his own opinions. The latter he gave freely on all subjects, whether praising the height of our door frames or extolling the virtues of the cabbage.

Unprepared to bear the burden of his conversation alone, I gave in to the darker side of my nature by inviting our guest to read to the girls.

"It would be my pleasure, Mr Bennet," he said, eyes glistening. "Perhaps I might choose a suitable tome from among your own magnificent collection of books?"

"Of course. I have many volumes of sermons I keep handy for just such an occasion."

"Wonderful, wonderful." He clapped his hands vigorously. It was not a sound I expected to hear very often that evening.

It took me a few minutes to find the mentioned volumes of sermons in the library.

I brushed away the dust and the fresh corpse of a spider who had lived under the strict morals of Anderson's *On the diversity of God's creation*. When pulled out of a forgotten corner, said book had, unfortunately, brought an abrupt end to the spider's enlightened existence. God's creation was a little less diverse than before.

One or two tomes smelled of freshly-turned soil, but I was sure Mr Collins would see past a little mustiness in the interest of bringing wisdom to the girls.

"Such a fine collection, Mr Bennet. It puts me in mind of—"

"The library at Rosings, perhaps?" The words tumbled from me before I could stop them. I had learnt many things of Mr Collins already. One was that the room or furniture had yet to be created that could not put him in mind of Rosings Park, the home of his beloved patron, Lady Catherine de Bourgh.

"Why, yes, you are perceptive indeed, sir. No doubt you have heard of the impressive nature of its clerical works?"

"Regrettably, no, but we should not discuss such things now. The girls will be waiting. We must not keep them from spiritual improvement."

He pressed a finger to his lips and I silently wished it might stay there. It did not. "*Diversity of Creation...Memoriae Ecclesiasticae... The Birds of the Welsh Marches.*" He looked up briefly. "Fordyce's *Sermons to Young Women!*" He waved the book in front of my face like a crusader brandishing the severed head of a heathen. "It will be most instructive for your daughters."

~ ~ ~

I felt the accusing stares of the girls even before Mr Collins had finished the first page. Fortunately for them, he made it no further than page three thanks to a most ill-mannered interruption by Lydia. I could not find the heart to chastise her.

~ ~ ~

Though I rose early, it was still not early enough to miss Mr Collins at breakfast. The coffee had barely touched my lips when Rosings was once more a topic of conversation. Apparently, one chimney piece had cost 800 pounds.

"800 pounds you say? That is quite a sum," I said, not knowing how best to react to such information.

"Indeed, sir, yet wisely invested. For it has produced a most elegant piece of architecture. As I told Lady Catherine herself, I have never seen smoke so cleverly and swiftly removed from a room."

"And this is but one of many fine examples, I presume?"

"One of very many. I do believe as many as…" He began counting on his fingers. "Yes, very many indeed, very many indeed."

I opened my newspaper, hopeful he might be too exhausted by his mathematical efforts to continue with conversation.

"And the fireplaces themselves. Such a size. I could not begin to describe their magnificence." Unfortunately, he then spent a good many minutes contradicting this very statement.

"I am curious as to their dimensions, Mr Collins. Would one be wide enough to fit a man inside?"

"Without a doubt, my dear Mr Bennet. Certainly the fireplace in the main drawing room. Though I cannot imagine a circumstance where that would be required."

"I can think of at least one." A glare from Lizzy persuaded me to change the topic of conversation. The girls had joined us and it gave me a rather splendid idea. "Mr Collins, is it not the duty of a clergyman to apply his wisdom and pastoral care to as many people as possible?"

"Indeed, as Lady Catherine often—"

"I wonder, then, if you might like to walk into Meryton with the girls?" To her credit, Kitty managed to conceal her cry of despair with some timely coughing. "The good folk of Meryton should not be left in ignorance just so I might have your company all day." I had not lived among a household of women without mastering a little of the dark arts of manipulation, even if it earned me another reproachful look from Lizzy.

"My good Mr Bennet, your selflessness does you much credit…much credit. It is also the wish of Lady Catherine that I should share words of comfort and conversation with as many people as possible. I would be remiss if I were not to travel to Meryton. Such elegant company will make the duty all the more pleasant." At this, he seemed to glance meaningfully toward the girls. Perhaps he thought some shared understanding had passed between us.

"The girls will not be happy, Mr Bennet," whispered my wife as we watched them all leave.

"Given a choice between my children's resentment and a day of Mr Collins, I will always favour daughterly damnation. It was fortunate for Job he never faced an obsequious clergyman with such an extraordinary affection for vegetables."

After returning, and despite the lateness of the hour, Mr Collins managed to find time to divulge further details of four more of Rosings' fireplaces. It would have been five had I not persuaded him to sample the Madmaidens. I left him sound asleep in an armchair.

In search of refuge

Another day of Mr Collins proved too much. I was in grave danger of inserting all three volumes of Goedart's *Metamorphosis Naturalis* up his most humble nether regions. All it would take is one more mention of the affability and condescension of Lady Catherine de Bourgh. Respect for Mr Collins's personal safety and my peace of mind forced me to flee to London. I claimed urgent business, intending to return in time for the next Society meeting and the ball at Netherfield. My decision also opened the possibility of meeting John and helping him search for Miss Hayter.

I could never become used to the cacophony that seeped through the walls of the coach whenever I entered England's greatest city. My ears and nose alerted me to shops, stalls, and stables, not to mention the people, rushing around like ants on a midden heap. I was exhausted on arrival, with bruises to tell a tale of every stray cobblestone between Meryton and Cheapside.

Gracious as ever, Mr Gardiner did not hesitate to extend the hand of hospitality on the unexpected arrival of his brother-in-law. Their townhouse was a keep whose stone walls refused to be breached by the clamour and chaos outside. It became even quieter once the children had retreated upstairs like crows departing to roost.

"You look tired. Is it only the journey?" said my host after dinner. Mrs Gardiner had left us, busy as she was planning a family trip to the north. I thought of joining them on it, of exchanging the shades of Longbourn for the shale of Derbyshire.

"I am recovering from a difficult house guest. My cousin, Mr Collins. He turns all conversation into a reminder of the inestimable qualities of his patron and the glory and grandeur of that great lady's residence. Not to mention her propensity to dispense advice on household matters and furniture. Were she not already one of the richest ladies in England, she might make her fortune as a carpenter. The only pleasure gained from his visit is to soundly thrash him at backgammon."

"And Mr Collins is all that troubles you?"

"Not all, no. But what father is never troubled, my dear brother? My ill humour will soon pass, once there are fewer daughters and one less Collins at home."

"You sound like a man in need of more wine." He reached for a bottle and two fresh glasses.

"You are wise and perceptive, Gardiner." After accepting a glass, I waved a solicitous finger at him. "You will remember my words when your children are of an age to marry and the talk is all of balls, bonnets, and young men."

"How *are* my nieces? Mrs Gardiner looks forward to seeing them at Christmas. She can swap the company of one husband for that of six ladies. It is a decent exchange."

"That it is. My daughters are well and not lacking in

entertainment. We have the presence of the militia to thank for that."

He filled our glasses, then settled back into his chair. "Tell me, do you have plans for your stay? I am pleased to share my wine with you, but my time flows less freely. Business has first call on me tomorrow, but perhaps we might take supper together?"

"You need make no provision for me. The note I received before dinner was from my friend, Mr John Barton. I should like to spend tomorrow with him."

"Ah, the fellow you mentioned? I remember him as a boy. A little clumsy with words, but he had a real talent for drawing. We have his sketch of Mrs Gardiner somewhere. A remarkable likeness. To think he could not have been more than, what, eleven?"

I had forgotten the Gardiners knew the Bartons from previous visits to Longbourn. "He paints now. Very well, too, though he will not admit it. He is quite the artist."

"Since you mention him, I have been remiss in not replying to your letter concerning his interests in a certain family. Though now I can at least save myself the cost of paper and you the cost of postage."

"You have news?" I leant forward in my chair.

"A little. Twenty years of purchasing gifts for you and your ladies has left me well acquainted with many grateful booksellers. It took some delicacy—I cannot expect tradesmen to be so free with information. I would be disappointed if they were."

"And?"

"It seems the Hayter family is not unknown among London's book community. They are partial to the Temple and other establishments around Finsbury Square, particularly your favourite." Brecknell's was, indeed, my Aladdin's cave.

"Might they be in London now?"

"That I could not say."

"Well, my thanks for your efforts. The information is most helpful."

Mr Gardiner nodded. "If you will allow me a question, brother?"

"Of course."

"You spoke so well of Mr Barton in your letter. Would he not make a suitable partner for Jane or Lizzy?"

"He would. A more than suitable partner." I took a sip of Mr Gardiner's fine red. "But his interest lies elsewhere and he has placed me in his trust. And where there is trust, there is obligation."

"He is accounted for, then? His prospects of an understanding are reasonable?"

I shook my head. "His *interest* is accounted for, but his prospects are imperfect, his position impossible, and his plans impractical. His rivals have society on their side; he has merely hope, without even reciprocated interest to let that bloom for long."

Mr Gardiner's face combined a frown with puzzlement. "If the lady does not find affection for him, then he had best give up this hope, lest he suffer like others have done." A memory flared again, though I knew he could not have meant me.

"The lady has not yet even met him. The question of her affection is one we now seek to answer by arranging an encounter." Mr Gardiner's expression reminded me of the foolishness of John's situation and my willing participation in prolonging it. "It does seem a little absurd when I hear myself speak of it. But young men will be fools in love. And I am fond of the boy."

"And am I right to suppose that the lady in question belongs to the Hayter family? That the interest you wrote of is amorous in nature?" He sat back at my nod of acknowledgement. "Well, then you must throw the dice tomorrow and win fortune's favour. We will send a servant with a note to Mr Barton suggesting a rendezvous outside Brecknell's. And if I can be of any other service, I will be glad to help. An old school friend of mine has a house in Bath and dines with me shortly. I will write should I learn anything more of interest about the family."

"You are a kind brother to us, and a generous one." I raised my glass to my host. "Though I fear what John needs is neither kindness nor generosity, but a miracle."

Decisions

Breakfast was glorious, all the more so because it reminded nobody of any repasts at Rosings Park. Afterwards, I took the ten-minute stroll up Bishopsgate and then west to Finsbury Square. The smoke of the chimneys slid quickly to the east, but the buildings kept the worst of the wind off. I was tightly wrapped in my greatcoat anyway, and warmed by anticipation of fresh delights from the capital's printing presses.

Around the corner and there it was: Brecknell's Book Merchants, purveyors of the finest volumes of education and enlightenment this side of the English Channel. John stood outside, as arranged. His boots shone with the gleam of fresh leather and a new coat hung a little loosely on his frame. Land for clothes—a bitter exchange.

"I don't suppose…" I said.

He shook his head. "Already looked inside." After a brief pause, we both laughed at our own ridiculousness. "I have spent more time in bookstores this month than in my own bed. I bought or borrowed enough poetry to woo half the ladies of Bath and never repeat myself." He must have sensed my confusion.

"Slim volumes are cheap and the payment rids me of the guilt I feel at spending so much time browsing."

"Well, let us walk, John, and see whether we might find your Miss Hayter among the other booksellers." He did not move. "John?"

"I will gladly walk with you, but it will be my last turn of the card. I leave for Yorkshire this very afternoon."

"But what about—"

"Mr Bennet," he said, straightening himself. "I do not believe myself a fool, but I have allowed myself to act foolishly. What kind of man walks the same streets again and again in the hope of a chance meeting?" A mild blush squeezed its way onto my cheeks. "You see, even you are embarrassed for me. And what if such an encounter took place? Supposing we could converse in some bookstore. I would mumble some bland comment. She would reply in kind and move on, as ignorant of me as before. I am driven to distraction by a notion. An absurd notion. It is time to replace the dream of a painter with the reason of an heir to a poor estate."

I felt strangely disappointed, as if an actor had forgotten his lines and broken the theatre's spell. "But—"

"I have made my decision."

I stared at him for a short while, his arms folded, face set in apparent determination. "Then you have lied to me or to yourself, John. Neither does you honour."

"Sir?" He seemed taken aback, but I was not minded to spare him a little vexation after all the hours I had spent weighing up the wisdom of my intervention in his affairs.

"You made your feelings for Miss Hayter very clear back in

Longbourn. Did you paint a false picture for me, or was your affection nothing more than a passing fancy, a false interpretation of your heart?"

"It was neither, I assure you."

"Then how am I to understand your decision?"

"I am merely seeing my situation for what it is—untenable, silly, foolish. You must agree."

"Untenable? Probably. Silly? Undoubtedly. Foolish? Quite possibly. And what of it?" My raised voice attracted a few stares, but a little of the lunacy of my youth had taken hold. "Of course you have nothing but a wild hope. Of course you will likely be disappointed. But the pain of disappointment is no worse than that of *regret*. The pain of rejection, of failure, is strong. But no more than the pain of wondering what might have happened had you only tried. You may give up eventually, but not so early and not so easily. Do not abandon hope, however foolish it may be. At least not yet. Why, she may be waiting for you in the very next bookstore."

"We both know that is highly unlikely."

"John, I know the pain of rejection *and* the pain of regret. Do not imagine the former greater than the latter."

He was silent.

"Well?" I said.

"I thank you, but my mind is made up. I leave for Yorkshire in a few hours."

I turned away from him to see a street more crowded than at a Meryton summer market. A couple passed us arm-in-arm, heads close together, lost in their own conversation. "Very well. To your relatives, I presume?" It was hard to keep the chill from my voice.

"Eventually. My finances will demand it. They will be surprised to hear from me, but the climate and countryside there will bring me further to reason. Come spring, I will endeavour to reach Austria, though the French do not make such an undertaking easy."

"Will you not visit Longbourn, then?"

He had the decency to look embarrassed. "Please allow me to delay that visit. I ask for your forgiveness and understanding. You cannot imagine how many hours I have wasted wandering our estate, possessed by thoughts of Bath. I made a small studio out of one of our rooms and it is filled with nothing but portraits of Miss Hayter and imaginative landscapes where eagles soar above sunlit meadows. I even carved her face into an old beech tree deep within the woods behind the western gate, where hopefully nobody can see it and suspect my madness. It is enough. I must put distance between myself and the foolishness of the past few weeks."

"That may be so, but your own father proves that distance does not allow escape. I do not believe your affection for Miss Hayter is so shallow that it can be swiftly forgotten. And as for forgiveness and understanding...I can offer the first, but not the second. You allow feelings to overcome sense."

"On the contrary, I allow sense to overcome feelings."

"If you had any *sense*, John, you would have saved your money for Bath, as I once recommended."

"But she was not *in* Bath."

"Not now, but later...oh, I suppose I should not blame you for rushed decisions. Men in love are not renowned for their acts of rationality. But, my dear boy, you know you have many in

Hertfordshire who wish you well. Spend time with us, allow the ladies of Longbourn to improve your spirits."

"I am sorry, but I cannot. Yet I would not part from you on poor terms. Your kindness has been very great indeed. I must prevail on it once more in asking you to accept my decision."

"I will accept it, but not particularly *like* it." I took his outstretched hand. "Well, it seems today is not to be as merry as I had expected. Still, let us not waste it on arguments. Or on bookstores. I know an excellent inn. It is quite a walk away, but near your lodgings and worth the effort for the quality of their roast fowl. At least allow me to send you off to the north with a full stomach. And you will make me a promise you *must* keep— that you will write to us once you settle."

And so it ended. "Much Ado About Nothing," as Shakespeare might have said.

A familiar scent

I knew John was right, yet his decision still left a gnawing disappointment within me. After we parted, I retraced our steps with a mind to buy my daughters some more leather-bound gifts.

Brecknell's was not like its neighbours, with their tidy shelves and open spaces. Inside was a forest of books, thick stumps of scientific tomes, tall stems of poetry, and religious pamphlets scattered about the tables like autumn leaves.

Scampering between them was Mr Brecknell, pot-bellied and balding, with spectacles perched on a thin nose. I often wondered whether he was not some cold Prussian aristocrat. Neither his voice nor demeanour ever gave a hint of pleasure, whatever the words he might use. He was alone in his store, but for a middle-aged lady half-buried under a preposterous hat.

"Mr Bennet, welcome. So soon after your last visit, too. May I recommend new volumes from Prowse, Wilshire, and Dunston? In the usual place."

The gifts would have to wait. I nodded my thanks before hurrying to the rear, where the musty scents of wood and leather were at their strongest.

The prospect of Wilshire's new volume on butterflies sent my distress at John's plans fluttering away into the rafters. I pulled it from the shelf like an explorer prising loose a gemstone from some ancient tomb.

"James Bennet? It is you, is it not?" A metaphorical musket ball struck home, driving all breath from my body, leaving me unable to move. "I recall you a little livelier than this, last time we spoke. And a little younger."

With some effort, I lifted my head from my book to look at her. I imagined lustrous black where flecks of silver now prevailed, smoothed the lines around the eyes, followed the curve of a cheek down to lips I had only kissed in my desperate imagination. She still had that single freckle on her chin. The blemish made her perfection more human, less divine.

"James? Can you hear me?" the voice said.

"Abigail…Miss Abigail Spencer…Mrs Abigail Trott."

The words fell like a heavy weight, dragging my stomach with them. Even then, I recalled my manners, as any good Englishman would, and bowed.

"You remember me. How delightful."

A second lady came around the bookcase, head half hidden behind an open book. With her came salvation and, ironically, the scent of lavender. There had been a sister—Emily? Amelia? I focused on her, anything to divert my eyes from Abigail.

"Ah, there you are, my dear. I was just renewing an old friendship. Mr Bennet and I knew each other many years ago in Bath, long before I married your father. James, may I introduce my daughter, Miss Anne Hayter?"

I steadied myself on a bookcase. "Hayter?"

"My second husband. You did not know?"

We stood in silence, Abigail wearing an amused smile, Miss Hayter expressionless, and myself paralysed by a mixture of terror and delight.

"Are you well, James? Or perhaps just a little surprised?"

"Very well, very well. And yourself? Good, I hope." My gaze latched onto a familiar object. "My apologies, Miss Hayter…but your book." She held it up. As I suspected, Smythe's *On the Path of Marco Polo.* "I would not read any further."

"No?"

"Mr Smythe never got beyond the London docks. Made the whole thing up." I dabbed at my forehead with a sleeve, still feeling like a soldier on his first view of the battlefield—fascinated, horrified, struggling to stay sensible. My gaze shifted from daughter to mother and back again. Then the clouds broke above Brecknell's, pouring afternoon light through the back window. And I understood, finally, what John had meant that day back in Hertfordshire.

Miss Hayter was not a ballroom beauty, pressed and pinned into shape with corsets, bright gowns and brighter jewellery. But she looked easy to love. A figure from a Greek myth. Andromeda. Ariadne. Anne. And then there were her eyes. Teasing, almost judging, drawing me in like open skies call the lark's song. They were not new to me, for they were just like her mother's. Azure blue.

I floundered like a man determined to deny the existence of ghosts even as one stood before him. But when a man finds himself struggling in a flood of remembrance and confusion, he grasps at any passing branch. Mine was John Barton and the task in hand.

"Miss Hayter, my daughter Elizabeth enjoys books on travel, too. She talks often of Mr Pullar and Mr Strecker's volumes on Vienna. Perhaps they might be of interest to you? I believe the authors have actually spent time in that city."

"I *love* tales of Vienna—it is on my list of places to visit as soon as the war allows." My heart would have skipped the required beat had it not been pumping so furiously.

"I *am* pleased. Now, what else can I recommend to you? Are you, perhaps, interested in art…in painting?" I tried to keep hope out of my voice.

"Oh, I have no interest in that at all, Mr Bennet. Nor in painters. They are all much too vain for my taste."

I swallowed hard. "A high self-regard and talent with a brush are often intertwined, but it is not always so, Miss Hayter. I know many a modest artist who paints out of joy for what he sees, simply wishing to capture beauty for later admiration. And Brecknell's does offer some excellent books on the topic, as you likely know. The very best of society can be found browsing the art section."

"And yet here you are, Mr Bennet, in natural history." Her quick mind reminded me of Elizabeth.

"You must permit a country gentleman varied interests," I said.

"Like butterflies?" She pointed at the book in my hand. "They are wonderful creatures. So delicate. It is a shame some gentlemen seek to pin them down in boxes, don't you think? Things of beauty should be left free, not chased and captured for a man's amusement."

"Ah."

"My favourite bookstore in Bath has a number of excellent volumes on butterflies. Should you ever be in town, Mr Tavistock takes delivery from his London suppliers on Fridays. It is the best day to visit."

"I shall remember your advice, thank you."

All this time, Abigail had been watching me with a wry smile. Now she spoke. "Anne, we must leave if we are to join Aunt Emily as arranged. It is our last chance before we return home. James…" Her voice faded and seemed to soften as we held each other's gaze. "It was a pleasure after so long."

And so they departed, leaving behind a hint in the air of summer days and purple blooms. I rushed to John's lodgings, cursing the timing of his departure, but he had already left.

Objections and resolutions

I told the driver to take his time and spare my flesh and bones the worst of the ride back to Longbourn. Perhaps it was my imagination, but the fragrance of lavender seemed still to cling to my clothes. And as the shadows lengthened and the view outside the carriage dwindled into darkness, the steady drumming of hooves lulled me into further introspection.

Fielding's words came back to me as we left London. "*Perhaps one of us also regrets his own choices and would see another man joined with the lady he truly loves, to have the pleasure once denied him.*"

Then the memories returned in full. Sitting in a coach to Bath, nervous but determined, rehearsing the question every man hopes to one day ask, repeating it again and again in my mind. Then hearing her name spoken out loud. *"Have you heard? Miss Abigail Spencer. She is newly engaged to a local gentleman of wealth and standing."*

It was not my choice I regretted, but *hers*.

I carried the loss like a stone around my neck, never finding much goodness in the world, often disappointed with a life that could never compete with what might have been. I had still admired, even loved, but the recipients of this admiration or love were few and far between. Lizzy, Jane, Fielding, one or two others. And now also John in all his youthful innocence.

It was hard to cast off this world-weary mantle, sewn on that journey to Bath and worn for so many years. But, as Longbourn neared, I finally accepted my mistakes, my selfishness, my frustration. And I chose to believe I might find solace and, perhaps, some redemption in the happiness of another. As my carriage finally reached home, I determined to see how I might move beyond obligation and sincerely help my young friend find the joy once denied me.

Miss Hayter was clearly worth the gamble, even if we had a poor hand. And if John's affection proved ephemeral or hers illusive, well, at least I would have tried. My first task was to engage again the help of my friends and then write to John with suggestions as to how he might proceed. The thought of his surprise at the news of my bookstore encounter brought an unapologetic grin to my face. It does a young man good to learn that his elders are not always fools.

This newfound resolve I attributed to one moment: when the Hayters—mother and daughter—both stopped just before the door out to Finsbury Square, turned back to me, and lit up Brecknell's with the same smile. One reminded me of what I had lost, the other of what I would not let John lose.

~ ~ ~

Those smiles seemed all too far away the next day. I knew not which was darker, the cloud overhead or my mood in the carriage as I rode to Meryton. We rocked from side to side, beaten by wind and rain such that conversation was barely possible. Which was some kind of blessing, since Mr Collins accompanied me on my journey.

It seemed Mrs Bennet had alerted him to my pending visit to the Society and assured him I would be *delighted* to have him join me. Swift revenge for my London absence.

Introducing the ignominious Mr Collins to good friends risked the possibility of their no longer being so. Nor could I now discuss John with them; the situation would quickly become unbearable if news of it were to reach the ears of my wife.

The warmth of the inn was all the more welcoming for the poor weather. The crackle of a hearty fire and the clink of plates filled with cake and pastries helped drown out the pelt of raindrops on the window.

We were the last to arrive, delayed by Mr Collins's unerring ability to mislay his hat which, showing admirable judgement, seemed reluctant to stay on his head. I made the necessary introductions, with Mr Collins bowing deeper and deeper at each new name, until I feared he would bang his head on the floor.

"The natural world is most dear to me. My garden at Hunsford is a source of considerable pleasure, small though it is, and dwarfed in both size and magnificence by the extensive gardens of my neighbour. Mr Bennet has perhaps not informed you, but I am lucky enough to enjoy the patronage of Lady Catherine de Bourgh." Mr Collins paused, clearly waiting for a reaction.

Fielding was aware enough to murmur his appreciation of

such a good position, but then there was a bemused silence.

"De Bourgh? Of Rosings Park?" Jackson put an end to the embarrassment.

"Indeed." My guest stood like a child before an unopened gift. "Are you, sir, familiar with that great estate and that most elegant and condescending of ladies?"

"Visited with my uncle. Was only a young lad. Lots of paths and forest walks and such. Remember throwing stones at the parsonage. Awful little building. Got chased away by the parson."

Mr Collins's smile trembled a little at the edge. I intervened before it could collapse entirely. "Well, gentlemen, let us proceed with the meeting, shall we?"

There was little for us to discuss. Plans to invite a Mr Hayward to give a talk on potatoes, and a brief review of the accounts.

Then we came to "other business", which of late meant "Barton business." I held my breath.

"Any news on John Barton, Bennet? Is he of good spirits?" I would normally have welcomed Jackson's questions, but not on this occasion.

"Oh, my dear Mr Bennet," said Mr Collins, turning to me and clasping his hands. "Is someone in need of help? I would be most happy to offer spiritual guidance in any way possible. It is my duty to offer succour to those less fortunate than myself, of which there are many."

"You might pray for divine intervention, Mr Collins," said Stanhope, "Mr Barton has fallen for a lady, but a lack of prospects means, well…"

"Objections from the lady's family?" said Mr Collins.

"That is for Mr Bennet to say," said Stanhope, looking at me with a hint of embarrassment.

"There is nothing further to be discussed on *that* subject." I folded my arms.

"Very wise, Mr Bennet, very wise indeed." Mr Collins's head bobbed up and down as he spoke. "An excellent decision."

To ensure my guest learnt nothing more, I took advantage of the Hertfordshire weather. "Gentlemen, look out the window. The weather worsens and we must all find our way home while there is still light enough to do so safely. Let us end our happy gathering early."

John would have to wait.

Balls and other trials

"Mr Collins!" Lizzy's tone was somewhere between admonishment and desperation. Beside her, our guest twisted like a kite in a tempest.

"The joy of our heart is ceased; our dance is turned into mourning." Mr Murden appeared at my shoulder in smart regimental attire, looking across to where Mr Collins struggled to master his feet.

"Lamentations 5:15," I said. "You surprise me, Mr Murden. I did not believe you a religious man."

"I have prayed to God enough times, like any soldier. Mr Collins is very attentive to Miss Elizabeth tonight."

"You are an observer, as well as a soldier, Mr Murden? Let us walk a while together. Perhaps we might observe the spectacle that is the Netherfield ball, and you can tell me what you see?"

"A test, Mr Bennet?" A hint of a smile formed across his face. "You wish, perhaps, to use my observations to make your own as to my character. I can well understand it; officers are a disreputable lot."

"If that were so, then you will surely make those observations that give the best impression of that character."

"And so we are at an impasse."

Mr Bingley had transformed Netherfield into a fairy tale for the ball. Coloured foliage twisted through its staircases, over doorways and across ceilings, silk flowers adding bursts of colour to the autumnal reds and greens. Hundreds of candles lit bright paths through the interior, drawing us around tables heaving with sweet delights, past ladies encased in glowing jewels that caught the light and begged for attention.

We stopped before a room filled with guests at leisure. The dancers sat with their chairs pulled back from the tables, legs extended and drinks in hand. The others sat in clusters, heads bobbing forward and back with the tide of conversation. Raised fans hid whispered insults, and the chink of glasses masked the passage of gossip.

Mr Murden viewed the scene before him as if surveying the terrain before battle. Or perhaps he searched for bodies with the greatest promise of loot.

He turned to me. "I see many fine folk of Meryton enjoying the generosity of a charming host."

"Most diplomatic, Mr Murden."

"If you will excuse me, Mr Bennet, one of your daughters promised me the next dance and I must away before she gives her affections to a less deserving officer."

"Lydia or Kitty, I presume?"

"Miss Jane Bennet. Mr Bingley is as generous with his time as he is with his food and drink. He must dance with many a guest tonight. I hate to think of your daughter left unattended while he sees to his duties."

"I thank you, sir," was all I could manage as he departed. I hoped my wife was otherwise engaged. She did not take kindly to anyone dancing with Jane who was not old, ugly, or Mr Bingley.

Mr Murden and Jane were not the only unexpected couple that evening. It seemed someone shamed Mr Darcy and Lizzy into dancing. I could not imagine either would have volunteered for the task and the dance seemed to delight neither of them. Even at a distance I could see Lizzy haughty with aggression; it must have tried her patience to keep the conversation pleasant.

After they finished, I was about to ask her what they talked about when Mary took it upon herself to sing at the piano. Her performance was industrious, but hardly suited to the Netherfield stage. She would have continued had I not intervened, even though several ladies stood near her, waiting their turn to impress the crowd. Lizzy seemed to think I had committed some grievous sin by interrupting her sister's singing. If so, then I sacrificed my honour for the good of all present. I spared their ears. In return, perhaps they could spare my reputation.

~ ~ ~

At the breakfast table next day, the Netherfield punch took revenge for its mistreatment by Mrs Bennet. Happily lacking in conversation, she sat with a pale face and a paler liquid, poured from a suspiciously small bottle. She clearly hoped the mixture might reverse the damage of the night before. It did not, so she banished it to the shelf of nerve tonics in the parlour, the ones that reduced my wealth but, sadly, not the afflictions they claimed to assuage.

"I see Mr Murden stood up with you, Jane?" Kitty's head whipped round at my question. "Is his dancing as careful as his conversation?"

"He was a considerate partner, very polite, but he saved his enthusiasm for others." Her eyes flicked briefly at Kitty.

"Did he pay you much attention, Kitty? I would hardly think him your sort of man, what with his scar." Nor did she strike me as his kind of woman.

"His scar is quite dashing. And he tells such wonderful stories." She rested her head on her hands and stared into the distance.

"I am sure he does. Some of them may even be true. Well, if we are to hear reports from each of the girls—Lydia, do tell us who you danced with."

Lydia looked up and yawned deeply. "I danced with every officer, at least all the ones worth dancing with. Including Mr Murden." She stuck her tongue out at Kitty. "Though I was disappointed Wickham was not there."

"Wickham?" I said.

"An officer whose acquaintance we made just the other day, Papa," said Jane.

"Another one? There are so many. Now, what about you, Lizzy. I saw you stand up with Mr Darcy. Could it be you have revised your opinion of the man?"

Lizzy continued buttering a roll. "Not at all. I was simply being polite. I would hardly dance with him out of choice." She shuddered and stuffed a piece of bread into her mouth.

I returned my attention to my plate, adding another slice of ham and an apple, not yet wrinkled by the passage of winter.

"Does nobody want to know who *I* danced with?" said Mary.

We all looked at each other. "Of course," I said. "Which officers were kind enough to stand up with you?"

Mary's back stiffened and she held her hands tightly on her lap. "I did not dance with *any* officers. They are brutish. I did, however, dance with Mr Spigott."

"My dear Mary," I said. "Did I notice a coquettish turn of the head as you spoke? How astonishing. Tell me, did Mr Spigott regale you with stories as well?"

"Only parables, but they are the very best sort of stories. He dances better than Mr Toke."

"Mary! You surprise us all," I said. "With practice, you may become as silly as your younger sisters."

"I find Mr Spigott improves with acquaintance, Papa."

"How fortunate. The alternative does not bear thinking about. See, my dear, there is hope for all the girls. It will soon be just the two of us here in Longbourn. Now there's a thought, eh? What say you?"

The silence was marred only by the soft groans emanating from Mrs Bennet's end of the table.

~ ~ ~

The following day began ominously. The rain got in and ruined my copy of the *Chronicle*. Then Peggy took ill and Froggat spent all morning nursing her. Presumably it was something she ate, since our pig would eat anything and everything. The time she got hold of some rum cake was still a fresh memory for us all. We pursued her across the meadows all the way to Meryton, where she put a small gathering of officers to flight. Discretion appeared to be the better part of *their* valour when confronted with two hundred pounds of drunk sow.

Then Mr Collins proposed to Lizzy.

I was not privileged to hear the exact words he used, but he likely managed to mention the name of his patron and express his affection in as insulting a manner as possible. Lizzy turned him down, of course.

Such a marriage would have solved many problems. But Mr Collins as a son-in-law? I would rather have dined with Peggy, who at least would be silent on the topic of Lady Catherine and fireplaces.

Naturally, Mrs Bennet saw the proposal differently. Once I refused to intercede on Mr Collins's behalf, I knew the future would soon contain the words "my nerves" and "vexing." The study seemed the best place to retreat to.

Lizzy found me there, hunched over my desk, gripping a pinned dragonfly. She rested her hands on my shoulders and leant down to whisper, "Thank you."

I stared up at her, all deep brown eyes and high cheekbones. She had much of Mrs Bennet in her looks, but, fortunately, less in her character. "Today has not been an easy one for us all, especially your mother."

"And you seek refuge from her anger in your collections?"

"Some men flee their cares through drink or a mistress, but for me there is nothing better than sending colours cascading across a set of wings as they turn in the sunlight. Insects interest me far more than any loosed cork or looser woman. Also, your mother does not like the smell in here."

Lizzy nodded and then moved to leave. Before she reached

the door, she turned. "May I ask why you said no?"

"I could not imagine you having to listen to descriptions of fireplaces every night for the rest of your life."

She smiled, waiting for more.

"My dear, there are so many rational reasons why a match with Mr Collins would be advantageous and I will not question your sensibility by listing them." My new resolve, forged in the fire of the Hayters' smiles in London, pulled more words from me, though I hesitated before continuing, glancing at the wings of the dragonfly in my hand. "I have seen what it is to live with someone you neither love nor respect. I wish such a fate for none, least of all a favourite daughter. Some say that love can grow with time. Respect, too. This may be so, but not between two people so unequal in intelligence and character as you and Mr Collins."

"I could not learn to love Mr Collins." It was half a question.

"Love needs a foundation to prosper, good soil to plant its roots. Mr Collins is rock and sand—love will never grow there, excepting his own love for himself."

"Does a marriage need love to succeed?"

"No, but a marriage without love cannot bring true happiness. And I would wish such happiness for you, Lizzy. Your mother is fond of saying that Jane's beauty cannot be for nothing. I believe the same of your intelligence. It will find its reward, though it will take a special kind of man, of that I have no doubt. Mr Collins is certainly special, but not in *that* way." I returned her smile. "And there, now you have witnessed my romantic side. Let us not talk of it again. I have a reputation to keep and it will do no good to expose myself so."

She nodded and left, passing her mother on the way out. The

two did not acknowledge each other. I sat back in my chair and took a deep breath.

Mrs Bennet's head shook from side to side, her hands clasped in supplication. There was no anger in her face, though I suspected it was in her heart. "Oh, Mr Bennet!"

Seeing my silence, she continued: "It is so very cruel! We shall all be thrown on the generosity of my brother before you are cold in your grave. Why can you not accept Mr Collins's offer?"

"I cannot have Lizzy marry Mr Collins. The happiness of others, however great, could not compensate for the misery that would bring her. That is all. Besides, my dear, I am convinced your good efforts will soon bear fruit. Mr Bingley is sure to make an offer, and both Kitty and Mary look to have admirers. You may be rescued from the gutter yet, should I die soon."

"Mr Bingley, indeed." Her forced laugh seemed to echo around the room. "Mr Bingley has gone to London and is not expected back. You will get no help from Mr Bingley!"

~ ~ ~

The misgivings of Mrs Bennet on the inconstancy of men dominated the evening conversation. She spared nobody. Even John was accused of unfaithfulness. "He has not visited. And he promised to paint Kitty and all the girls. But what are promises to men? They hand them out like ribbons at a fair. But do they keep them? It is most vexing."

Jane remained in good spirits. If she had been stranded Crusoe-like on an island, she would have blessed the shipwreck that sent her to such a delightful beach.

Lizzy blamed Mr Bingley's sisters and I was inclined to agree.

My initial impressions of both were not felicitous, but it seemed they had enough sense not to wish their brother burdened with an inappropriate match. "I do not rue the loss of *their* company," I told Lizzy. "But Mr Bingley I *will* miss."

It is a truth universally acknowledged that a married man in possession of a single daughter must be in want of a brandy. That night, with five such offspring, I felt the need for a whole bottle.

~ ~ ~

Mr Collins's departure not two days later ensured some kind of peace once again found a resting place at Longbourn. Only his promise to visit again tempered my relief. There was some more unpleasantness, though, when Sir William called to announce the engagement of our former guest to his eldest daughter. It was fair to say Mrs Bennet was vexed, both by the loss of Mr Collins as a suitor, and by the gain of Charlotte as the future mistress of Longbourn.

I did not wish Mr Collins for Lizzy, but then I did not wish him for anyone. Except, perhaps, as an ideal match for Mr Bingley's unmarried sister. It would have been a fine combination of arrogance and obsequiousness that would know no equal. Charlotte had always been a true friend to Lizzy, with a most sensible disposition. Perhaps too sensible. I was both sad and happy for the girl.

Sir William made no secret of *his* happiness. To his inestimable credit, the disbelief his announcement caused among the girls did not appear to give offence.

"I hope the girls did not disgrace themselves too much, Sir William. They are young and romantic, and have not seen enough of the world to properly understand it. You will forgive the surprise and wonder in their response to your news?"

"Why, of course, there is nothing to forgive. Nothing at all!" Sir William shifted in his chair. Outside my library we could still hear excited chatter punctuated by shrill cries.

"Mr Bennet," he continued, pausing to take a sip of port, then returning the glass to the table slowly. "I know Mr Collins is a strange kind of fellow. But a man would have to be a mighty fool not to give him his blessing. He has so much to offer a wife. A good home." He looked away, and his voice dropped a little. "Capital prospects."

Turning back to face me, he continued. "We are friends, Bennet. I know you must feel disappointment that Miss Elizabeth did not accept Mr Collins's offer. And I know that as a good and sensible father you will have tried to persuade her otherwise." I forced a smile. "But I feel sure you will soon share in equal happiness. There is Mr Bingley, for example." The smile fought briefly with my feelings, but managed to maintain a steady presence on my face. "And I understand Mr Murden shows much interest in Miss Catherine. Why, the church bells will barely stop ringing!"

War and peace

We celebrated Mr Collins's absence quietly, like the few survivors of an abandoned siege. His timely departure, combined with Lydia's regular absences at Colonel Forster's, meant December began peacefully enough.

I woke one morning to find the windows painted in ice and the gardens sculpted in crystal. Early risers had left their trails on the frosted ground. I soon added mine, leading all the way to Meryton on business.

By chance, Fielding met me in Weintraub's and persuaded me to join him in the Flighted Duck. In truth, I was happy to delay the journey home in a frozen carriage. Tincton's beef and potato broth would also tide me over until Longbourn.

We found the same quiet niche once used by Jackson and me, sitting snug behind its oak column. It still seemed best suited to discussions of dark deeds, but we were men of Meryton, not merry men of Sherwood. So we talked only of books, horses and the delights of sponge cake. Our conversation faded, though, as full stomachs and a fat fire pulled us into drowsiness, at least until familiar voices urged us back to wakefulness.

Had I not known the tones of Murden, Denny, and Wickham from dinners at Longbourn, I would still have recognised the sound of officers. Boisterous. Loud. Entitled. And seemingly thirsty.

In the army, we would curl up like ferns when the cold seeped through our tents and clothes and watch the ice form over our weak stew. The thought returned every time I saw Meryton officers feasting on Tincton's fine offerings.

I was grateful the young men were there, though, safe in Hertfordshire and not with Lord Wellington, even if Portuguese winters were likely warmer than ours. If nothing else, they allowed our nervous spinsters to roam the streets safely, free from the threat of rioting workers from factories we did not have.

I hunched lower in my seat, not wishing the burden of polite conversation.

"Mr Bennet!" I had not hunched low enough. "Are you well, sir?" asked Mr Murden. "Does your back trouble you in the cold? We have liniment in our quarters."

I straightened, assured Mr Murden of my good health, and then introduced Fielding to the assembled men of the militia.

"Would you care to join us? There is space enough at our table. We can provide the warmth of good company and spiced wine on this chill day." Fielding's hospitable spirit drew a silent curse from my lips.

"That is an offer neither an officer, nor a gentleman, may refuse."

Mr Murden took a seat opposite me, flanked by his two colleagues. "Your family is well, Mr Bennet? Mrs Bennet and your daughters?"

"Very well, thank you, Mr Murden. Kitty is a little bored. She misses the distraction visitors bring." He merely nodded.

"And Miss Elizabeth Bennet?" said Wickham. "With her curiosity and vigour for life, I cannot imagine she could ever be bored."

"Indeed not, though she suffers in winter when shorter days make reading less easy and visitors less likely." A nod from Mr Wickham. They would all have made excellent donkeys. "We have not seen you all in some time. You might join us again soon at Longbourn...for dinner?" The girls, at least, always longed for military entertainment.

"I would very much like that," said Mr Denny.

"As would we all, though our duties are onerous at the moment." I might have given Mr Murden's words more credence had he not spoken them between sips of wine in an inn.

Mr Wickham chuckled. "Most onerous, my friend, keeping you up so late, so often. Such stamina."

"You have many calls on your time, Mr Murden?" I said.

He stared into his wine a while before answering. "Like your daughters, I seek distraction, Mr Bennet. The militia is military by name only. We have no walls to repair, no fortifications to build. No hills to patrol, no enemy to watch. No deserters to chase or prisoners to guard. No threat to hold our attention and keep us lively. So we must seek our own entertainment. Here in the inn, or among the people of Meryton. Fear is not our constant companion in this town, Mr Bennet; boredom is. So we drink, and gamble, and dance, and tell stories, and find relief among the families of gentlemen, travelling from one to the next, for a soldier seldom settles in one place when out campaigning."

He drained his glass without any sign of pleasure.

"Your mood is blacker than usual," I said.

"Too much wine, perhaps." Mr Murden raised his empty glass. "Or not enough. Forgive me, I am not myself today. Your invitation is a kind one. Perhaps nearer Christmas, if the weather permits?"

We settled on the seventeenth. I suggested to Fielding that he might join us at Longbourn, but he was sensible enough to have a prior engagement. The officers left shortly after to attend to their various obligations, encouraged by little attempt at conversation on my part.

"Forgive me the observation, Bennet," said Fielding. "But for a former army man you show no great love for the company of soldiers."

"I meant no harm. Besides, we must distinguish between the military and those who serve in it. One is admirable, the other subject to the same diversity of character and morals as any collection of men."

"Still, your manner was cooler than usual."

"My lack of warmth was perhaps caused by frustration. From what Mr Murden said, my Kitty can no longer entertain any hope of his exclusive attention. Another daughter knocked aside from the path to the altar. It is a sad state of affairs when all that now remains of Mrs Bennet's matrimonial ambitions is a curate's brief interest in Mary at a ball." Fielding looked unsure whether to laugh.

~ ~ ~

Despite the intentions born on my recent carriage ride from London, I soon found my old cynicism knocking at the door to my soul like a returning beggar.

There was little joy at Longbourn. Perhaps it was the way Mrs Bennet's lips tightened at any mention of Mr Collins, or how one or other daughter could often be found staring bleakly into the distance, hands closed over a volume of poetry.

My mood was not helped by the clouds that spread a wet blanket over days dulled further by the arrival of a letter from Hunsford's paragon of obsequiousness.

"Read it, dear Lizzy, and rejoice in your lucky escape," I said, when alone with my daughter. She wrinkled her nose and shook her head. "It is easily summarised. He takes five lines to express his gratitude for his first visit here, and another ten to announce the next one. The plague returns to Longbourn. Shall we both leave for London and find comfort and safety within the walls of Brecknell's leather-bound treasures? No book will berate me for choosing your happiness over that of your mother. Nor will any book spend thirty minutes apologising for dropping a soup spoon."

There was nothing to be done but to take long winter walks and cover myself in books, port and a sprinkling of self-pity until I could begin to work on John's behalf.

That task began with the next Society meeting. The capricious Hertfordshire winter teased us with clear skies, so I rode forth to the Flighted Duck in better spirits than of late.

With little Society business of note in December, we used the time to sail through the trusted conversational waters of politics, the war, pigeons and partridges. Then we dined on those two very birds, our bowls and plates filled with steaming soups, stews, and pies.

Fielding's sigh of satisfaction at the meal seemed greater than my own, perhaps because he enjoyed little game at home. His wisdom was rich, but his aim poor. The wildlife had little to fear from the landowner's gun on Fielding's manor.

I finished my wine, drummed a few bars of a Beethoven piano sonata on my stomach, then stood, tapping my glass with a spoon. Jackson was the last to give me his full attention, since that required dragging it from a promising slice of Mrs Tincton's sponge cake.

"Gentlemen! You remember my friend John Barton and the enigmatic Miss Hayter?"

"The fellow who is Yorkshire?" said Stanhope. "As I recall, Jackson provided all the information needed to bring about the desired meeting?"

"I did at that. Duty complete and problem solved. Now pass the cake."

My good humour began to slip away like one of Fielding's beaters, fearful of another wayward shot from his master. "Well, yes, Jackson's intelligence was of considerable help, but John has not yet met the lady." That brought groans from around the table. "I, on the other hand, *have*. In London. Just over a fortnight ago."

"And you did not think to tell any of us before?" I knew Fielding well enough to hear the disappointment in his voice. I could have told him when we met a week ago, but it would have meant discussing Abigail, too.

"I felt it only fair to first report my experience to you all."

"And?" Fielding leaned forward in his chair.

"Miss Hayter is particularly handsome and remarkably quick-witted. Easy to feel affection for, I would say, though perhaps a little, well, *forward*."

"Who was with her?" said Elliston.

"What do you mean?"

"I cannot imagine you had a private tête-à-tête," said Elliston. "Was it the mother? From what Jackson says, she has quite a reputation. Bit of a harridan."

"I do not see what *that* has to do with anything. We are talking about Miss Hayter."

"No need to get upset, Bennet. I was only curious." Elliston sniffed and seemed a little put out.

"Of course, my apologies."

"So?" said Fielding.

"So what?"

"Did she have company?" said Jackson.

"Yes, she did. Her mother. She was with her mother. Who was perfectly amiable. Not a harridan at all, nothing like one. On the contrary." I took a deep breath, then rubbed my face. "Anyway, may we return to my story?"

Nobody spoke, but their faces looked surprised at my vehemence.

"Please continue," said Fielding, eventually.

"As regards *Miss* Hayter…I am no stranger to women, but when she smiled, well…I am even more sure than before that she is not short of admirers, all armed with money or position. Or both."

"So your friend, lacking cash and connections…" Jackson looked almost sad.

"Must find some other way to distinguish himself, if he is not already too late. I am resolved to continue to help John. All is not lost. When I say she is forward, some might interpret her behaviour as…challenging. I cannot imagine she tolerates fools easily, which will eliminate much of the competition. Unfortunately, John has largely given up hope and is now up north."

"Whereabouts?" said Stanhope.

"Ironically, Yorkshire." I gave him a frown dressed as a smile.

"Oh."

"So, we need a fresh plan to tempt him back south. I would, again, welcome your advice in this matter." None was forthcoming. Jackson began to eye up the cake again. "I should also bring to your attention that the young lady has a particular interest in…butterflies."

At Longbourn, I could look out a bay window across to the hills at dawn and wait for the rising sun to find a crack in the morning cloud. When it did, a flood of light fell across the meadows, changing the world in a moment. The word 'butterflies' had a similar effect.

Jackson's fork paused halfway to his mouth. Elliston put down his glass and straightened himself in his chair. Stanhope just stared, eyes wide and unblinking.

Fielding's smile was an earnest one. "Bennet, we must help this young man. One does not simply give up a Lepidopteran lady." Mumbled assent came from around the table.

"I am glad you all agree. And I thank you for it. So, let us apply our wisdom and understanding, once again, to the simple task of bringing one gentleman together with one lady." I looked around, eyebrows raised in question and hope.

All I could hear was Stanhope humming some Italian opera. Perhaps he sought inspiration from Pollarolo and Scarlatti.

Then Jackson rose slowly from his seat like Cetus emerging

from the sea. "I faced a similar challenge once. In the Americas. Dispute with the locals. How to bring our two sides together. Neutral ground, gentlemen, neutral ground. That is the key. Let them spend time in each other's company. Recognise shared interests and come to a satisfactory arrangement." He sat down again and rewarded himself with the patient piece of cake.

"You will recall we *lost* that particular argument," said Elliston. Jackson ignored him, addressing all his attention instead to the sugared delight before him.

"The idea has merit," I said. "Let us only hope for a better outcome. I can easily arrange for John to be anywhere, given sufficient incentive, but ensuring Miss Hayter's presence for any length of time seems something of a hurdle. Perhaps in London."

"Or at Longbourn," said Fielding. "What we need is for her to befriend one of your daughters. Then you can invite her to your home and have your friend along at the same time. From your description of Miss Hayter, Miss Elizabeth would make the perfect foil in our little plan. What say you, Bennet?"

"But how do we bring the two together? An encounter between two ladies is a sight easier to arrange than between a lady and a gentleman, but still…"

"If we cannot bring Miss Hayter to Longbourn to plant the seeds of such a friendship, then we must take Longbourn to Miss Hayter. My dear friend," said Fielding, "it is time for you to return to Bath."

Travel plans

The Bath proposal, conceived so diligently by committee, seemed considerably less attractive in the morning light. We lacked the resources to finance an extended stay in the city. Nor was I sure how to engage the attention of Miss Hayter. To call on her mother would be possible, but hardly advisable with Mrs Bennet in tow.

If Jackson was right, the Hayters' lack of enthusiasm for Bath's assemblies and similar would not make chance encounters easy, either. And yet, even as I pondered the problem, I recalled Miss Hayter's words: *My favourite bookstore in Bath has a number of excellent volumes on butterflies. Should you ever be in town, Mr Tavistock takes delivery from his London suppliers on Fridays.* It was worth a roll of the dice. And if all else failed, I could always rely on the girls' ability to bury themselves in Bath society and dig their way to Miss Hayter.

Regardless, I wrote to Mr Gardiner. Perhaps his friend from Bath had some knowledge we could use.

~ ~ ~

The world might have rebuked the Gardiner family for giving it Mrs Bennet, but it could not doubt the value of her brother. Knowing of my wish to visit Bath, he quickly found us accommodation on Gay Street at a very reasonable rent. Business would keep his friend in London through to the summer, and the fellow was happy to allow us to use his empty townhouse at any time for a small consideration. I accepted the offer in principle by letter. The details would wait until the Gardiners joined us at Christmas.

I rode over to Fielding's to tell him the news and seek his advice on one remaining obstacle. He was in his lower fields, giving full rein to a horse.

"She flies like the wind," I called as he approached.

"Silly of me really, all this riding at my age." He patted his chestnut steed as it stood snorting and pawing at the ground. "My legs fail me slowly, Bennet. But my horse does not. It feels good to get up speed once more."

"Time is an enemy we will never defeat." We set off slowly back to his stables. "I have secured accommodation in Bath. I thought you would like to know."

"Hah! I am pleased to hear it. But I sense you are not entirely happy."

I pulled my horse to a stop. "There is one problem that concerns me."

"Go on."

"Returning to Bath might unleash a demon or two of regret. I feel trapped between good intentions and certain memories." He knew of my history with Abigail, but not that she was Mrs Hayter. That was a conversation for another day.

Fielding pointed further down the trail we rode along. "When I was much younger and at a loss, I used to sit on an old grey stump at the edge of Three Stone Copse. We will pass it. I would watch the wood ants about their work, follow the lines of movement that all led back to a twisted pine and a great pile of needles and litter that was the nest.

"I always envied the insects their single-minded purpose. And their courage—a passing invader would see them thrust themselves into the fray in selfless sacrifice. For their queen and colony, as you and I might say.

"My friend, romantic disappointment never bothers an ant when there is work to be done. It is a lesson you should have learned by now. You must not allow a past grievance to cloud the present."

We rode on in silence until I could see the copse he mentioned appear above the rise. "You are right, Fielding. Besides, Bath holds pleasant memories, too."

"Think only of your motivation to help a young friend. I am sure you can spend time in that city without significant discomfort."

"I shall convince myself of it before we leave. All that remains, then, is to enlist the support of my family. And that will require some delicacy."

~ ~ ~

I did not wish to request Lizzy's help directly. She was too proud and principled to seek a friendship that was not genuine. Nor could I risk word of the whole business reaching Mrs Bennet's ears. There would be trouble enough when it did, but the longer I could delay that trouble, the better for us all.

Passing the kitchen after my return from Fielding's, I heard the lamentations of the listless within. A peek inside revealed piles of twigs, leaves and berries awaiting transformation into winter decorations. Above each pile was a sullen face. The arrival of rain had trapped the girls inside the house, forcing their mother to find occupation for restless minds and fingers. I gave everyone a smile of encouragement from the doorway.

Their poor spirits presented a timely opportunity.

"I saw you all working on arrangements for Christmas. How diligent. I am pleased to find you engaged in such amusements. When will you be finished?" So began the game of verbal chess at dinner.

"Quite soon, Papa, we are nearly done," said Jane.

"And you would all be very much done had Lydia not dragged her feet so!" said Mrs Bennet.

Lydia's bored frown migrated into a pout. "We are not a workhouse, Mama. I *long* for the sun. When can we go to Meryton again?"

"You must wait for the weather to turn," I said, "Or until Tuesday. Then the officers will dine with us once more." Lydia smiled at Kitty, who seemed to avoid her gaze.

"And do not forget, we expect Mr Collins on Monday, which should provide considerable entertainment for all of you." To my family's credit, only Lydia gave any clear sign of disappointment.

"And to think Mr Collins could have…" Mrs Bennet shook her head and sought consolation in a glass of Portuguese wine.

"You all seem quite despondent. Perhaps I have some news to lift your mood?" I sipped at my wine to allow curiosity to build.

"Is John to visit again?" cried Lydia. "I do so want him to

paint me. I promised my portrait to Denny so all the other officers would be jealous."

"That is *not* my news." I dabbed my mouth with the napkin.

"Papa, do not keep us in suspense." Jane was the first to speak.

"I am of a mind to take us away for a week or two." Had I thrown an apple core into the pig pen I could not have witnessed a greater tumult of excitement. "Now, now, it is but an idea."

"Is it to be Brighton? Oh, Papa, might we see the Pavilion?" Lydia appeared to be shaking with excitement.

"And the Prince?" said Mrs Bennet, winking as she did.

"It cannot be the seaside. If we are to travel then it must be in January and I am not minded to visit the coast in winter. Besides, Parliament will likely have opened, so Brighton will be empty. I cannot imagine architectural delights compensating for a lack of society. Is that not so, Lydia? Kitty? My dear?" None of them blessed me with an answer, but Lydia's frown returned.

"What about Bath, Papa?" said Lizzy. "Society in Bath is said to be pleasant at any time of year and there would be much to amuse all of us."

"I am told the book merchants there are second only to London," said Jane.

"Are they indeed?" I sat back as if lost in thought. "And Bath is inland enough to assure us of at least reasonable weather."

"How right you are, Mr Bennet. We will have so much fun. A friend of my sister's once visited the Pump Room. She spoke of a very large gathering that included a number of amiable young gentlemen. Imagine, Lydia!"

"We could simply go to London. It is nearer and offers more

diverse entertainments. I should like to visit the churches that Symonds speaks of in his guide," said Mary, potentially condemning herself to a year without sheet music for her interruption. Lizzy glanced at Jane. Of course, Mr Bingley was in London.

"Oh, yes!" cried Lydia, "So many balls, we will be quite giddy. And we can—"

"London is quite out of the question," I said, before the wild mare of Lydia's mind could get up a gallop. I hoped the strength of my voice and fatherly authority would suffice, for I had no justification for the statement.

"But why, Papa?" I determined to check how much Lydia spent on ribbons and halve the amount.

"Yes, Papa, why?" Kitty's allowance also hung in the balance.

"It does not suit me to visit London," said Mrs Bennet, offering unexpected help. "You are wise, husband, in choosing Bath." Her folded arms brooked no quarrel. Checkmate.

It was only later she revealed to me her true objections. "London is full of the likes of the Bingley sisters and the girls will face far too much competition. We may show them to the better in Bath, and there will be plenty enough men there. Of that I have no doubt."

Despite the city's failure to be Brighton or London, the decision pleased the girls and so I basked in that cloak of approval so rarely bestowed on fathers by their daughters.

The plan was not without flaws. I had to ensure Lizzy met Miss Hayter quickly and then protect any friendship that might blossom from sisterly interference. There was much work ahead.

The joys of the arena

Togas may have given way to tailcoats, but that did not stop audiences enjoying a decent fight. In my case, though, the only conflict I enjoyed was verbal in nature—the cut and thrust of conversation where wine flowed freely, not blood.

Two armies assembled at dinner. Occupying the high ground, the Bennet sisters, sharp of tongue but liable to ill discipline in the ranks. Advancing on their lofty position were Mr Denny, Mr Wickham, and Mr Murden, equally well-armed with conversational *bon mots*, but reluctant to land a killing blow where ladies were concerned. And in among them, Mr Collins—ever fearful of action without orders from his patron and switching sides like a disloyal Spanish noble.

"*Ave Caesar.* Those about to dine salute you," I said to nobody in particular.

As expected, my cousin had arrived the previous day. His engagement had improved his position, but not his character. Fortunately, we expected to see little of him during his stay, given his declared wish to spend as much time as possible at Lucas Lodge.

Approaching the table, there was a general rush to avoid sitting next to Mr Collins, a task made no easier by his own indecision. Certain girls wished to sit near particular officers, and certain officers near particular girls.

It made for a most diverting sight, all conducted with the utmost politeness, as men and women bobbed up and down, shuffled left and right, squeezed and pushed. We could have gone on all night, but for Mrs Bennet. "Oh, do be seated, you are giving me the most dreadful headache. Have pity on my poor nerves."

There followed many apologies and a last dash for the best seats. Few words accompanied the soup, just an occasional giggle and the inevitable compliment from Mr Collins. "Such an elegant liquid, Mrs Bennet. And possessed of the perfect temperature, being neither too hot as to scald the unprepared tongue nor too cold as to cause unpleasant curling of the lips."

He followed that nonsense with that little look he had, where his eyes squeezed tight as he smiled. Like a new-born kitten, but without the charm.

"It must be a frustrating time for you gentlemen soldiers," I suggested. "The poor weather prevents much in the way of manoeuvres, and the opportunity for society must be few and far between, what with many families laid low by poor health or trapped within their homes by the cold."

"I will concede only in part," said Mr Wickham. "It may require more effort, but we manage to find ways to entertain ourselves and others. Is not one of our duties to ensure congeniality and relief in dark times?"

"And keep the wine merchants in business throughout the winter," said Mr Murden.

"Yes, they will be excessively disappointed once you depart, as will others no doubt." None of the officers took advantage of my words to fan the flames of hope in any lady present.

"Do not say you will leave soon," said Lydia. "Meryton will be so dull when you do."

"And our lives the duller for the loss of your company. All of you," said Mr Wickham. "But we are here at least through the spring."

"There's a thought to warm us, Wickham," said Mr Murden.

"You have been a rarity at Longbourn of late," said Lizzy. "Have we fallen so far in your favour, or are your duties in winter more onerous than you have admitted?"

"Life in Meryton is full of distractions," said Mr Murden.

"Like Miss Smith, eh?" said Mr Denny, earning himself dark looks from more than one person at the table.

"And we are most grateful for your reassuring presence, gentlemen," said Mr Collins. "As I have said to Lady Catherine on more than one occasion, it is to those who bear arms that we may give thanks for that which our arms carry." I lingered at my glass in the vain hope that getting drunk might help me understand his words. The wine was full-bodied, but left a sour taste. Not unlike Mr Collins. I called for a fresh bottle.

"Who is Miss Smith?" Kitty's voice was a little higher than usual. The officers looked at each other. None seemed in a hurry to answer her question. "We hope to receive our friend, John Barton, soon. He has promised to paint me." She looked at Mr Murden as she spoke.

"And me." Lydia would not allow Kitty to claim centre stage alone.

"He is a fine young man," said Mrs Bennet. "Most attentive to the girls. I grew to like him very much. It is a shame he does not visit more often."

"A painter, you say?" There was the hint of a grin on Mr Murden's face.

"It is not a fit occupation for a gentleman, if you ask me," answered my wife. "And some might question his position, what with his father's estate being what it is." She paused to give us a sad smile. "But his manners and conversation endeared him to me. I have no objection to him at all."

"How lucky for John," I mumbled through my napkin.

"Most generous of you, Mrs Bennet," said Mr Collins. "To allow his good character to allay your well-founded concerns for the standing of your daughters. As I always say—"

"Do you paint, Mr Collins?" Lizzy's question was all innocence.

"Goodness me, no, I am a man of words, as you will undoubtedly have noticed. Though I do paint a pretty floral portrait with the roses alongside my laurel hedge. You might say I am the Gainsborough of garden art." Only Mr Denny rewarded him with something approaching a laugh.

"Never thought much of painters," said Mr Murden, helping himself to more potatoes. "Happy enough to portray a battle, but not to help win one. They prey on the vanity of the superior officers for work. But I am sure your Mr Barton is a fine character, for he has your approval, Mrs Bennet. And yours, Miss Catherine."

"He does." Kitty lifted her chin.

"And what do you think of Mr Barton, Miss Elizabeth?" said

Mr Wickham, turning to Lizzy. "I would trust your judgement above all others."

"I like John very much indeed, as a sister might like a brother."

"How fortunate," said Mr Collins.

"He is reliable in his constancy of character," continued Lizzy.

"Reliable?" laughed Mr Murden. "That is a compliment indeed. What more can you want from a man than reliability?"

"Do not underestimate reliability as a virtue," said Lizzy. "What use is love, loyalty or liveliness, if they cannot be relied on?"

"In that case, perhaps he would make a good soldier after all. If we ever meet, I shall invite him to exchange his brush for a blade."

Mr Collins broke the silence that then descended. "What excellent parsnips…"

~ ~ ~

My cousin's departure from Longbourn was as welcome as spring or a new volume of *Papilio Litterae*. Shortly after, I received a more agreeable arrival in the form of Christmas wishes from John, together with a reliable address to send correspondence to. His spirits seemed as damp and dull as the northern climate. Whether they remained so would depend on how he regarded my reply, particularly the following lines:

> *It was army life that forged my friendship with your father. It taught us that honesty trumps propriety when the only judges are God and the enemy. This friendship and honesty I extend to you as his son. In so doing, I now*

ask that you do not abandon hope as regards Miss Hayter.

I met the lady and her mother in Brecknell's, the very day you left for the north, and urge you to visit us as soon as possible. Plans are afoot that may bring Miss Hayter to Longbourn. If you would prefer silence on this matter, you will find no reproach from me. But I believe your cause may not yet be lost.

I left out further detail to save paper, but also in the hope that curiosity might help drive him south again.

A change in year

The Gardiners' Christmas visit brought laughter and comfort to our home. Mrs Gardiner was a Hertfordshire Bifröst, a bridge between the realms of the young and old. She was young enough to chatter away with the girls, but old enough to talk as an equal with their mother. If only we could have persuaded her to leave her children behind in London. They behaved well enough for their age, but not well enough for mine.

Mr Gardiner's presence in the house was a particular pleasure. We walked parts of the estate on Christmas Eve, enjoying a few hours of quiet before the coming entertainments.

The first bites of wind were painful, but its bluster soon dulled to playful nips. The further we went, the more at peace we seemed to become.

"Our exertions have earned us an extra slice of goose at tomorrow's table," I said as we reached the top of a small hill. "Froggat was fattening the beast for years, but it has finally met its seasonal—and well-seasoned—end. You should see its size. We will be eating goose in one form or another for weeks to come."

I led my brother-in-law behind the old spinney so he might see some of the new tenant buildings. The trees were all dull browns and greys, branches bare and extended in supplication to a pale-yellow sun. Only an orange-red flash broke the monotony, a robin who paid us little heed.

Mr Gardiner talked of machines and other inventions that seemed set to change our world, though there was little sign of it in Hertfordshire.

"Your land looks well set for the future, too, brother." My guest pointed with his hat down to the outhouse by Boulder farm, the fresh stones yet to suffer the sharp caress of a full winter. "And your girls also seem in good health."

"In good health, but still unmarried."

"My wife tells me there were hopes of a young man and Jane. Is this no longer so?"

"He is lost to us and his departure gave Jane's heart quite a beating. It is unfortunate, for the gentleman in question was a good sort and I cannot say that of many men."

"And the other girls?"

"Hints and sighs and dances, but nothing close to certain. Mrs Bennet is vexed. You heard of the incident with Mr Collins?" My guest was kind enough not to venture an opinion and merely nodded.

"I always find travel a useful distraction in times of disappointment." Gardiner stopped walking and turned to me. "Should we invite Jane to London? There are enough distractions there for a hundred broken hearts."

"That is a kind offer, brother. Let it come from your wife, though. It will fall on more willing ears that way."

"Mrs Gardiner would enjoy Jane's conversation of an evening. Varied company is good for the soul. Indeed, my sister has been most kind in arranging so many guests and amusements for our visit."

"I fear you will see more officers in the coming days than in a London gambling club."

"Such fine gentlemen. Excellent manners." He paused. "Always telling interesting stories."

"Yes, they are full of good tales, particularly when full of *my* best port. The Meryton officers are harmless enough; Colonel Forster is a credit to Whitehall."

"There is much talk among the ladies of a Mr Murden. A lively fellow apparently."

"If they say so."

"You have no opinion of the man?"

"Not for lack of trying. He plays a game with all of us. But what kind of game?" I pulled my coat tighter around me as the wind picked up. "He is certainly engaging company. You will like him. Everyone seems to."

~ ~ ~

Cook's plum pudding could have fed the five thousand and spared our Lord the miracle of the bread and fish. But the last piece had disappeared by the time New Year's Eve had arrived.

The Gardiners were also no more, having left earlier with our eldest. We had company most every day they were here, and only now could the servants clean the house. Jane would miss our Bath trip, but London would provide its own consolations.

The rest of us were glad to spend much of the last day of the year in quiet reflection. All except Lydia, of course, who spent most of the time looking quietly at *her* reflection, admiring every curve and curl.

Later, as we sat waiting to welcome the new year and say farewell to the old, a rare moment of philosophical enlightenment struck Mrs Bennet: "What shall we wish for in 1812?"

"Oh, yes, let us all say," said Lydia, "And now that Jane is in London, she shall not shame us into saying something noble."

"Yes," I said. "Let us rejoice in her absence. We may now express all our selfishness and poor judgement without fear of rebuke."

"I would have relief from my nerves. And see all my girls married to gentlemen with large fortunes and great estates. But all nearby, so I may visit often and make Lady Lucas very jealous indeed."

"What about you, Lydia?" I said. "Do you wish to improve yourself with extensive reading? Perhaps retire to a life of contemplation in a small Cornish abbey?"

"Whatever gave you such strange notions, Papa? That might do for Mary, but not for me. I would be happy with an officer to wed. He must enjoy dancing and plays. And travel. Give parties every day when we are home. And buy me new hats and gowns every week. And he must be excessively handsome, of course, so all my sisters die of envy."

"I am not sure such a man exists, but, if he does, I hope he finds you," I said. "And you, Kitty, how will you make your sisters jealous?"

Kitty cupped her face in her hands and sighed. "I daresay an offer from an officer would be charming, but I would be more than happy with the attentions of any young man. I do declare I would be quite content with another visit from Mr Barton, so…"

"…he might paint you," I finished for her.

"He will paint you all," said my wife.

"Yes, but he will paint *me* so beautifully that every officer will ask, 'Who is that most beautiful of ladies hanging on your wall?' I will outshine all my sisters."

"Well, yours is one wish that may come true, Kitty. I hope John will visit soon. I wrote to him recently encouraging just that."

"I have no wishes for next year. What will come will come. We must accept the fate that God has prepared for us."

"Thank you, Mary," I said. "At least you will not be making anyone jealous. And you, Lizzy, I can rely on you for something more sensible?"

Lizzy spoke softly, perhaps feeling some sadness at the loss of Jane to London and the loss of Mr Bingley that made that absence necessary. "I would see all your wishes come true, though perhaps John might paint me equally as well as he would Kitty."

"But for yourself, Lizzy?" said Lydia. "Just because Jane is gone does not mean you must take her place in conversation."

Lizzy looked out the window, seemingly lost in thought beyond the borders of Longbourn. "I would simply like a man who loved me and who I might love back. A man of warmth and compassion, at ease at a ball or in a bookstore. He should have a sad smile, one that only I can turn merry." She pursed her lips and nodded gently. "And if he is excessively handsome, too, I shall not complain!"

"And you, Papa," said Kitty, "You have not yet told us your wishes."

"My wishes?" How much I might have said in that moment. That I might wake one day and find I had a son. That Longbourn might be secured for the family, and no wife or daughter need worry for their future. That Miss Hayter might fall irrevocably in love with John. That Abigail might be happy with the match. That I might forgive and forget more easily. That I might once more chance upon the glorious wings of another Silver-washed Fritillary.

"Papa?" I came to my senses to find them all watching me, concern on their faces.

"A warm fire and a good book will do me, Kitty, and perhaps less of your silliness."

"Oh, Papa!"

John's return

My letter to John received a swift answer. He followed in person only a day or two later.

As on his last visit, I chose to meet him in Meryton. A pearl blue sky beckoned, so I sent his bags on ahead and we walked back to Longbourn along the banks of the stream, heedless of the muddy reminders of the previous day's rain. A few weeks in the north had not changed him. He was a little fatter around the cheeks, certainly, but that might apply to almost any gentleman in the days following Christmas.

"You are not too tired from your journey?"

"Tired, yes. But happy to stretch my legs again, and happier still to be away from my fellow passengers. Their chatter was my constant companion south of Coventry. There is no escaping gossip in a carriage."

"A truer word was never said." We walked in silence for a few moments. "You are curious, no doubt, as to the details of my encounter with Miss Hayter?"

"I cannot deny some interest."

I began counting on my fingers. John's eyes narrowed. "Well, by my reckoning, you must have started your journey south some, let me see, five, perhaps as many as six, minutes after receiving my letter."

"It was half a day. It took that long to pack and arrange transport."

"It is a wonder you did not arrive before your letter. Either your hosts were so abominable that my note gave you an excuse to leave immediately, or you have a little more than 'some' interest."

"They were gracious hosts. It was not on their account that I left in haste." I smiled at him but he kept a stern face.

"I did warn you, John. It takes more than a few miles of road to remove the barbs of affection from a stricken heart. Perhaps you now regret your early departure from London?"

"Interest and regret are not the same, Mr Bennet. One may lead to the other, but much depends on what you have to say. You lit a candle, but I am still largely in darkness."

"If you say so, John, if you say so."

Our path took us away from the stream and we crested a small rise to see Longbourn in the distance. I fancied I could hear the girls' squeals, no doubt having seen an easel emerge from the carriage that bore our guest's belongings.

John stood on the ridge, arms folded and coat flapping in the breeze, one boot tapping out an irregular staccato on the ground. We held each other's stare for a few seconds, then the wind carried our raucous laughter out and across the fields.

"Very well, John…I will keep you in suspense no longer. She is very handsome indeed." The response a snort of disappointment. "Forgive me, dear boy, it has been many years since I last paid attention to a young lady. I do not have the words and, frankly, I was a little distracted at the time."

"Tell me simply, how did she make you feel?" He was all earnestness now, like a dog waiting at the door for his master's return.

I walked on and called back to him over my shoulder. "When she smiled, she brought summer into Brecknell's."

He caught up with me. "You see it, too? And her conversation? What did she say? How were you even introduced?"

"Ah," I said, turning away from him again.

"My apologies. I ask too many questions."

"It is not your questions that trouble me, John, but *my* answers. Miss Hayter was with her mother, you see. Mrs Hayter as is, Abigail Spencer as was. Perhaps you have heard the name from your father?" He shook his head. "Then Henry was more discreet than necessary with his own kin." I looked long and hard at him. He was so young. "You see, John, well, I once thought of Abigail Spencer much as you now think of Miss Hayter. She refused me. No, let me be fair to her—she found another before she had the opportunity to refuse me. As I discovered that day in London, she eventually married the late Mr Hayter."

John touched my arm briefly, unexpectedly, concern gracing his face, all sign of his own hopes removed in concern for mine. "I am sorry. Was it not difficult for you?"

"A little awkward, I grant, particularly as *she* recognised *me*, too. But perhaps we can turn this connection to our advantage in some way. As long as you do not oblige me to call on the mother." I waved a finger at him. "The past is best left undisturbed, especially *my* past."

"Ah," said John. "I understand. Though a wise man once told me that distance does not allow escape."

"I could not possibly say," I said, avoiding his gaze. Perceptive company does not always make for comfortable conversations. Life is sometimes far easier when surrounded by ignorance. "Now come, let us hurry to Longbourn." I strode forward, not waiting to see if he caught up. "By the way, I hope you have plenty of paint with you. There are many eager to have you flatter them in a portrait. If you are one of those that paints his subjects with faithful honesty, I would advise against it. Unless you wish to spend your stay shivering in icy stares of disapproval. And no word of the Hayters to anyone. Our hopes rest on the ladies knowing nothing. Absolutely nothing. I will explain all to you later. And that reminds me: if there is time tomorrow, I would like to introduce you to my friends at the Meryton Natural History Society. I hope you like butterflies. Miss Hayter does."

~ ~ ~

The call of sunlight and impatient girls brought John out early from his bed. He had barely time to breakfast before they dragged him toward the drawing room. There the light was best, even if winter's long reach dulled its brightness.

As promised, he painted Kitty first. He treated his canvas kindly, with the light strokes and tender touches of a mother seeing to a bruised child. All the while he kept his subject content with stories of Vienna and Prague, sweetened with regular compliments on her poise and patience.

When he was done, after but two hours, we all crowded round to praise the results.

"Such a pretty face, I can barely recognise you, Kitty," I said.

"I am not sure I wish for my own portrait now," said Lizzy.

"Is my work so shameful?"

"On the contrary, dearest John, you have captured Kitty's looks *and* her character. For my part, I merely fear what you might reveal of my soul."

"Goodness knows what he will make of Lydia," I said.

"And now it is my turn," said the subject of my jest, hurrying over to the chair by the window.

"It is a very pleasing picture, John," said my wife. "And quite enough for one day, I think. I have errands for the girls in Meryton. The day is dry, but the weather may turn at any time, so they must be off this very moment." The protestations were both loud and long. "No, you must be off. Now. All of you. Except for Kitty."

"Mama?" said Kitty.

"With your sore ankle, you must remain here. You may look after John, so he is not alone while your sisters are in Meryton."

"My sore ankle?"

"Yes. The left one." We all followed her outstretched finger.

I had no wish to condemn our guest to an afternoon entertaining Kitty. "John is otherwise engaged, my dear. If he is not to paint, then he must come with me. I wish to introduce him to the Society. They are eager to meet him."

"You cannot leave Kitty *alone*," said Mrs Bennet.

"But she is not alone, is she? What better company can a daughter ask for than that of her mother? There, we are all spoken for now. Let us meet again in the evening. We shall take the carriage, and the girls will walk."

When it was not a market day, Meryton had the sleepy countenance of some fairy-tale hamlet. We were a little early for the Society, so I took John for a turn around the town, curious as to what his painter's eye might discover that lay hidden to me. As we finally entered the square, I saw a familiar group ahead of us: three red coats and the same number of bonnets. The girls had found themselves some officers.

"Well, John, I had hoped to spare you the formality of too many new acquaintances this afternoon, but it appears you are to meet the militia in the form of—let me see—Messrs Wickham, Denny, and Murden, the trio that have made merry around our dinner table on several occasions." I hailed the group from a distance to allow Lizzy time to make John's status and character known to her companions.

"Well, gentlemen, no riots to quell?" I called as we approached.

"Not today," replied Mr Murden. "But we remain ever vigilant."

"I should not like you to quell any riots; you might spoil your beautiful jackets," said Lydia.

The light of day gave me the first chance to see Mr Murden properly. Candlelight confers a sallow, haunted look, so I did not like to judge people at my dinner table or at an inn. Even without the shako, tucked beneath his arm, he was a tall man, three or four inches taller than John, and broader with it. His high cheekbones put me in mind of classical heroes, a vision supported by his tight curls.

The officers each greeted John in their own particular way. Mr Wickham was a picture of amiability, his every word meant as much for the audience as his direct opposite. Mr Denny was open and brief, Mr Murden polite, welcoming, and impossible to read.

"What happy coincidence that we should meet," said Mr Wickham. "Shall we all retire to the inn? I am growing cold and seek good wine and conversation to bring life to my limbs."

Taking up Mr Wickham's suggestion, we repaired to that fine establishment; John and I had a good hour to pass before the committee would begin to arrive.

I asked for a private room, where bread—still hot from the ovens—and mulled wine warmed us until the fire found its strength.

"You know nothing of weather, Wickham, if you think this cold," said Mr Murden.

"I must protest," said his colleague-in-arms. "Derbyshire winters can be harsh and many is the time I have—"

"But you have no experience of a Russian winter! There your breath freezes in the air and the icy ground steals the very life from your toes." Mr Murden turned to John. "I imagine you are glad of the Gloucestershire climate, Mr Barton, all sun and rich country harvests."

Lizzy answered for him. "Mr Barton lived most recently in Austria. I understand the mountains in winter are very fierce, is that not so?"

"Colder than home, to be sure," said John. "But not comparable with Russia, as I think Napoleon will discover should he turn his attention to the Tsar."

"Ah, Wickham," said Mr Murden, clapping his companion on the shoulder. "We are in the presence of a learned man. We must watch ourselves, or he will expose us for the fools we are."

"If you are fools, you are very handsome ones." Lydia's intervention saved John from the need to respond.

Mr Wickham's shiver spilled bright drops of wine from his glass.

"You are still cold, man? Then we need more fuel. This fire is a disgrace." Mr Murden turned about himself. "Where is the serving girl?"

I leant toward Mary and whispered. "Please fetch Jenny and ask her for more firewood. We do not wish our brave officers to face unwarranted hardship."

"Are you enjoying Meryton, gentlemen?" said John.

"We are," said Mr Wickham. "The townsfolk are generous with their hospitality and have been kind enough to remain peaceful, though I did see two ladies raise their voices over a ribbon at Frederick's. I almost had to call for the cavalry." We all laughed dutifully.

"You have forgotten the chief source of delights in Meryton, Wickham." Mr Murden, standing, swept his arm around the table. "I have travelled through much of Europe, seen all that the courts of St Petersburg and Stockholm can offer, but nothing can compare with the beauty of the Meryton ladies." He bowed deeply and the recipients of his flattery rewarded him with generous applause. "I'm sure you would agree, Mr Barton, no?"

John took a moment to answer. "The ladies I have met do their parents great honour. It must come as a relief to enjoy such a peaceful shire, Mr Murden. Or were your previous assignments equally enviable?"

"They were not, sir. We were recently in the north, where we taught the local population a few sharp lessons concerning respect for the law." He lifted the hilt of his sword.

"Do tell us, Mr Murden," said Lizzy. "What great battles raged in the moors and vales of the northern counties? What sieges? What desperate actions in the face of a well-armed enemy?" I found it hard not to smirk.

"Hardly well-armed, Miss Bennet. Sticks and pitchforks make a poor argument against solid steel blades. And we had law and righteousness on *our* side."

"Is that where you got your…" Lydia ran her finger down her cheek.

"No, for that you can blame a Russian officer, unable to handle his drink or his loss at cards."

"I hope you made him pay for his insolence," said Lydia.

"Have no fear on that account."

"How lacking in diversion you must find Hertfordshire in comparison," said Lizzy.

"I am the happier for it. Besides, there is plenty enough to amuse me. Today, for instance, I have made a new acquaintance in Mr Barton." He turned to my friend. "Tell me, what passes for amusement in Gloucester?"

"I cannot say for I am rarely there. I have been abroad for most of my life."

"A fellow soldier, perhaps, never long in one place?" Mr Murden looked John up and down.

"No. While you collected fame, fortune and victories, I collected memories. Travelling with my father through the Caribbean and the great cities of the Austrian Empire."

"Not a soldier. Yes, as I now recall, a painter, no?"

"Of sorts," said John.

Mr Murden turned back to the rest of our party. "I once knew a countess from Bohemia."

"Ah," said Mr Wickham, "I daresay there is a pretty story to be told there."

"Indeed, there is. More wine and I will tell it. Where is that serving girl?"

I looked at Mary. She rolled her eyes, but rose and left to fetch Jenny again. The latter's arrival a few minutes later proved a double blessing. There was more wine for the officers and a message from Fielding that the committee awaited John and me in another room. We made our excuses immediately, and to the obvious relief of everybody. The officers liked any audience, but preferred a female one, and the girls could now sigh and swoon without risking fatherly censure.

My friends greeted John like the return of a comrade believed lost at sea. For his part, John was clearly surprised at the generosity of the welcome. Of course, he had no knowledge of the Society's involvement in his affairs.

"John, these gentlemen have been greatly supportive of my endeavours on your behalf. Mr Jackson alerted me to Miss Hayter's presence in London, for example, and Mr Fielding here is the architect of our forthcoming Bath adventure."

I watched John closely, unsure how he would take to the inclusion of my friends in his amorous tale. I had meant what I had written to him about friendship and *honesty*, but openness is not always rewarded with approval.

"Mr Bennet has been most discreet in his reports. Nevertheless, I hope you do not object to our interventions. They are all well-meant," said Fielding.

"I must thank you all for your kindness," said John, to my relief. "I am glad to find support in a country where I am a stranger."

This led to numerous enquiries about his Caribbean and other travels, John dealing as best he could with questions on fish, insects, and the finer aspects of Imperial garden architecture.

"This butterfly lady of yours, Mr Barton—" said Stanhope.

"She is not *mine*, Mr Stanhope, but please do continue."

"She must be a lovely creature…"

"More than you can imagine." John closed his eyes briefly, then walked over to where Stanhope sat and bent down to look him in the eye. "Mr Stanhope, her skin is as soft as, well, as soft as a Swallowtail's wings."

"Goodness me."

John straightened and stepped behind Stanhope's chair. Placing both hands on its back, he looked directly across at Jackson. "She has all the grace of a Glanville Fritillary."

"My," said Jackson.

John lifted his arm, turned to face Elliston, then waved his hand gently across my friend's view, like a conductor demanding tenderness from the violins. "Her movements are as delicate as a Small Tortoiseshell."

"Tortoiseshell," repeated Elliston, as if hypnotised.

"And yet, gentlemen, she is possessed of the rare majesty of a Purple Emperor."

They all sat open-mouthed for a moment, then broke into riotous applause.

~ ~ ~

Sitting with John in the library that evening, I scolded my young friend. "You have never revealed any knowledge of butterflies."

"Alas, I possess none. But foreign travel has taught me many things, Mr Bennet. First and foremost, the importance of learning the local language. I took the liberty of borrowing a 'dictionary' last night." He pointed to the shelf where I kept my books on butterflies. It was only then I noticed the gap.

~ ~ ~

John intended to leave for his estate mid-morning, so we all rose early, keen to make the most of his company before his departure.

"Are you in discomfort, dear Lydia?" I asked. She had been squirming in her seat all through breakfast.

"No, Papa, I am simply aggrieved that Mr Barton is leaving."

"That is kind of you to say, Miss Lydia," said John.

"Oh, I do not mind you going, just that you have not painted me. I do not see why Kitty should be the only one to enjoy such a privilege. Mama, tell John he must stay until he has kept his promise to us."

Mrs Bennet's mouth seemed fully occupied with a resilient piece of cold pork.

"Lydia, mind your manners," I said. "John is here as a friend and guest, not a tradesman."

"Sorry, Papa." She nodded in apology to John, who merely smiled.

"I must attend to business at home. Perhaps I might visit again after your return from Bath?"

"But that will not be for at least another month," wailed Lydia. "It is so unfair."

"I cannot help it if Mr Barton prefers me," said Kitty. "He simply has an eye for beauty."

"Papa?" said Lizzy. "Might John not join us in Bath? You said yourself our lodgings are ample enough for two families. And it is not so far from Gloucestershire as Longbourn. John, would that not please you, too? Please do say yes."

The thought had not crossed my mind, but seemed obvious in hindsight. "John, we would be glad of your company on our expedition. You could join us after we have had a day or two to settle, seen the lay of the land, perhaps made a few *acquaintances*." I hoped he understood my meaning.

"I would not wish to intrude on such a family occasion." I rolled my eyes at the triumph of manners over need.

"Please say yes," said Kitty. "Mama, persuade him."

The pork having surrendered, my wife entered the conversation. "Of course you must join us, John. But you must bring your easel. And introduce us all to other young men."

"Very well, I shall look forward to it, though I cannot promise to meet all your expectations, Mrs Bennet." He clapped his hands. "I have many pleasant memories of Bath."

"As does Mr Bennet, do you not, husband?" It seemed an honest question; there was no hint of guile in my wife's expression.

"It has been so long, my dear, I have quite forgot the place. And the people."

Back to the past

The days before Bath passed slowly, but, as long as there were insects, books, and port, I was rarely short of something to do.

On this day, though, as the house echoed to the renewed assault of rain clouds, I chose to review the estate books with Mrs Bennet, a task made all the more urgent by our impending trip. Before we left, I wanted to know just how much I dared let the girls spend in Bath's stores.

The matter of finances set my wife off on a long tirade against inheritance laws and the English justice system. Her diatribe wound its way through its emotional hills and valleys to land at the feet of the chief object of her anger.

"To think Mr Collins has married Charlotte Lucas," she said, wringing her hands.

"I kept an eye out for locusts and seven-headed beasts outside the church. None appeared. It seems the world is not yet to end just because Lizzie refused her cousin."

"Wedlock is a fine thing for *Mrs Collins*. Oh, Lady Lucas was very happy. And did she not show it?"

"Well you can hardly blame her, my dear. Charlotte has

ensured a home of her own, wealth, the approval of society, relief for her family, a view of Rosings Park, dinners with the great Lady Catherine de Bourgh and, of course, the companionship of a spouse. Though you know my thoughts—all the former is inadequate compensation for the chatter of *that* particular spouse."

"Oh, you delight in vexing me, husband. I will not have it. Let us read the accounts and then see how you feel."

All men are equal in battle and bookkeeping. It does not matter how rich or poor you are, but only whether your income exceeds your outgoings. Our finances were not so extremely parlous, but I still feared the task before us. It would reveal all too much about the nature of our expenditures.

"How many ribbons does a family need? Does cook use them in baking?"

Mrs Bennet assumed her usual stance when conversing on household matters with me, arms folded, head shaking gently from side to side, each sentence preceded by a weary sigh. "Do not talk such nonsense, Mr Bennet. The girls must look their best if they are to get husbands, and so their ribbons must always match the latest fashions."

"And the subscription to *La Belle Assemblee*?"

"We cannot know the latest fashions from Meryton gossip alone."

"A wonder, since there is so much of it. What about the muslin?" I waved a fistful of invoices at my dear companion.

"Mr Bennet, you know very well that the muslin is for your butterfly nets."

"I might concur with you, dear, if butterflies were the size of whales."

"There may have been a yard or two for the girls."

"And how is our tapestry business going? Given the length of thread ordered in the last three months alone, I can only assume we intend to embroider the very walls of Versailles."

"Do not be silly, husband. And besides…" Her haughty look foretold unpleasantness.

"Besides what, dear?" My courage held.

She pointed at the boxes alongside my desk. "Will I ever understand what you need all those pins for?"

"Of course not, you are not a collector."

"And you have never sewn. Do not suppose to understand embroidery."

My hand circled over a morass of papers before falling on one particular sheet. "And what, pray, is *White Imperial Powder* and why do we purchase so much of it?"

"With five daughters, Mr Bennet, I hardly need explain why."

"No?"

"No." The shape of her lips indicated there would be no more information on that subject. "Is that Hill calling? I hope she has not ruined the drapes. I must go and see."

~ ~ ~

A week later and the memories came cascading back. My delight at discovering a Bennet Street. The sumptuous buns I used to buy by the dozen, their fragrance tormenting me until I reached my lodgings. The bookstores on Bond Street. The young ladies taking walks across the Crescent Fields and on through Cow Lane to Weston. I wondered if they would remember me, some twenty years later. That young man so in love with life and with Abigail, when one smile would send me tumbling into breathlessness.

We were in Bath, safely arrived at the house on Gay Street, perfectly placed to reach all the establishments the girls wished to see and be seen in.

I hoped to find some time to visit old haunts, since there would be entertainment enough to keep the rest of the family occupied. Bath offered all the benefits of London, but with less dirt, danger, and damage to your purse. Although, like in any English city, the best comedy, tragedy, and romance was always found among the audience, not on the stage or dance floor. Here, the ladies grazed on scandal and hearsay, while young bucks clashed horns in pursuit of bonnet-clad does. What connections might be made at a Haydn recital. What prospects ruined by a misplaced word or hasty gesture.

It was only as we first saw the city, spread out before us like an Italian landscape painting, that I truly knew how I felt at returning. My fears faded. I was happy, an emotion I found surprising.

~ ~ ~

As a servant of Cupid, my initial task was to prepare the ground for a meeting between Lizzy and Miss Hayter. Despite the chill wind, we took our first turn about the town the very day we arrived. And so my campaign began.

Memories truly were everywhere in the city. They clung like ivy, drawing my gaze to what was and, less pleasurably, what might have been. I stood on the same corner I used to wait at again and again, all trembling impatience, hoping for a glimpse of a pretty face edged in dark curls. I could still see where my nervous fingers had worn a patch in the brickwork all those years ago.

"I thought I might visit Tavistock's tomorrow. I understand he expects a large delivery of books. Perhaps I shall find something new on Prussia. I know so little of that country, an ignorance I fully intend to remedy." I resisted the urge to look directly at Lizzy as we walked along Quiet Street, her arm linked in mine.

"Might I join you, Papa?" said Lizzy. "Perhaps there is something new from Parses. His stories from Sicily were a treat." I smiled at my immediate success.

"But Lizzy, we were going to visit the shops on Milsom Street? Maria says they are quite the best for new fashions and I do so need your advice. You did promise." The Gods had sent Lydia to punish me for my hubris.

Books could not beat bonnets and the promise of an admiring look from a young man, but I knew of something that might.

"There is a teashop opposite Tavistock's that makes the most delightful sponge cakes. I am of a mind to call in there first and still the rumblings of my stomach before finding nourishment for my mind." This time I *did* look pointedly at Lizzy. Cake is a powerful weapon in the hands of the wise.

"Books and sponge cake. You would spoil me so, Papa. I am grievously tempted to break my promise to Lydia."

"Did we not say we would take tea afterwards at Curran's?" said the tool of the Gods. "Maria says their scones are to die for." It was a shame that was only a turn of phrase. Maria Lucas's advice was becoming quite unwelcome.

Army life, fortunately, had taught me to turn my enemy's tactics against them. "I am quite partial to scones myself. What say I treat you all to tea there tomorrow? Lizzy and I can meet you in the afternoon, after you have enjoyed all that Milsom Street has to offer young ladies with less sense than money." Lydia pouted but made no objection. "There, Lizzy, it is decided. You shall dine on sponge cake in the morning, scones in the afternoon. Can we not persuade you to join us, Lydia? Tavistock has a wonderful selection of philosophical treatises."

As we came out of New Bond Street, the tip of the Abbey came into view and I whispered a prayer that He might bless my endeavours. If my plan failed, then my only other option was to enter the seventh circle of Hell that was society to track down Miss Hayter. No doubt Mrs Bennet would have had all details of the young lady's movements within hours. But this task was mine alone for the time being. I resolved to keep my wife and girls in reserve, ready for deployment as a last resort should the battle appear hopeless. Besides, the longer they remained ignorant of the former identity of *Mrs* Hayter, the better.

Chance encounters

Lizzy and I sat in the teashop among the maiden aunts, all seeking safety in numbers for the nieces in their charge. The chink of spoons and teacups accompanied the steady hum of gossip.

We sat near a window, well-placed to keep an eye on the street and the entrance to Tavistock's.

"You seem distracted, Papa, are you well?"

"Quite well, thank you. I merely delight in observation. The ladies flit from one shop to the next, drinking in the nectar of fashion. They never stop long unless caught in the net of company. It feels like watching a meadow of butterflies. A most enlivening experience. More tea?"

"No, thank you."

"More cake, perhaps?" I pointed at the plate in front of us.

She fixed me with a stare. "Might we visit the bookstore now? Mama will fret if we take too long."

There was still no sign of Miss Hayter and too much tea was having an unwelcome, but inevitable, effect on me. Then, with an exquisite timing that had my legs skipping with delight beneath the table, a figure appeared beyond the window with a grace of movement I recognised from London. "Heaven forbid your mother should fret. It will only lead her down the rocky path to vexation and unpleasantness. Let us be away, Lizzy, and leave the teashop to the unmarried and the hopeful."

Tavistock's reminded me of Brecknell's. A place of dark corners that revealed its mysteries slowly, wrapped in the promising perfume of leather, glue, and expectation. I was happier here than in the cold orderliness of a typical circulating library. The smells called forth memories of winter evenings, feet warmed by slippers, imagination fired by Simpson, Raleigh, and my other favourite authors.

"Miss Hayter?" I was rather pleased with the note of surprise in my voice.

She lifted her head. Confusion turned into a smile of warmth I would have walked any street fifty times for three decades ago.

"Mama!" she called deeper into the shop. "Imagine, it is your old friend, Mr Bennet. Who we met in Brecknell's. The hero who saved me from the ignorance of Smythe." I ignored Lizzy's questioning glance, busy as I was trying to relax various parts of my body while clenching one part in particular.

"You flatter me, Miss Hayter. But I am delighted to see you again. And in a bookstore. If travel broadens the mind, then a bookshop is its own ship, is it not? Or carriage." Fumbling, foolish words, yet I received another smile for my trouble. It was difficult to stay sensible, hopping from foot to foot, regretting that last cup of tea, aware of the impending presence of Abigail.

Then she appeared.

I wanted to be resolute and steady of purpose, even believed myself master of my own mind and thoughts. But, just as in London, I was a lost man the moment I saw her.

If Abigail was troubled by our meeting, there was no sign of it. "James Bennet," she said, after introductions were over. "Almost thirty years apart, yet our paths cross twice in two months. I might almost suspect you are following me. What would your wife say?"

Lizzy saved me. "Mama knows Papa's eye falls only on beetles and butterflies. Though sometimes I think she is a little jealous of both in summer."

"Ah, yes, as I recall he was always one for pursuing butterflies across the fields here in Bath. But with little success." Abigail lowered her voice. "I believe he enjoyed the chase most."

"Is that so, Papa?"

I felt an urge to be somewhere else, and not just because of the tea.

"Do you enjoy travel books, Miss Bennet?" Miss Hayter's words were a timely distraction.

"I do. I find a journey in the mind as refreshing as one in the world. I am certainly enjoying Bath more than I anticipated after reading Mr Craven's guide. I am not convinced he has ever been to the city."

"Then he has much in common with Mr Smythe. It is your first time here?" said Miss Hayter.

"It is," said Lizzy.

"Then I hope your father allows you to visit more than just the bookstores."

"He does, but every corner reminds him of his own memories, leaving me little time to collect some of my own."

At this, Miss Hayter turned to her mother. "Mama, may I invite Miss Bennet to join us tomorrow? We might show her the Circus and I feel sure she would enjoy seeing the river."

I could barely breathe.

"I am not sure her father…" Abigail looked at me, her eyebrows raised just slightly.

"I would have no objection," I said, perhaps a little too hastily. "If you will indulge the daughter of an old…" I hesitated before settling on "acquaintance."

"Of course. You are most welcome to join us, Miss Bennet." Abigail addressed the words to Lizzy, but her eyes stayed on me.

~ ~ ~

Later, as I sat with my family before a mountain of scones, Lizzy interrupted my reverie of self-satisfaction.

"May I ask you a question, Papa?"

"As I recall, you claim it a privilege of your sex, though I also recall I am under no obligation to answer."

"It is about Mrs Hayter."

"Ah, there is no question you can ask there that I can easily answer. I knew her briefly many years ago, one of many acquaintances in Bath, but remember little." I put down the butter knife and tucked my hands under the table to hide the trembling.

"Who is Mrs Hayter? Do you have a mistress, Papa?" While Lizzy had the intelligence to navigate a conversation into safe waters, this was a reminder that Lydia did not.

"A mistress indeed! As if Longbourn could afford one." Mrs Bennet smiled.

"Lydia?"

"Yes, Papa?"

"Did you enjoy last week's assembly?"

"Oh, yes. I stood up for every dance. I was quite the prettiest girl there. Everyone thought so, didn't they, Mama?" My wife nodded her agreement.

"I am glad you did. But ask any more silly questions and it will be your last."

On pride and prejudice

The following day I took tea alone at the same table used to spy on Tavistock's. I would have preferred to sit with John, but a note from him that morning had warned us of delayed travel plans. My time was not wasted, though, as Lizzy and Miss Hayter saw me on returning from their walk. Abigail was not with them, a state of affairs that left me pleased *and* disappointed.

Looking at the recipient of John's admiration, I felt some pity for her plight. Her mother had wealth and independence, which would, fortuitously, pass to her daughter. As a result, she was 'blessed' with the opportunity to marry for love, should she and her mother wish it.

Were it standing or income she wanted, she could have had her pick of lords and landowners eager to decorate their great estates with a wife of equal value. But, if she sought love, she could not simply browse a line of ball guests and pick out her favourite. She could not find love by comparing incomes and titles, or reading society magazines. Instead, love would have to find her.

In such circumstances, poor Miss Hayter would be forced to

rebuff and delay, hoping for that one day when a man might break through her defences and then love her in return. Sadly for John, it seemed she had built her castle walls very high.

According to Sproggat's *Avians of the Americas*, there is a bird whose female sits quietly on a branch while a queue of males hop, flutter, and parade past, each attempting to draw her attention with ostentatious displays of plumage. Tea with Miss Hayter was similar. Barely a bun was eaten before some young gentleman was there to nod, bow, and preen as he sought to win her affections. She was a skilled duellist, though, turning praise aside or drawing blood with a word to send the would-be suitor fleeing, wings thoroughly clipped.

The confident ones she dealt with in conversation, the others through a lack of it.

"Miss Hayter, I have not had the pleasure of seeing you for some time." This fellow was a Mr Pearson.

"Nor I you."

"We see you little at the theatre or dances." He hesitated. "You are well?"

"Quite well."

"And your mother?"

"Yes."

"And you are enjoying tea?"

"Yes."

Few men could maintain an offensive in the face of such resistance.

"Well, I must be on my way. I wish you all a good day." An honourable retreat.

Her smile allowed her to skirt the edges of impertinence

without offending. Though she was all sweetness with Lizzy and myself.

"Miss Hayter!"

This one seemed a little surer of himself, less intimidated by Miss Hayter's finances. Introductions over, he contemplated the spare chair at our table like a pickpocket spying a mark.

"I find myself at a loss this morning, Miss Hayter. I have nothing to do and the cold of winter does not invite a long walk or ride."

"I had not believed you so susceptible to the whims of the weather, Mr Huddlestone. Surely a little chill in the air would prove no hindrance to a man of your robust character?" She was masterful.

"Perhaps you are right, though I do long for company. I find a walk or ride all the more diverting when taken in good company."

"How very true. Your friend, Mr Thorpe, was here but a moment ago. He expressed similar sentiments. I believe he left in the direction of Union Street. If you are quick, you should catch him."

"Would it be easier for you if I removed the chair?" I said, after Mr Huddlestone had left. She nodded her approval, smiling as she did so. "What rich society you have in Bath. You are acquainted with so many families, so many young gentlemen."

"Papa!" said Lizzy, but Miss Hayter laughed, seeming to take my statement as intended.

"Mr Bennet, I am a young lady of good family with a large income. Bath is a wasp's nest and *I* am sugared water."

"I admire your fortitude. But your mother must worry about your future?"

"You do not know Mama, Mr Bennet." That brought a

rueful smile to my face. "She would see me happy and, so, only married if such a state contributed to that happiness."

"And how might that happen?"

"Mr Bennet, such an interest in a young lady's feelings? I would think you a rake were you not already happily married. Let us say I do not seek a partner for wealth and position."

"Love, then?" said Lizzy, but Miss Hayter just smiled in reply. "Then we must pity the poor men who come to our table. Perhaps you could point out some worthy ones to me. I have four sisters all in need of husbands."

"Much depends on what you find worthy, Miss Bennet. Few men fulfil my understanding of the word."

"There we must differ, Miss Hayter. I believe all men are good and worthy, then allow individuals to demonstrate otherwise. It is my sister Jane's influence."

"Whereas I assume all men are foolish and allow individuals to surprise me. It is Bath's influence."

"You are very…direct, Miss Hayter," I said. "Is there not a risk in such judgments that you both look for signs that confirm your expectations and ignore those that would defy them? Does pride allow for a change of opinion?"

"I have little pride, I hope." Miss Hayter reached for a scone.

"And there we differ again," said Lizzy. "I have too much. I know this for Mama constantly berates me for it." As she spoke, my daughter's eyes drifted around the room, likely measuring up characters in that way of hers. "Oh…John! John!" She beckoned. "Over here."

My young friend waved to her, then wove a path through the packed seats.

"Mr Bennet! Elizabeth!"

"John, we thought you delayed."

"I was, but not as much as I believed. Mrs Bennet was kind enough to direct me here. How pleasing that you are here, too, Elizabeth." He stood before us like an innocent puppy.

"John." I rubbed my hands. "May I introduce you to a new acquaintance." He turned to look. "Miss—"

"Hayter," he whispered. "I assume...from what Mrs Bennet said about Elizabeth...Miss Bennet." His face seemed uncertain whether to turn pale or a deep red.

"Miss Hayter, this is Mr Barton, a family friend down from Gloucestershire. Lizzy, do retrieve that chair for us, there's a good girl. John, you must join us."

"How good that you could come earlier than expected," said Lizzy.

"I was delayed by an illness of a servant. I did not wish to leave until I could be sure he was in no danger." As he spoke, his glance flicked toward Miss Hayter.

"And he is well now?" He nodded at my question.

"John, you are trembling. Are *you* well?" There was concern in Lizzy's voice.

"I am fine. A little tired, that is all."

"Might I ask the nature of the servant's affliction?" I said.

"The apothecary suggested otherwise but *I* would have said a broken heart." John's eyes wandered briefly to Miss Hayter again.

Lizzy laughed. "I thought that disease the sole domain of *our* sex, John."

"Only in books. I think we may suffer so, too, but perhaps we show it less."

"Are you suggesting ladies exaggerate their feelings in such matters, Mr Barton?" said Miss Hayter.

"Not at all, Miss Hayter, rather that men moderate theirs, even assuming we know them for what they are."

"You are harsh on your sex. Though I am no great admirer of such men as Wordsworth, Byron, or Shelley, you cannot accuse them of reluctance in expressing their feelings more than adequately."

"But they are poets. Few men possess their command of thought and word."

"Thank goodness," I muttered, drawing a look of reproach from Lizzy. I fell silent again as the duel continued.

"True heartbreak would need no words," said Miss Hayter. "It would be evident in a man's bearing and mood. Like true love, it cannot be so easily disguised or hidden."

"Can it not? Now *you* are harsh on my sex, Miss Hayter. Fear of ridicule or rejection might drive a man to hide even the strongest of emotions. We are insecure at the best of times. How much more insecure we become when we love, but do not know if we are loved in return."

"And yet Shakespeare wrote *They do not love that do not show their love.*"

"Shakespeare was a playwright, not a peddler of indisputable truths."

"But are his plays not based on experience? Are they not a summary of what it is to be a man or woman? Is that not the foundation of their popularity?"

"He talks of witches, ghosts, faeries, and baking your enemies into pies. I beg to suggest experience is *not* the defining element in his work."

"You do not like Shakespeare, Mr Barton?"

I suddenly felt very tired. "John, Miss Hayter, let us not—"

"I have the greatest respect for Shakespeare, Miss Hayter. But we cannot all be Romeo."

"John is more of a painter," said Lizzy, no doubt trying to be helpful.

"Oh no," I whispered.

"A painter?" said Miss Hayter. "And what do you paint, Mr Barton. Let me guess—light and movement and colour, no?" I hoped John noticed the hint of sarcasm in her voice.

"Light and colour, mostly." He did not. Or chose to ignore it.

"And what light and colour does our Bath shop offer a man who paints?" Miss Hayter spread her arms. "What shines brightly in among all the tea and cake?"

John sat back somewhat and little creases crossed his brow. "Why…you do, Miss Hayter." He spoke as if it was the most obvious thing in the world. "You shine."

For the first time since making her acquaintance, I found Miss Hayter at a loss for words.

"Well," said John. "I believe I should be going. Errands and, yes, things to do."

"We will see you later?" said Lizzy.

"Of course. Elizabeth, Mr Bennet…Miss Hayter."

Abigail's daughter stared after him as he left. Almost out of the door, he stopped to look back and half raised his hand as if to bid farewell.

"Painters," I said, with a wan smile. Miss Hayter remained silent.

~ ~ ~

After delivering Lizzy and her new friend to the latter's home, I set off in search of John. He sat in an inn near our lodgings, head in hands, a half-empty bottle of red nearby.

"John?"

He looked up, then grimaced. "Was I a complete fool or just half a fool?"

"I'm not sure." I sat down and helped myself to his wine. "You did question her appreciation of literature. And cast doubt on her understanding of human nature. Then you embarrassed her publicly with a compliment that was entirely unsuitable, given you had only met her ten minutes earlier."

"I did not know what I was saying. She...disconcerts me." He groaned. "Is my cause already lost?"

"It could have been worse. You did manage not to insult her family. And there is some good news. As I left, she mentioned that you were...interesting."

"Oh, hell."

"Come now, John. Interesting is good."

"Beetles are *interesting*." He was right. "Reports of a recent trip to Yorkshire are *interesting*. But Hermia did not declare herself swept away by Lysander's *interesting* character. Interesting is how you describe a book you dislike when you know the author personally." He managed to slump even lower in his chair. "She is too beautiful for any man."

"Oh, I would not say that. A whole stream of young men paid their compliments while we took tea." He did not look reassured. "If I might give you one piece of advice?" He nodded. "Should you...*when* you speak to her again, do not talk about literature. Or painting." I paused. "Or butterfly collecting."

"Butterfly collecting?"

"Trust me, avoid that topic. But see, you have had your meeting at last. And I think you are still very much in love with Miss Hayter, no?" His look was all I needed to confirm my opinion. "I will see you later, John."

As I turned to go, he caught my sleeve. "Is she not wonderful?"

"She certainly takes one's breath away." I thought back to that first meeting in Brecknell's. "She is easy to love, John, temper notwithstanding. But I do not think she will find it easy to love in return. Be patient and do not expect a miracle."

~ ~ ~

Lizzy lay on the sofa, head back, almost purring in delight. "I do so love Bath."

I peeked out from behind my book. "I take it your day with Miss Hayter was enjoyable?"

"It was. She has a small library she takes with her everywhere. I am quite jealous."

"No doubt full of plays and poetry," I said.

"She even has a book on butterflies."

"How unfortunate I am not twenty years younger. And single. She sounds perfect, though her tongue can be a little sharp."

"In her position, I wonder it is not sharper. Men of greed and poor character beset her on all sides."

"Though you paint a poor picture of my fellow man, Lizzy, I shall not argue with you. But I hope you do not count John among those wretches."

"Of course not. Though if he had not left, they would likely still be arguing." Lizzy sat up, hand beneath her chin, a puzzled look on her face. "Mrs Hayter asked after you, Papa."

"Did she now?" I was careful to keep my head firmly behind the book this time. A sidelong glance found Mrs Bennet absorbed in her embroidery, enjoying the last of the daylight.

"She said she knew you in Bath many years ago."

"Did she?"

"Is that true, Papa?" Kitty called from across the room. "Did she know you?"

"She did, albeit briefly. As I said, she was one of many," I allowed my voice to grow a little louder.

"You have kept it secret from us," said Lizzy.

"It is no secret. The acquaintance was of no consequence. Besides, since Miss Hayter has no eligible brothers, cousins, fathers, or uncles that I know of, I assumed the information was of little relevance to you all."

"Did you—" began Lydia.

I closed my book abruptly. "If I wished to be tormented by endless questions, I would have taken us to Spain."

"Why Spain, Papa?" said Kitty.

Lizzy mouthed "the Inquisition" at her and Kitty mouthed back "the what?"

"I would like to go to Spain," said Lydia, standing and twirling before us with her head raised and eyes closed. "All those regiments. I would never run out of officers to dance with."

A clash of conversation

I felt a little like Wellington, poring over a map of Bath, pushing around little models of Lizzy, Miss Hayter, John, and the rest. I could almost sense the lead weight of Abigail, heavy in my hand.

The Pump Room would play host to the next skirmish. Miss Hayter and her mother were to make a rare visit there in the afternoon and sent a note to ask if Lizzy might join them. It seemed my daughter's company tempted Miss Hayter out into the sunlight of society.

"The Pump Room, yes, what a good idea, Lizzy." Like a mother hen, Mrs Bennet began gathering her chicks in preparation for a grand excursion.

"But there is no need for all to attend, Mama. Papa can escort me until I meet with Miss Hayter and her mother." Lizzy looked to me for support, but I knew my wife.

"We shall all go, Lizzy," I said. "Why are we in Bath, if not to enjoy its pleasures? I shall not disturb your new friendship, and your mother and sisters will be too busy enjoying the spectacle to interfere. John, you will join us?"

"I do not feel much like society. Perhaps afterwards." He was still in mourning. At least his face had resumed a natural colour, albeit tinged with green from too much wine the day before.

"Very well," I said. "Meet me outside the Pump Room around three. We may take the air, talk a little of those things that interest only gentlemen."

The ladies all dressed up warm in bright shawls and pelisses; I wore my blue greatcoat. Suitably braced for the chill of Bath and the discerning eyes of its inhabitants, we stepped out to walk down to the Pump Room. The trickle of people became a stream as we neared our destination.

~ ~ ~

"Miss Bennet!"

I looked over Miss Hayter's shoulder and relaxed. There was no sign of her mother.

Lizzy introduced her new friend to the rest of the family, who paid polite attention to Miss Hayter, but no more than that. They were like children at their first circus, lost in a whirlpool of strange sights and desperate not to miss a passing juggler.

Lizzy and Miss Hayter drifted away into a quiet corner for earnest conversation, while Mrs Bennet and the others threw themselves into the midst of Bath society.

I was left to myself, an abandoned general waiting for news from the front. Would it be defeat or glory?

"Tea or coffee?"

The ghost from the past returned, plunging me into the same maelstrom of emotion that had trapped my tongue back in Brecknell's and Tavistock's.

"If I recall correctly, James, you are a tea man, with only a little milk and one of those small, round biscuits Cottersham's used to sell. Though no longer, I fear. Various continental inventions are all the rage in Bath now. It becomes harder to indulge in past loves."

I could not remember how *she* took her tea. Only how she looked when doing so.

"Your daughter is a blessing. She has enraptured Anne. They have much in common: an interest in books, a keen eye for observation. They also share an alarming impatience with arrogance or stupidity. They will see plenty of that here." She drew an imaginary circle around the room with a twist of her finger. "Your wife must be an excellent woman to have brought up such a daughter." She paused, but I was still struggling to find the right words, or *any* words in her company. "You have grown silent with age."

"My apologies, Mrs Hayter…Abigail…it has been a long day." She arched an eyebrow.

Out of the corner of my eye I could see Mrs Bennet approaching with two glasses of water. Her look suggested she was burdened with vital gossip to impart and, with Mrs Philips back in Meryton, it would fall to me to receive it.

"Lady Reynolds!" Abigail swept off. I did not know who the good Lady Reynolds was, but offered up a silent prayer to thank the Lord for having sent her.

After a few minutes of trivial conversation with my wife, I stepped outside to see if John had arrived. He was waiting, eyes a little puffed, a few stray strands of hair dancing across his forehead in the wind.

"You know, John, you will find it easier to encourage a lady's interest if you are at least in the same room as her."

"I thought I would wait, see what more you might discover."

"That sounds exciting," said Lizzy, surprising us. "Have I discovered some plot?"

"Lizzy. And Miss Hayter," I said. "How...delightful. John and I were about to take a walk...up past the theatre."

"We are going that way ourselves, since Miss Hayter wishes to show me some of her favourite shops, at least from the outside. There is no need for the rest to accompany us, then, if you will do so instead?" I nodded. "I shall tell them at once. They will not be unhappy to stay longer in the Pump Room." And off Lizzy went, leaving John, Miss Hayter, and myself to stand in a silence as stony as the colonnade we found shelter under.

Just as I was beginning to feel a prickle of discomfort climb my back, Miss Hayter spoke. "It is refreshing to be out of the wind, is it not?" My relief was great. John could not possibly give offence on such a topic.

"Yes," he said. "Although I find a gale often reminds me that I am alive."

Miss Hayter placed her hands on her hips. "Do you often forget that you are alive, Mr Barton?" My prickle returned.

"Not often, no." John's right leg began to shake slightly. "Do you?"

"I am fortunate enough to have a daily reminder when I wake."

"I think, perhaps, what I meant was that a good wind can bring us out of a reverie or black spirits, especially if it is also raining."

"The people of Scotland must be a merry folk indeed." I

winced at her remark and ran a nervous finger around the inside of my cravat.

"May I ask, Miss Hayter, what makes *you* smile?" said John.

"Intelligent conversation, Mr Barton."

He swallowed hard. "Then you must have little cause to smile at all, especially around men."

"You are very harsh on your sex, Mr Barton. Once again." She folded her arms.

"In our eagerness to impress, we fall easily into flattery and foolishness. That is all."

"How would you then advise your fellow man to give intelligence to their flattery?"

"They might quote the poets. Perhaps Wordsworth?" In his nervousness, he must have forgotten yesterday's conversation.

"If you quote Wordsworth to me, how am I to know whether you are truly intelligent or merely a good reader?"

"The two commonly go together," said John.

"Besides," said Miss Hayter, "poetry cannot substitute for one's own thoughts. Especially Wordsworth, who I cannot abide."

"But if those thoughts are foolish, then is it not better to use those of others? Of poets or other masters of language."

"Miss Hayter, Mr Barton, I beg of you both." I might as well have stayed silent.

"Since you quote no poetry yourself, Mr Barton, am I to understand you have no wish to flatter me?"

"All men wish to impress, but not all wish to flatter. I have enough intelligence to know that flattery would not impress *you.*"

"Miss Hayter, you must come." Lizzy saved us all from further conversational toil. "I have found an old acquaintance and promised to introduce you. She must leave in an instant. Papa and John must wait for us a little longer."

After they went back inside, my young friend turned to me. "I am not myself when I am around her."

"I had not noticed. Come, John, it was not all that bad." I returned his questioning stare. "Perhaps you should try less conversation." A thought sprang from my memory of post-assembly discussions. "Or you might try a compliment. Only a small one, mind."

The two ladies soon returned, hurrying to reach the safety of the colonnade's arch as the grey skies darkened and growled above.

"It is beginning to rain," said Miss Hayter. "How pleased you must be, Mr Barton." I had to hide my smile.

"My thoughts on the wind and the rain may have come out badly," said John. "I become a little confused in the presence of beauty." Miss Hayter's eyebrows formed little arches of their own.

A return to the dance floor

The next day I claimed for myself.

Mrs Bennet and the girls visited the shops with Miss Hayter, eager to find the fashions that little Meryton could not provide. Since they were just as eager to see those same fashions worn by the rich and titled, or by those who aspired to join them, they planned another visit to the Pump Room.

That was the very last place I wanted to visit, in case *she* was there. Though a part of me yearned for the chance to see Abigail again, a larger part dreaded the feelings such a meeting would bring.

Instead, I treated myself to one slow walk up and along to the Crescent, where memories became real before me. The feel of the cobbles through my boots. The cries of the waggon drivers as they made their way out of Corsham's, loaded with wine and ale for the inns. All that was missing was the smell of fresh loaves outside Lancaster's, but it seemed Lancaster had moved on. Rolls of fabric now lay where once there were rolls of bread.

Later, despite my intentions, I found myself in a teashop with John, Lizzy, and Miss Hayter, who had somehow met each other—

and me—in town. Perhaps John had followed my practice of lurking on street corners in the hope of a serendipitous meeting. I braced myself for the next conversational faux pas my friend would come up with. Perhaps a contrary comment about cats? Something dismissive about the colour blue?

I had become a little tired of tea. Ever since we had been in Bath, we seemed to follow an eleventh commandment curiously ignored in the Bible. *Thou shalt honour the tea bush and drink of no other beverage.*

Lizzy, perhaps sensing John's insecurity, did much of the talking. She had clearly found a kindred spirit in Miss Hayter, who was her equal in wit and intelligence, if more scarred by her experience of society. They dealt with passing men with deft slices of conversation. It felt like John and I were condemned prisoners, forced to watch the brutal execution of our fellow gentlemen. It was hard to feel sympathy, though, since most of them stalked Miss Hayter without finesse or charm, as if hunting rabbits. Eventually, though, the shooting parties found a better manor to bless with their buffoonery and we were able to enjoy crumpets and tea without disturbance.

"You talk very little of your travels, Mr Barton. Most men I know are only too keen to boast of their experiences abroad and the strange ways of all who are not English," said Miss Hayter.

"Yes, John," added Lizzy, "Do amuse us with tales of bizarre dinner rituals and the worst excesses of the Viennese aristocracy."

"I fear I can only disappoint," said John. "I lived abroad so long that the bizarre has become normal. Now it is English rituals and behaviour that appear amusing."

"Is that so?" said Miss Hayter. I prayed John would not seek to expand on his previous comment.

"Take the waltz," he said. "In Vienna, it is just a dance, an amusement. Here it is talked about as a threat to the purity and innocence of our womenfolk. We imply too much in a touch on the dance floor."

"But our beliefs beget rules, and rules give us certainty, do they not?" said Miss Hayter.

"Some certainty," said John. "But so much is still implied. So much depends on correct interpretation. Is a touch an accident or a promise? It would be better if we could speak plainly."

"Better, perhaps, but much less diverting," said Lizzy. "What would we ladies have to talk about after a ball if not a thousand different explanations for a look, a word or…a touch?"

"I would not wish to deny you that pleasure," said John, smiling.

"And how are we to interpret *your* words, Mr Barton?" said Miss Hayter.

John spread his palms in front of him. "I am not skilled with words. Perhaps that is why I enjoy painting. It allows me to express myself more clearly."

"Perhaps you might simply speak plainly."

"I think it is my plain speech that is the problem. People are not used to it, so look for nuances that are not there."

"So when you spoke of me shining…?"

"You shone."

They held each other's gaze, faces expressionless, each waiting for the other to blink. I could not say what was going through their minds.

Just as I was preparing a righteous cough to end the standoff, a small disturbance at the door attracted our attention. A rather portly young gentleman was easing his way through the tearoom carrying a small book. The scraping of chairs, little exclamations of surprise and a multitude of apologies marked his passage.

"Mr Jameson," whispered Miss Hayter. "He is very amiable but a little clumsy and a *lot* shy. Our mothers are great friends so he will feel the need to greet us, though he may be terrified of doing so."

"Is he…?" said Lizzy.

"Single? Yes and no. He adores a Miss Whitworth, a distant cousin of mine. He would make her a wonderful husband. His shyness hides a kindness few men possess. Unfortunately, it is this very shyness that prevents him from expressing his admiration. I do not think he knows where to start. It is perhaps time that someone intervened."

During introductions, Mr Jameson mopped his brow with a handkerchief, casting occasional looks behind him.

"Can I offer you a crumpet?" said John. "We are quite full and it would be a shame to waste the hard work of the baker. We have tea, too." He pulled out a chair, near the window and away from other tables.

I expected Miss Hayter to find a clever excuse to withdraw the invitation. Instead, she confirmed it. "Yes, Mr Jameson, do come and sit with us. I have not seen you for so long. What is it you are reading?"

Mr Jameson mumbled his thanks. One hand held up the book so we could see the title, the other fiddled with his jacket buttons.

"Wordsworth, how delightful!" said Miss Hayter. I looked

straight at her, surprised at her praising the very poet she had derided so strongly the day before, shocked when she began to quote verse.

A Violet by a mossy stone
Half-hidden from the eye!
—Fair as a star, when only one
Is shining in the sky.

"All good men should read Wordsworth," she said. "So they may make our lives more pleasant with his flattering lines. I think you will enjoy the book. Only the other day, I was saying to my cousin Miss Whitworth—"

"You know Miss Whitworth?" said Jameson.

"Yes, we are related. She delights in poetry, but only when read out loud. I believe she would fall in love with the first man to recite Wordsworth to her." She winked at Lizzy and took a bite of crumpet.

"I did not reckon you a follower of Wordsworth," said John, voicing my feelings.

"There is a time and a place for Wordsworth, Mr Barton. Do you enjoy his work?"

"Very much. I find quoting his poetry helps ensure intelligent conversation."

~ ~ ~

"My experience of such matters is somewhat limited of late, but it seems unlikely you can dance with Miss Hayter without first talking to her, John. And if I am any judge of Bath society, if you do not talk to her *soon*, her card will be full and you will have to spend the evening dancing with my daughters."

"You make the prospect sound like a penance," said John.

"You have not seen Mary in a quadrille. Now, see if you can dance with her twice. Apparently, that is all it takes; my wife is adamant on that point. Though, on reflection, it turns out she may have been misled."

To the delight of all but myself, we found ourselves at a dance in the evening. Compared to the Netherfield ball, the rooms had less decoration, but the people more. In a city full of colourful birds, nobody could afford to wear drab plumage.

I had spent the first minutes musing on all the places I would rather be, but the list was too long. Besides, as a follower on the battlefield of romance, I had little choice if I was to offer John support.

At that moment, Lizzy and Miss Hayter appeared at our table. "Papa, I have seen you happier at one of Mr Toke's sermons. Will you not dance?"

"Lizzy, you know me well enough to discern the answer. Besides, I cannot imagine either of you short of partners. Or is there still space on your card for one more?" I gave John a little glance.

"I have an empty space for the next dance, Mr Bennet, and would be delighted to fill the gap with your name," said Miss Hayter. She gave me a smile that all fathers knew. The kind that ensured a new ribbon, or merely mild censure for even the most heinous of improprieties.

"I fear my old legs are past dancing. But…" I turned to John. "I am sure Mr Barton would happily take my place. Can I prevail on you, John, if Miss Hayter is willing?" For a moment, he looked like a young fawn surprised on a woodland walk, all trembling nerves and uncertainty. But he recovered well.

"If Miss Hayter would honour me with a dance, I would be…most honoured."

She held his look in silence for long enough to induce a familiar feeling on the back of my neck. "It would be…" She paused, seemingly searching for the right expression. "Illuminating."

John and I must have looked uncomprehending. "That is a yes, John," said Lizzy.

As soon as they were gone, John fled in the direction of the punch bowl for a sip of courage before the dance started. On the far side of the room, Kitty and Lydia had tracked down and captured the only officers in sight, while Mrs Bennet was engaged in trading gossip with a lady she had met earlier at the Pump Room. It was a moment of quiet isolation among the hum of conversation, disturbed only by the occasional raucous titter or the discordant tones of a musician tuning his instrument.

"The James Bennet I knew never rested, not while there were pretty girls to dance with and good wine to drink. Has time aged you, James, or has my daughter's company tired you so?"

She was magnificent in a yellow silk gown, a pattern of roses drawing the gaze up to her face…and those eyes. Pretty as a field of daffodils. I was close to quoting Wordsworth, a sure sign of trouble.

"Will you save me, James? Nobody will dance with an old widow. Except perhaps an old friend?"

My mouth responded before my brain. "I would be delighted." I had never regretted four words more comprehensively, unless you count "Will you marry me?"

I was sure I would have all the grace of a drunk bluebottle.

Worse, there would be a torrent of teasing and a host of questions from the girls after. All for a few minutes dancing with Abigail. A part of me knew it was worth it.

I offered her my arm and together we moved out on to the dance floor.

"I am surprised to see you here. I was told the Hayters kept away from the Pump Room and assemblies. Was the gossip wrong?"

"Not entirely. But Anne has enjoyed showing Miss Bennet around Bath, and I have found my own reason to enter society more often." Her hand seemed to grow heavier.

Hearing the music begin, I was back in Bath as it once was. A young man, charming, and mischievous. "I do not see an old widow, Abigail. I see—" I caught myself in time.

She laughed. "For a moment, you were almost the James Bennet of old. You must be careful."

We lined up, her daughter and John on one side, Lizzy and a gentleman I did not know on the other. Regrettably, that meant too many conversations for one man to follow, though I was interested in all three.

"How are you enjoying Bath, Mr Barton? Have you found anything in need of painting?" said Miss Hayter.

"There are some shop fronts on Milsom Street that…oh you mean…well, yes," said John.

"You are distracted, James. Do my charms no longer have the hold they once did?"

"No. I mean, yes. Or no." I hoped Lizzy was not listening closely.

"I owe you an apology, Miss Hayter. My opinions may

sometimes come across as criticism of those who hold different ones. I blame it on Austria. My grasp of German is not strong enough for me to add nuance to my speech. As I have said, I often speak too plainly."

"But you are in England, now, Mr Barton. Perhaps I should ask my old governess to offer you English lessons?"

"What is so amusing, James?"

"Nothing. I was merely thinking of the last time we danced."

"Ouch!" Lizzy's partner, it seemed, was even worse at dancing than Mr Collins. I would not have to worry about his name, income or character. If he could not dance, then no Bennet girl would marry him. Though Jane would express sympathy for his plight.

"Again, James, it seems your thoughts are elsewhere. A happier place, I hope?" The words were soft but a tight smile suggested otherwise.

"My apologies, Abigail. It has been a while since I was on the dance floor. I had quite forgotten what it was like." The dance took us away from the others. "Lizzy is delighted by your daughter."

"But you are not?" Unfortunately, she twirled away from me before I could give an immediate answer.

"Of course I am," I said on her return. "But my opinion of young ladies is of little interest to anyone." The music stopped, so we moved away from the other couples. "Miss Hayter is certainly very popular in Bath. Every time we take tea, the men come swarming like flies."

"They do." She pointed to the table serving punch. I recognised Mr Huddlestone, standing with another gentleman, both trying to offer a silvered cup to Miss Hayter. John was nowhere to be seen.

Abigail looked me in the eye, all humour gone from her face. "I will not see her happiness sacrificed on the altar of comfort and position. I have seen to it she will need neither from a partner."

"For many, such comfort and position *is* happiness."

"But not for everyone, James. Not if you can neither love nor respect your husband. Or your wife. Is that not so?"

I did not reply immediately. "I cannot say."

"Cannot? Or will not? Do not look so stern. Your sense of propriety prevents you answering. It is to your credit."

"You always were free with your opinion, Abigail."

"And you should have been freer with yours. It might have prevented much suffering." I did not dare ask her meaning, my courage failing me when needed.

"Thank you for the dance. It was a delight," she said, lifting her gown and moving swiftly away. Before she had gone more than two or three feet, though, she spun around. "Those should have been your words, James. For a moment, before we reached the dance floor, I thought I saw your old self. But I was wrong. You are much changed."

I wanted to reach out, offer some protest with a word or a gesture, but she had turned away and the moment was lost.

Departures and revelations

With our time in Bath drawing to a close, I took Lizzy down to meet Miss Hayter one last time. I had wanted to visit Madiston's anyway, where I hoped to buy a copy of *Quod vero de Papilionibus*. I could have had it sent from London, but it provided a useful excuse to stroll through the city again.

As we walked, we exchanged little witticisms about some of the people we passed. It was unkind of us, perhaps, but the young men in particular were wont to make fools of themselves in public. It seemed a shame to waste the opportunity.

Miss Hayter was waiting for us with her mother outside a milliner's shop on Milsom Street.

"You go on ahead, Lizzy," I said, waving to the Hayters and preparing to make a hasty withdrawment.

"Will you not join us for a moment, Mr Bennet? We see so much of the daughter, yet so little of the father," called Abigail.

I felt the now familiar tug of long-lost feelings returning to haunt my presence of mind. "It would be my...pleasure," I said as we approached, taking care not to hold the eyes of Abigail. I feared what mine would reveal.

~ ~ ~

"Are you scared of me, James?" My cup rattled against its saucer as I placed it on the table. On the other side of the tearoom, Miss Hayter was introducing Lizzy to some acquaintance.

I was terrified. "Do not be silly, Abigail," I replied, before stuffing myself with cake to excuse further elaboration.

"If you say so." She stretched her arms out on the table until they almost touched my hand. "I loved you, you know."

I swallowed, but could not speak.

She pulled her hands away. "Why did you never ask me to marry you? I quite expected it. Hoped for it."

Now it was my turn to pull my hands away, gripping the table to steady myself. Moments passed before I found my voice. "I...I did not ask you because you were not there to be asked." I sought Lizzy out in the crowded room. She was still engaged in conversation. "If you must know, I came back to Bath with the express intention of speaking with your father, only to discover from a gossip on the coach that Miss Abigail Spencer was newly engaged to a local landowner of great wealth and promise. I did not even disembark."

"You did not write to me," she said. "I heard nothing more from you."

"It would not have been seemly."

Her face hardened. "And then you married Mrs Bennet. How fortunate that your affection for me was so easily—and so quickly—replaced."

"Papa?" The girls had returned. "Are you well? You have a strange colour about you." Lizzy put her hands on my shoulders.

"I am perfectly fine. Perhaps I have eaten too much and should take to the fresh air."

"What a wonderful idea!" said Abigail. "We shall all walk together up to the Circus."

~ ~ ~

Lizzy and Miss Hayter kept far enough ahead to stay out of earshot. Abigail and I walked without talking at first, her hands firmly entrenched in a muff, mine fixed at my sides.

I stopped and turned to her. "It was neither easy nor quick."

"So what did you do to bridge your disappointment? If I had to guess, I would say you retreated into drink, books, or travel."

"America," I said, quietly.

"But there was all that fighting?" She paused for a moment. "Oh, I see."

"I only caught the tail end. No battles. Just the odd skirmish, nothing recorded in newspapers or books. We were not even officially fighting anymore. But I saw enough blood for a lifetime. Just not enough to drive away the memories of Bath, memories of…" I looked away from her for a moment, glad that the clatter of a passing carriage excused me from finishing the sentence. "We should catch up with the girls. It is getting late and I must attend to matters in Gay Street. Abigail—Mrs Hayter—I beg your pardon but I must abandon you. My thanks again for your kindness to Lizzy."

I could not read her face and feared, again, what she might read in mine. But on leaving, I did not forget the purpose of my Bath visit.

"I am pleased your daughter and Lizzy have found each other. It has the makings of a fine friendship." After a few paces, I turned back to her. "In my experience, those who have lost in love often become cynics, finding relief in the barbs of conversation. They are all too keen to build walls around themselves."

"Are we talking about you…or me?" she asked, holding her bonnet to prevent it blowing away.

I did not answer, but went on my way, bidding Miss Hayter farewell and taking the long way back to our lodgings.

~ ~ ~

John left for Gloucestershire in the afternoon, but I managed to draw him to one side before he departed.

"And?" I said, gripping his arm. I had not been able to speak to him alone since the dance.

"I am still in love, if that is what you ask."

"Of that I am sure, John. But is there hope that I and my friends might go back to talking about other matters? Spring will be here and we need to plan our collecting trips." I was half serious. Ever since that first letter from John I had become altogether too distracted.

"At the dance, well, I believe she may now only dislike me. It is an improvement. Before last night I was convinced she must hate me."

"Progress indeed. In a few years, we may persuade her to be merely indifferent to you."

"Did Elizabeth invite her to visit Longbourn?" Now it was *his* turn to grasp *my* arm. "Was the invitation accepted?"

I gently removed his hand from my sleeve. "I have not yet seen to it, but believe Lizzy will be amenable to the idea. One step at a time."

"Thank you, sir, for all you have done."

"Yes, well, we shall see where it all leads us. Hopefully not to more disappointment. Leave it with me. Return to your estate and await my news."

"I shall do so, with more optimism than when I left."

His words reminded me of Jane, so my thoughts turned to London and whether the Gardiners had helped her recover her spirits. I hoped so. One broken heart was enough in the Bennet family.

~ ~ ~

The whole family enjoyed a small supper together at the end of our last full day in Bath. Tucking into an excellent soup and even better wine, I looked forward to a quiet read by candlelight.

Lizzy put down her spoon. "Papa, do you think we might invite Anne Hayter to stay with us at Longbourn?"

In my sudden excitement, the hot soup escaped down the wrong channel. All I could do was cough and splutter.

"My apologies, Papa, you think it too soon. It is only that I feel a strong attachment to her. We are already almost as close as sisters."

Still spluttering, I waved my spoon-free hand in an effort to dismiss her objections.

"Yes, you are right, Papa," said Mary. "We should not be hasty in pursuing further acquaintance until we are all more familiar with each other."

"Give your father a glass of water, Mary, he is quite beside himself," said my wife.

I managed to gasp "no" before another bout of coughing.

"Your father has spoken, children. Let that be the last word on the matter."

They continued eating while I removed the last traces of the itinerant soup. "Perhaps your idea has merit, Lizzy, despite my initial reservations. Although you have not known Miss Hayter long, one should never stand in the way of a good acquaintance, especially one which might throw all you girls into the paths of eligible bachelors." I may not have been the best spouse in England, but I did know where my wife was ticklish.

"How am I to understand you, husband?" Mrs Bennet cocked her head to one side like a magpie espying silver. "You said the Hayters have no male relatives."

"Miss Hayter did say that gentlemen are always calling and that several seem determined to marry her," said Kitty.

"There you go," I said. Then I remembered who I was trying to help. "Several? How many exactly?"

"I think it would be unsupportable to seek Miss Hayter's company solely for the sake of her connections, though," said Lizzy.

"Besides," added Lydia, "I have heard talk of Mrs Hayter."

"How so?" I asked.

"Yes," said Kitty, leaning forward and looking across at Lydia. "I have heard things, too."

"What things?" I said.

"It is not seemly to gossip," said Lizzy, as Kitty seemed poised to answer my question.

"Not seemly at all, Kitty," said my wife. "I abhor gossip. I should not like people to gossip about us." She frowned. "Not that we give them reason to do so. But tell us," she ventured after a brief silence. "What exactly *do* they say about Mrs Hayter?"

I watched the conversation like a condemned man.

"Apparently, she was quite the beauty when she was younger," said Lydia. "Is that true, Papa?"

"I could not possibly say."

Lydia's eyes gleamed. "They say dozens of men sought her hand, for she was also wealthy." They all looked at me but I merely shrugged my shoulders. "They even say that Miss Hayter may be…"

"Enough! I will not hear any more. I will not tolerate innuendo and supposition in this family. And as far as this Mrs Hayter goes, Lizzy is as fine a judge of character as I know. Besides, if there was any doubt about her she would not be seen so freely in the Pump Room or elsewhere. Why, back in the day, there were three other men who would have gladly married your mother. Are we to condemn her as quickly, merely for having looks and a dowry?"

Mrs Bennet mumbled something through her wine glass.

"What is that, dear?"

"Five, husband. There were five other suitors. I believe you may have forgotten the Mayhew brothers…though I have not." She smiled. "Now I think upon it, it was six. I am sure Captain Greenwich would have made an offer if you had not."

"It does not matter if it was five, six or six hundred. Lizzy, you will invite Miss Hayter to visit at Longbourn. And that is truly my last word on the matter."

Back to Longbourn

The family deemed the trip to Bath a triumph. Lizzy's new friend lightened the loss of Charlotte. Mrs Bennet returned bearing enough gossip to last several suppers with Lady Lucas and Mrs Philips. And all saw enough of society to desire some temporary relief in the tedium of home.

Most importantly, Miss Hayter soon accepted our invitation and, weather permitting, would join us a few days later. All that was needed was to ensure John visited at the same time.

Bath was still close enough in memory to ensure good spirits as we walked home from the morning service. Toke's sermon on generosity set the right mood for broaching the topic of another guest. Even Mary was less grim-faced than usual, perhaps because of a look or two exchanged with Mr Spigott.

"John Barton will pass through Meryton shortly. I thought we might ask him to stay. You all seemed to enjoy his company so much, both here and in Bath."

"Of course we must ask him, even if he did forget his easel last month," said my wife. "He is not as amiable as Mr Bingley and was a little morose in Bath. But such fine manners and a handsome face, is that not so, Kitty?" My daughter smiled in agreement.

"Will he be here at the same time as Miss Hayter?" said Lizzy.

I paused for a moment. "Let me think. Yes, he will at that."

"Would that be wise?" said Mary. "Miss Hayter might consider it improper." She looked to me for confirmation.

"There is nothing in the idea to suggest impropriety, Mary," I said.

"Though from what I heard, the two did not get on in Bath," said Lydia.

"I grant they enjoyed some robust conversations," I said. "But nothing unpleasant. Lizzy?"

She took her time replying as she stepped carefully around a small puddle that sat indelicately in the middle of our path. "I do not believe there was any animosity. Simply a difference of opinion on some matters. Well, if I am honest, on *many* matters. John is normally so open and eager to please, but with Miss Hayter, he seemed almost argumentative. I expected him to be more amiable around a young lady."

"Perhaps that tells us something about Miss Hayter, Lizzy. She is…spirited," I said.

"Forgive me, Papa, but you must allow a woman of education and standing to hold opinions. It is not so improper."

"It is not her opinions as such that concern me, Lizzy, merely her way of expressing them."

"Perhaps if men were more inclined to listen, she would not have to express them so forcibly."

"Lizzy!" said her mother. "Do not get above yourself."

"We should ask her mother, though? About Mr Barton's

presence." Mary's question ended any further argument.

"There is no need to trouble the mother." I picked up my pace.

"Did you not find her company amenable while dancing?" called Kitty.

"You danced, Mr Bennet?"

"Yes, briefly." I looked back over my shoulder at my wife. "Do not look so surprised. It was against my better judgement, forced upon me by duty and obligation."

"How extraordinary. When was this? It must have been on the Monday. Do tell, girls. Your father was *very* fleet of foot during our courtship. How does he now dance?"

I held one palm up for all to see and to ensure my wife's question remained unanswered. "Since we were much engaged with her daughter, I felt duty bound to extend my compliments to Mrs Hayter by asking her to dance. It gave me no pleasure. And how I dance is not a topic for a Sunday, or for any other day. And that is an opinion you would all do well to listen to."

Without thinking, I touched my arm where Abigail had held it.

~ ~ ~

With John and Miss Hayter circling toward each other slowly, like two leaves caught in the gentle swirl of a pond's eddy, the Fates decided to place a little worm in the apple of my plans. It seemed Mr and Mrs Collins would be visiting Meryton at the same time as our guests. Mr Collins's unerring knack of wreaking verbal havoc was a dangerous card in the game of lovers' whist. The only comfort was that he would stay at Lucas Lodge, not Longbourn.

"I shall have to hope they never meet," I said, staring out of one of the Flighted Duck's windows at the end of a Society meeting. The others had long dispersed in search of home comforts and warmer fireplaces, but Fielding, as was traditional, still lingered.

"This Mr Collins seemed harmless enough when we met him last year," he said.

I tapped the bottle between us. "A drop of wine is harmless enough, dear friend, but too much of it and you soon find yourself head down in a ditch missing your breeches. I am serious. We should drop Mr Collins in Paris. He would drive away the French faster than any army."

"At least our Bath plan was a success. But tell me, Bennet, what does the future now hold for your young bachelor? Does our Miss Hayter show any sign of attachment?"

"He seems to set her aflame at each encounter."

"Well that is good news, indeed. A toast to your Mr Barton!"

I put my hand over his glass before he could lift it. "The fires might well be anger, not affection."

"Ah. Still, let Longbourn weave its magic and then we shall see. Jackson was right: neutral ground may prove more fertile for love to blossom. And since we are on that very subject, I have another question for you." Fielding folded his hands in his lap and seemed to search for the right words.

I raised my eyebrows. "Yes?"

"What of her mother?"

"What of her?"

He stared at me like a mother at an errant child. "I was curious and looked up the family history. Mrs Abigail Hayter was once Mrs Abigail Trott and, before that, a *Miss* Abigail Spencer. That name is familiar to me. You mentioned it many times when we were younger, nearly always after a considerable amount of port."

I shifted in my seat.

"So, you *did* see her? I knew there was something missing from your accounts of Bath and London. So, tell me…is she still as engaging? Still as 'easy to love' as her daughter?"

"You go too far." Outside the window, shouting filled the silence. Two drivers, disputing the right of way. "I am faithful to my wife."

"That was never in question, dear friend." He patted me on the hand. "You know, they say true love never dies."

My thoughts wandered back to our trip to Bath, to how she took my arm at the dance, prettier than ever before. I lifted my eyes to catch his. "We can all imagine a better life, Fielding. Yet we may also accept our current one, leave that better life to daydreams tucked away for long walks on winter mornings." My voice caught in my throat. "You understand?"

Fielding nodded gently, then filled my glass with wine. "Let us drink to a handsome lady and what might have been." His eyes softened. "Then you should go home and drink to what must be."

A coming together

"The fish is not to your taste, John?" I said.

"It is fine. But I am not." He let his fork fall on his plate.

"She will be here later this afternoon. It will do no good to mope in this manner; you must give a strong impression of yourself."

We ended our conversation as Lydia joined us in the dining room. "I am quite famished. Though it gives me a pale, romantic look, like a heroine from one of Mrs Edgeworth's novels. Perhaps I should starve myself until Mr Barton paints me." Her harsh look made no impression on John.

"What a fine idea, Lydia," I said. "And if you should starve yourself to death, we will at least have the consolation of one less mouth to feed." Her frown made no impression on me.

"You seem glum today, Mr Barton," she said. "When are you to paint me?"

"Now, Lydia, John is an artist and you should not hurry them."

"My apologies, Miss Lydia, I am somewhat distracted today." John threw a glance at the window. "Besides, there is too much cloud. It would reflect badly on the painter *and* his subject if I chose the wrong colours in such poor light."

"We cannot have me looking anything other than my best. I shall be patient, then. But not so *very* patient."

"What you need, John, is a spot of fresh air," I said. "The rain has stopped. Let my man take you shooting. It will focus your mind and make the time pass *faster*."

John sighed. "Perhaps you are right, Mr Bennet."

~ ~ ~

An hour after John had disappeared into Longbourn's copses, carriage wheels rattled outside.

"That will be Miss Hayter, girls," cried Mrs Bennet from upstairs. "Let us all go and sit quietly in the drawing room. She must not find our country manners wanting."

Moments later, Hill announced our visitor. "Mr Jackson for you, sir."

"Good day, Bennet!" The call came from the hall, so I went out to meet him. "Thought I would drop in. Bring you that pamphlet." His breeches were new and his cravat tied in a manner I would have thought beyond a man of his years. He seemed to be on his way to some meeting of import.

"An unexpected pleasure, Jackson, though I forget this pamphlet you mention."

He grabbed my arm. His voice fell to a whisper. "Well, where is she?"

"Where is who?"

"Miss H of course."

I drew him away into the study, then closed the door behind

us. Once inside, I turned to him. "Jackson, am I to surmise that the sole reason for your visit is to spy on Miss Hayter?"

"Lay of the land and all that, Bennet." He tapped his nose, then settled into the armchair nearest the drinks table. "Wars are won with information."

"Right, yes, thank you." I found it impossible to blame the fellow for his interest, having encouraged it these past weeks. "She is not yet here. You know the roads from the west can be a devil in winter."

There was a knock at the door. Hill again. "Beg your pardon, sir, but you have another visitor."

Jackson stood, adjusting his hair and necktie.

"Mr Stanhope, sir."

"Jackson?" He merely shrugged at me as he sat down again.

"Bennet, so pleased I caught you," said Stanhope, entering the room. "I was close to Longbourn and thought about that book you promised to lend me."

"What book?" I said.

"Jackson! What a surprise." Stanhope's voice suggested quite the opposite was true.

"Sit yourself down, Stanhope. Is that a new jacket? Bennet here was about to offer us a drink." Jackson tipped his head at the bottles next to him.

"Of course," I said. "I'll organise some *tea*."

I left the study not quite knowing if I should be annoyed or pleased. Mrs Bennet made her own feelings clear outside. "Mr Bennet, Hill is most inconvenienced. Did you not think to warn us your committee would meet here today? As if we do not have enough guests. Still, I am sure we will manage somehow." She almost collided with our housekeeper coming the other way.

"Begging your pardon, but another visitor has arrived."

"How unexpected." I strode toward our front door. "I have no more books to lend and no time for pamphlets...oh...Miss Hayter."

"Do not mind my husband, Miss Hayter. He has not been himself of late." My wife gently pushed me to one side. "You are most welcome. Come through to see the girls. Hill, do bring tea."

With unmatched timing, Fielding then appeared behind Miss Hayter, shaking drops of fresh rain from his coat. Jackson and Stanhope emerged from the study behind me, their faces a mixture of awe and admiration. After introductions, Stanhope held up a book. "Butterflies," he stammered.

"We have heard so much about you," said Fielding.

"You have?" Miss Hayter offered him an uncertain smile.

Hill then coughed in the way of an experienced housekeeper, a noise both loud *and* discreet. An apparition stood in the doorway, hair decorated with skeletal leaves and mud, clothes dripping water onto the floor to punctuate the open-mouthed silence.

"John," I said, "You know everyone, I think."

"Mr Barton," said Miss Hayter. "You continue to surprise me. Were you lifting your spirits in the rain?"

~ ~ ~

While my unfortunate friend went to clean up, my wife led Miss Hayter to the girls. The committee returned to their horses and carriages, satisfied with the promise of a full report at the next meeting. After waving them goodbye, I hurried to the drawing room. The giggling within ceased on my entry.

John joined us, hair slick from washing, face tinged in red. Almost immediately, the girls—even Mary—collapsed in laughter. To his credit, John faced the humiliation with stoic fortitude, like a soldier who had made peace with his God.

"I have always wanted to become more familiar with the lakes around Longbourn, but may have taken the acquaintance a little too far." He held the edge of his palm to his chest. "About four feet too far."

"We are cruel," said Lizzy. "To find pleasure in the misfortune of others is shameful, especially when the burden of that misfortune falls on a much beloved friend. You will forgive us?" He smiled and nodded. "You did scare Miss Hayter, though, John. And that *we* cannot forgive. Your punishment will be to paint us all as soon as the light allows. Besides, Lydia talks of nothing else and we tire of her complaining."

"So you truly are a painter, Mr Barton," said Miss Hayter.

"As you know from Bath, I paint, but would not go so far as to claim to be a true painter."

"And why not?"

I steeled myself for another argument, but it was Lizzy who intervened. "It is certainly modesty."

"And you, Miss Hayter, is painting among your accomplishments?" said John.

"No, though I might call myself a painter."

"And how are we to understand that?" said Lizzy.

"When I was a child, I painted my father. He gave me sixpence for it."

John frowned. "You would not define a painter through his work, then, but through his success in selling it?"

"Can he be a true artist who does not live from his work?"

"A true painter perhaps lives *for* his work." John held Miss Hayter's gaze briefly before looking away.

She did not take her eyes off him. "And what do *you* live for, Mr Barton?"

He did not have the chance to answer as Mrs Bennet marched into the room, hands waving. "All the gentlemen seem to have left and now we have too much tea. It is all most confusing."

"That it is," I said, looking between John and Miss Hayter.

An unwanted reunion

The next afternoon, with the skies clear, Mrs Bennet persuaded Lizzy to take her friend to Meryton. Lydia and Mary she busied with sorting bits and bobs, leaving Kitty to entertain John. As on his last visit, I rescued him as soon as possible. "There is a volume of Italian engravings I would like your opinion of. Perhaps you might join me in the library? Kitty, go help your sisters." Kitty smiled at John, frowned at me, then skipped off towards the kitchen.

"Miss Catherine Bennet is a charming companion," said John, as we settled into the sanctuary of the library. He looked like he meant it.

"Though we know you would prefer the company of another lady in the house, no?"

John looked down at his feet. "Every word she speaks improves my opinion. She has a fire in her. But I fear my own words do me little credit."

"Do not be disheartened. We have enough time to work on her impression of you."

"I am paralysed by my affection. Would that I could talk to

beauty as well as I paint it. I did not fear the great gardens of Belvedere nor the majesty of the ocean, but Miss Hayter..."

"John, as always I say this with the best of intentions." He looked up. "Are you still sure of your affection? Miss Hayter seems, well..."

He looked me directly in the eyes. "She is prickly and defensive, but we both know the reason. Those who precede me must share the blame for that. I am not of their ilk. And my heart is still lost."

When a young man mentions his heart, then he is lost forever. A knock at the door prevented me responding. "A guest, sir. Mr Collins has been seen approaching and is expected at any moment."

"Cannot Mrs Bennet welcome him?"

"Begging pardon, sir, but Mrs Bennet says she and the girls are terribly indisposed and asks if *you* might, sir."

"Terribly indisposed?" I imagined what that would look like, certain they were hiding behind a locked kitchen door.

"Very well, send him through when he arrives." I turned to John and pressed my palms together. "My apologies, John. Imagine an affable gentleman of genuine humility, reserve, good education, and better conversation. Have you done that?"

"Yes."

"Now imagine quite the opposite. Whatever you do, do not mention buildings or gardens."

Moments later, Hill announced the latest guest to Longbourn.

"Mr Collins, what a pleasure to see you again."

"I found myself nearby on a morning stroll and could not resist paying my compliments." He made a show of looking around the library. "Your dear wife and daughters?"

"Indisposed, Mr Collins."

"How unfortunate," he said, shoulders relaxing.

"Mr Barton is staying with us from Gloucestershire." The two exchanged greetings. "Mr Collins is the parson at Hunsford and my cousin, lately married."

"My congratulations," said John. Mr Collins gave him the sort of nod that cannot decide if it should become a bow. "Hunsford? Is that near…" Behind Mr Collins's back, I shook my head vigorously. "…Rosings Park?"

"Indeed, sir, I am most fortunate to enjoy the patronage of that great estate, which my own humble abode adjoins. You are familiar with Rosings?"

"I have heard it has magnificent…" He hesitated, like a man unsure if he was taking the right path. "Fireplaces?"

A Collins enthused is like a foot wart—untreatable and most unpleasant. Yet the expected laudatory for Lady de Bourgh's architecture never came. Instead, he muttered to himself, head half-cocked to one side. "Barton, Barton, ah!"

John and I exchanged looks of bemusement.

"Mr Barton! Now that I recall, Mr Bennet spoke of your friendship not a few weeks ago in Meryton. As did Mrs Bennet. I am *most* pleased to see you here and in such welcoming circumstances." He twitched as if he had something in his eye. "But my! Dear Charlotte will worry at the length of my absence. I am blessed to have such a caring wife. It was she who suggested I take a walk alone. And no doubt you have much to discuss yourselves…" Another twitch. It seemed he had picked up some nervous affliction since the wedding. I would have believed it more likely of his wife.

He left us both somewhat befuddled and, in my case, grateful for the brevity of his visit. A little later, I entered the kitchen to exact my revenge.

"My dear, I took the liberty of inviting Mr Collins for dinner tonight. He does so look forward to seeing you all again. And I could not help but notice he was carrying a volume of sermons with him. If we are lucky, perhaps he will read to us all." I let them stew until dinner.

The misery of men

The morning heavens held the first promise of spring, the perfect day for fresh garlands of affection to embrace the hearts of young ladies. Unfortunately, it was also a perfect day for a walk to Meryton. Mrs Bennet had again sent Lizzy and Miss Hayter away, this time in search of new fabric for a damaged gown. Lydia accompanied them, though more in search of soldiers than silk.

"Miss Hayter will soon know the path to town far better than she will ever know you," I muttered to John in a moment alone.

My wife busied Mary and Kitty with some task, but rapidly grew irritated with the younger of the two. She insisted John and I take her out for a walk around the grounds, preventing John from following the other girls.

The constant calls of the crows seemed to mimic my own irritation at the hurdles placed in my friend's way. We had not gone far when cries of "Papa! Papa!" brought us to a stop.

"Whatever is the matter, Mary?" She had a coat on over her shift, but seemed uncomfortable in the cold.

"You are needed at once, Papa."

233

"What has happened?"

"I cannot say, but Mama insists you return. She is most vexed." And away she ran.

"We shall, of course, return as well, Mr Bennet," said John. "But do not tarry on our behalf." The urgency in Mary's voice compelled me to overlook the impropriety of leaving the other two alone, however briefly.

I set off in earnest, Mary far ahead, John and Kitty following a growing distance behind. On reaching the last bend before the house a shout caused me to stop and look back. Kitty rushed toward me, one hand held to her mouth, the other pressed against her bonnet.

"Kitty?" She ran on to the house, splashing through puddles without a care for her clothes.

John then strode past me, his back uncommonly straight. "John! What is all this?"

He turned back to face me, cheeks red, hands shaking. "Mr Bennet, it is only respect for your family and my father that prevents me from leaving your house immediately. I had always believed your advice was offered in friendship, an honest wish to help the son of an old comrade. Instead, I find this invitation, indeed all your efforts, were but a plan to throw me together with your daughter." I was speechless. "Amiable Miss Catherine may be, but she is *not* Miss Hayter. Can you explain yourself, sir?" My momentary hesitation set him off again. "You cannot. I thank you for at least having the honesty not to deny the charge, and bid you good day." And away he went, equally dismissive of the puddles.

The scene at the house was just as perplexing. My wife

embraced a tearful Kitty in the doorway, with a distraught Mary nearby. On my arrival, Kitty pulled herself from her mother's arms to run inside, followed by her sister. Doors banged upstairs.

"Oh, Mr Bennet, what have you done?" My wife shook her head.

I had the same question. "My dear, I am at a loss. Why is John under the impression he is the victim of some plot to marry Kitty?"

"Poor girl, how she suffers. She has been cruelly misled."

"Misled? Explain yourself."

"I was told only yesterday that an understanding had been reached for a match *I* have encouraged. You had objections that were now overcome, and John's current visit was to finalise the engagement." A vague memory tugged at me like a child wanting a treat. "Was that not so?"

"This is nonsense!"

"And now dear Kitty, in her innocence, gave a hint of her own satisfaction with the arrangement to John and was rebuffed most forcibly. It was ill done, leading her on so. Ill done by John and ill done by you. Have you no concern for your daughters? No concern for me?" She wiped away a tear.

Then I remembered. "Collins!" I shouted.

"Yes," whimpered Mrs Bennet, "I met him yesterday, as he was leaving. He congratulated me on such a fine catch."

"Where could he have got such a ridiculous notion?"

"It seems he first learned of John's interest at one of your committee meetings."

"And you never thought to talk with me, first?" I asked.

"Do not shout at me so, husband. Oh, Mr Bennet!"

"There has never been a wish on my part to see John married to one of the girls, desirable though such a prospect might seem. His interest lies elsewhere. Mr Collins has the perspicacity of one of the potatoes he so admires. You and Kitty have been misled by him and he has been misled by his own insufferable foolishness."

Now it was my turn to storm inside the house. The study door mimicked that of Kitty's room as it slammed shut behind me. Then I just stood there with my fists clenched, chest heaving. Anger and despair make poor companions, but they would keep me company for the rest of the day.

The meaning of affection

Dinner was a joyless occasion. John remained in his room, pleading a poor stomach. I had neither the courage nor the countenance to go up and talk to him. Understandably, Kitty also kept to her room. Lydia stayed in town with Mrs Forster and an importune storm prevented Lizzy and Miss Hayter's return. Mrs Philips kindly kept them safe and dry, though the same could not be said of the unfortunate boy who delivered the information to us. Mrs Bennet did not make it past the soup before her nerves forced her to retire early.

Dinner for one, then, and plenty of time to reflect on my failures. Eating alone gave me little peace, as the distant sound of crying accompanied each mouthful. Afterwards, I did what all good Englishmen would do. A bottle of fine red wine eventually dulled the pain of the day and the prospect of pain to come. But it did not silence Kitty's wailing.

~ ~ ~

If dinner yesterday had been uncomfortable, breakfast the next morning was almost intolerable. We all sat together in a silence interrupted only by Kitty's whimpers.

Eventually, I could bear it no longer. "Kitty, I will thank you to end this ceaseless noise. It is not appropriate behaviour." Her whimpering ceased, though the tears did not. Nobody spoke.

After some minutes, John put down his cutlery, then leant toward my wife.

"Mrs Bennet, it seems I have been the cause of much distress and injury through my behaviour, albeit inadvertent and with the best of intentions. My apologies, madam." He looked across to me. "And to avoid further discontent I intend to leave this morning for Gloucestershire."

I spoke before my wife had a chance to. "You have done no harm in this household, John, taken no action, spoken no words that require an apology. Kitty is young, impressionable, and the victim of a deep misunderstanding, one for which you carry *no* blame. But it is her youth that will allow her to recover with speed from her disappointment." There were enough officers in town to provide the necessary distraction. I turned to Kitty. "We have another guest returning soon, and I do not wish her unduly disturbed by what has passed. Is that clear?" Kitty nodded. "As to your wish to leave, John, I implore you to reconsider. At least do me the favour of speaking with me after breakfast. I believe you misled in apportioning blame for recent events and wish to speak with you about them."

"Very well, sir."

~ ~ ~

Soon after breakfast, John joined me in the study. He stood in the doorway, hands clasped in front of him, his head at an angle. Lizzy often had the same look, a mixture of resolve and defiance.

The box in my hands gave me the strength missing in my tired old bones.

"Sit down, John. Please." He walked over to perch on the edge of a chair. I held out the box to him with all the reverence it deserved. He took it, then let his hand run along the dark grain of the rosewood. "Go on," I said.

He opened the box and sat silent for a moment, face confused. "What…"

"Take it out."

The steel blade sent shafts of sunlight spinning across the far wall. He rubbed the broken end with his thumb. "What is it?" he said.

"That, dear John, is the reason why I could never do or say anything against the wishes of the son of Mr Henry Barton." I sat down in my chair and poured myself a drink from the decanter on the desk. "It is a little early, but still…" I held up an empty glass to John, but he shook his head.

"The sixteenth of October 1782, in woods whose name will not trouble the history books. Hostilities were more or less over, or so we are all told. True, there were no battles, no incidents deserving the word 'major' placed before them. But there were skirmishes, encounters, little conflicts barely worthy of the title. Forgotten by all but the unfortunate few who witnessed them." I paused to take a sip. The liquid ran slowly down my throat, burning its way back to the past. "I was knocked aside by a musket, left on my back like an upturned beetle. Never was much of a swordsman." I closed my eyes. I could smell the stale sweat of the man standing over me, weapon thrusting down, his face wreathed in terror. "They say time stops still in such moments, but I only remember how fast it all was. No time to think. No time to move, to react, to resist. I would have died if not for your father." I opened my eyes and put down my glass. "He turned the blow. The bayonet pierced only my sleeve and broke, left that piece stuck in the ground." John stared at me, the steel loose in his hand.

"And your assailant?"

"Your father dispatched him with his upstroke." John put the blade back in the box as I spoke. "Do you think I could ever sport with the son of the man who saved my life?"

"But then why did Miss Catherine...?"

"A misunderstanding, and there I must take some blame. As you know, I did not take Mrs Bennet into my confidence concerning Miss Hayter. I did not wish to put her in a difficult position. Single men are all potential sons-in-law for her. Unfortunately, she heard a misleading report from an acquaintance who himself misunderstood a comment or two, and then gave Kitty the wrong impression. The fault lies with me, though. I forgot my wife would follow her instincts, as is her right, and failed to recognise the signs. Will you forgive me, John? Will you stay?"

He rubbed his chin, again. "Of course. But only if you will forgive me for the unwarranted condemnation of your honour and word. It was foolish and unworthy."

"Nonsense," I replied. "It was merely the natural reaction of someone presented with the terrifying prospect of a lifetime with Kitty."

He was trying not to laugh; the tension was gone. "You are most hard on your daughters."

"When you have five daughters like mine, you may understand that I am all too soft."

After he left the room, I finished my glass, closed the box, and returned it to its resting place. My hands did not stop trembling until much later.

~ ~ ~

The next morning sat on the border between the chill of winter and the warmth of spring, when the leaves on the ash trees begin escaping their tight black prisons.

Mrs Bennet had the younger girls sorting dried herbs, while Lizzy and Miss Hayter looked through the former's clothes with an eye to sunnier days and changing fashions. I took John off into the gardens and down to the bottom stream. I felt sure he would enjoy the shy yellows and greens of the willows and daffodil buds.

We stood in silence a little while, watching birds skit on the light breeze. I fought the impulse to ask if the wind helped him feel alive.

"Your conversation with Miss Hayter has lost much of its previous harshness. I do believe there may be one or two subjects on which you actually agree." They had both stated that the breakfast ham was more than usually succulent and been equally of one mind in their praise of the cake.

"You jest with me, I think. We still argue, but at least she does not dismiss me like she did all those gentlemen in Bath. For that I must be grateful. Yet neither does she flatter or indulge in polite irrelevancies, breakfast fare notwithstanding. You have the wisdom of years, Mr Bennet. How am I to understand the lady?"

"As a friend of our family, perhaps you enjoy a unique status among the men she meets. It is no surprise, then, if she treats you differently."

"Her words give no indication of affection."

"Ah, I believe that is a topic we covered adequately in Bath. For my part, affection is evident in gestures and deeds: a blush, a glance, in all those ways we reveal ourselves when we act from instinct, when we act from the heart. Reveal a little more of yourself to her. Perhaps she simply needs encouragement."

Miss Hayter's voice called after us as we reached the bottom of a meadow. Though I looked behind her, I could catch no sight of Lizzy.

"I am glad to find you. Mrs Bennet said you would be here." She caught her breath and looked around at the view. "There is something about willow branches trailing in a stream, like a painting come to life. Don't you think, Mr Barton? All we need is a stray heifer, a cowherd, and a good sunrise and we shall have our landscape."

"Is Lizzy not following?" I said.

"She has taken to her bed."

"Is she unwell?" said John. "Should we return?"

"She complains of a headache and wishes to be left alone for a short while. It is not serious, I think. I had hoped to help Mrs Bennet with the herbs, but she was at a loss to find work for me. And so she suggested you might like female company. You do not mind? I have no wish to come between men discussing matters of great import."

I sensed a trap. John, too, seemed to be learning, as we both merely mumbled general approval of her presence.

"Perhaps you can help us, Miss Hayter," said John. "We were again discussing how one might recognise affection in another. Mr Bennet believes in gestures and deeds. You would agree with him, I think?"

She thought for a moment before replying. "I hear many sweet phrases in Bath and few move me. Some are said to tease, others out of politeness. Still others are out of affection for my mother or my wealth. Perhaps some are truly meant earnestly. But I would need more than words to know the honesty of the feelings so expressed. Is it not what we *do* that defines us best?"

"I would argue it is what we *feel*," said John. "And feelings provoke actions, except where one might fear the consequences of such feelings, however honourable they may be."

I could sense the conversation taking a familiar and unwanted turn.

"I know Elizabeth would be disappointed were we to leave her alone too long," I said. "*My* feelings of concern certainly require action. Let us walk back to the house."

The conversation moved to safer ground as Miss Hayter collected early spring flowers to give to Lizzy. She gave a little exclamation of joy each time she discovered a new bloom, delighting in the freshness of the season. I could not help but smile. It felt almost like walking with Abigail.

We found Lizzy waiting in the back garden with Mrs Bennet, Mary, Kitty, and Lydia.

"Are you recovered?" I said, as we all sat on the grass. It had long lost its morning dampness, despite the weakness of the sun.

"Yes, Papa. A little solitude and darkness does more for a

headache than any of Mr Jones's concoctions. Did you enjoy your walk?"

"Mr Barton and I had another argument," said Miss Hayter.

"John," said Lizzy. "I am disappointed. Why this great interest in picking arguments with young ladies?"

"I do not wish to contradict Miss Hayter, but it was a *debate*, not an argument. One leads to enlightenment, the other to a grievance."

"I am glad to hear it," said Lizzy. "Do tell me, though, what did you 'debate'?"

"How words alone are not enough to properly express affection for another," said Miss Hayter.

"Oh, yes," said Mrs Bennet. "I lost count of how many men made declarations of affection when I was young. I did not believe any of them." My wife wore her youthful popularity like a blanket, to keep her warm as she aged.

"Do tell us, Mama," said Lizzy. "What did Papa do to make his affection more worthy?"

"Yes, tell us, my dear, so we might warn young men."

"He showed me Longbourn."

"Mama!" chorused the girls.

"If a man is to declare his affection to me, then it should be in full regimentals while seated on a white charger, and in front of everyone so they know I have bewitched him." As Lydia spoke, Kitty nodded with enthusiasm. It seemed she had recovered quickly from her recent disappointment.

"He must not bring me flowers," said Mary. "It shows a lack of inspiration and an affinity for the ephemeral. He must bring me books."

"Books. A fine idea," I said.

"Thank you, Papa. Ecclesiastical tomes and moral lectures would be most suitable."

"How romantic," muttered Lydia.

"How about you, Lizzy?" I looked at her intently.

She sat back on the grass. "I cannot separate affection from respect. With all his words and actions, he must show I am more than some prize to be won at a fair. He must value my companionship *and* my opinion. His conduct must be to my wellbeing, but with no hope that I may discover his kindness, with no intention of seeking advantage through his behaviour. Then I can believe his actions selfless and anchored in true affection. And once assured of my affections in such a manner, he may then express his feelings through the giving of numerous presents. Volumes of poetry, exotic jewels and invitations to travel the world." She laughed.

"Well said, Lizzy. I wish you a man able to offer such affection. But we have not heard from Miss Hayter on this matter." I turned to her. "What do you require as a sign of affection? Surely you owe an explanation to Mr Barton?"

"Why me, sir?" said John, half rising from the ground.

"If Miss Hayter disagrees with your view, then she must present her alternative," I said.

"Of course." He settled back down.

"A grand gesture," said Miss Hayter. "That is all."

"I am surprised," said Lizzy. "I cannot see you waiting for some proud officer on a great stallion."

"That is not what I mean. He must do something out of character, something he is uncomfortable with, but with the hope of impressing me. The proud officer must come down from his stallion and bake a cake."

"And the baker?" I said.

"Must ride a white charger, of course."

"But what should a lawyer do, Miss Hayter? Or a doctor? Or an artist?" I did not think Lydia meant to embarrass John, though he froze at her final words.

"That is for them to decide," came the answer.

Conflict and conversation

As so often when guests were at Longbourn, Mrs Bennet had felt the need to invite officers for dinner. I was not overjoyed. As their stay in Meryton had continued, their stories had lost much of their novelty.

The usual tales of drink and daring soon bored me and left John on the periphery of the conversation. He sat patiently, like a wolf cub waiting for his elders to finish eating.

"Gentlemen," I said. "Have you seen Mr Barton's painting of Kitty? He has talent, no?"

"Mr Barton is clearly a man of great skill," said Mr Murden. "I envy him. Not least for the hours he must have spent admiring your daughter." Neither John or Kitty smiled at the comment. "But I cannot be too jealous. After all, we military men prefer to seek adventure in the real world, not hidden behind a canvas." Mr Wickham and Mr Denny chuckled.

Both Lizzy and Miss Hayter glanced at John, but he showed no outward reaction. Instead, it was Lydia who spoke. "Do tell, Murden. Have you more stories for us?"

I sighed. "Now, now, Lydia, let us not burden Mr Murden

with *all* the responsibility of conversation."

"I thank you, sir, both for your consideration and your fine wine, but what use would it be to endure the hot sweat of battle if I could not boast of doing so?" Mr Murden paused to refill his glass, then cleared his throat with unnecessary drama. "Let me think. Ah, yes, here is one I have yet to tell…

"It was the summer of 1809 and a small group of us were cut off from the main army. We were too late to join Wellesley at Talavera. Thousands of Frenchmen lay between us, with no means of circling round before battle commenced. It seemed we would have to sit this one out."

"How unfortunate," I murmured, attracting a "shush" from Mrs Bennet.

"Desperate to offer aid to our fellows, I set upon a plan. Had us all dress in peasants' clothes, shove fruit down our fronts, and march straight through the French lines disguised as Spanish washerwomen. We were too ugly to attract unwanted attention. An hour later, we were back in uniform and showing the French the wrong end of a bayonet."

"You are not serious, Mr Murden?" said Miss Hayter once the laughter had died down.

"Madam, I am *always* serious."

Miss Hayter smiled. "Such bravery. It is a wonder you were not promoted on the strength of that incident alone."

Mr Murden sighed. "Alas, Miss Hayter, bravery alone is insufficient qualification for a higher rank."

No," said Mr Wickham. "For that you need to consume large quantities of wine, thrash your fellow officers at cards, and compliment the colonel on the elegance of his wife."

After more laughter passed, Mr Murden continued. "As to the first, Wickham ..." He drained his glass, then waved the empty vessel at the table before helping himself to more wine. "Your debts in my favour speak to the second point." Mr Wickham raised his hands in mock surrender. "And for the third, anyone who has seen Mrs Forster can have no reluctance to express such admiration. She is a beauty."

Lydia put her hand to her mouth. "Mr Murden!"

"Though the same might be said of all the ladies present." Mr Murden gave each a brief nod, lingering a little too long on Miss Hayter for my liking.

"Mr Murden, I always say regimentals are a sign of great character," said Mrs Bennet.

"They are certainly a sign of *a* character," said Miss Hayter. "Though we should not judge a book by its cover. Perhaps by its words. Or actions." She looked across at John. "But we shall not bore the table with old disagreements."

A slight blush tinged my friend's cheeks. He seemed about to reply when Mr Murden, perhaps importuned by half a minute of conversation without his involvement, spoke up. "Wickham, you and I will never impress the ladies with modesty and mystery. Unlike our painter from Gloucester, we are fond of good, honest conversation and they must take us as we are." Again, John showed no reaction.

"And fine gentlemen you are, too," said Mrs Bennet.

"We are open books, Murden, ripe for reading," said Mr Wickham.

"But," said Lizzy. "Will we find you shelved as military history? Or mixed in with the worst of the novels?"

"Any book that a young lady would wish to consume, Miss Elizabeth," said Mr Murden. "And what about you, Mr Barton?" He twisted to look at my young friend. "We have entertained you with our stories, as officers must do. You are a painter. Will you not paint something for us, this very moment?"

"I am no master," said John. "Besides, I have no tools to hand."

Mr Murden flicked his hand dismissively. "A typical artist, then. In my experience, most of them are charlatans and wastrels."

Lizzy and Miss Hayter exchanged glances. Even Mrs Bennet seemed uncertain how to react.

"Steady on, Murden," said Mr Denny.

"Oh, I am only ragging you, Mr Barton. You are no doubt a splendid fellow. The exception that proves the rule."

"John," said Lizzy. "You are so quiet. Are you not provoked by Mr Murden's dreadful teasing?"

"Is that what it is?" said John. "No, I see no threat from Mr Murden. We do not play the same game."

"Ah, there you are mistaken," said Mr Murden. "All conversation is but a game, no? And ladies are present. Where there are ladies, there is competition. Will you leave the field clear for the military men?"

"I place my trust in those ladies, sir. They know the true worth of a man."

"Then you risk a brutal defeat. Take Miss Hayter." Everyone looked at our guest from Bath. "I wager she prefers a soldier. A man of strength and authority, more skilled with a sword than a paintbrush."

Miss Hayter seemed unperturbed. "You ask me to choose between brushes and blades, Mr Murden, when I have seen neither in action."

"You would like my blade, I think."

"Mr Murden, we edge away from respectable conversation," I said. "We soldiers forget ourselves sometimes. Let us talk of other things."

"Perhaps what you need from me, Mr Murden, is proof of *my* skill with a blade?" Once he had our attention, John picked up a knife and flourished it theatrically. "Do not be alarmed, ladies." He turned to my wife. "If I might have some flour, Mrs Bennet?" She nodded, sending Kitty to fetch some.

John pushed his plate and glass to one side. "I am a maker of pictures. If I use paint, they call me a painter. If stone, then a sculptor. If words, then a writer." All the time he was talking he collected items from around the table. "We all make pictures, Mr Murden. You, for example. Every story, every quip, every witticism builds a picture of how you would like us to see you. The amiable officer. Is the picture real? That is not for me to say."

"John?" I said, but fell silent at his look.

He unfolded a large, green napkin and, after Kitty's return, began placing small piles of flour on it, smoothing them out into shapes with his thumb. Everyone was silent, seemingly hypnotised by the rhythmic movements of his hands.

"Miss Elizabeth Bennet," he continued. "Now, she uses words to build a picture of others. She examines character like the carver tests the grain of the wood, noting its strength and direction. I envy her intelligence." He began placing dried leaves and fruits from the table centrepiece on the napkin, crushing some beneath his fingers, then spreading out the results with the flat of his knife. "Miss Hayter, she already has a picture in her mind and judges everything she sees in comparison. It is a beautiful picture, a masterpiece, and I fear the likes of myself appear dull and foolish beside it."

He stopped for a moment, and it seemed as if we all held our breath, wary of any noise breaking his spell. "One more thing." He reached over to pluck a handful of dried flower stalks, looking at Miss Hayter as he did so. "Lavender." He crushed the blossoms to release the faded purple florets. These he spread along one edge of the napkin. Finally, he used the end of his knife to make a few indentations.

"You wished me to paint, Mr Murden? I have done so as well as I can with the tools available to me." He turned the napkin around to face my end of the table.

"An autumn meadow," murmured Lizzy. I looked at Miss Hayter and saw her, perhaps for the first time, as unguarded as she might be when alone. Her fork hung loosely in one hand, her other hand clasped to her chest, her breathing fast.

The bottle did not break when it hit the table, but it released a stream of red wine that flowed into the meadow, plucking flowers from the soil and turning clouds of flour into a single, sticky mess.

"Oh, Mr Murden," said Kitty. "We have not had a proper look yet and now it is ruined."

"An unfortunate accident," said Mr Wickham, using his own napkin to contain the spreading scarlet stain.

"Most unfortunate," said John looking at Mr Murden.

"I say, Murden, have a care," said Mr Denny.

"It was just a picture. No harm done, eh, Mr Barton?" said Mr Murden, his tone affable enough.

John stood up. "Mr Murden, you may sneer at a man who wields a paintbrush, rather than a sword. But painting teaches many things. How the light betrays our vision, how colours change and how our eyes may deceive us. So I see you for what you really are."

"And what am I, Mr Barton?"

"A bully."

Everyone froze, except Mr Murden, who rose to his feet, though his hands remained by his sides.

"Withdraw your comment and we will say no more."

"You insult me beneath your veil of amiability. That I can forgive." John gave a slight shake to his head. "But you insulted Miss Hayter, too…"

"No," cried Miss Hayter, "No grand gestures, Mr Barton. Not on my behalf." She looked to me and Lizzy.

"Gentlemen," I said. "This is most improper. Will you not shake hands and be done with it? John?"

"I will not. I see your fear, Mr Murden. The fear of discovery. It hangs on you like a badly-fitting cloak."

Mr Murden shoved his chair back and strode over to John. "You know what I see, Mr Barton? Your bloodied face on the ground."

"Mr Bennet!" cried my wife.

"Not in my home, gentlemen. There will be *no* fighting. John, you will apologise at once. I insist. You are a guest in my house. As is Mr Murden." I half raised myself from my seat.

253

The two held each other's gaze for a moment, before John lowered himself back into his seat. "My apologies, Mr Murden." The soldier nodded. "And to you, Mr Bennet. To you all. I overstepped the mark."

The officers left quickly, Mr Wickham and Mr Denny making conciliatory noises on behalf of their hot-headed colleague. Miss Hayter fled the room, chest heaving, tears tracing ugly lines down her face. She was pursued by Lizzy, my other girls, and Mrs Bennet.

"John?" I said. "What on earth were you thinking?"

He shook like a new-born lamb, but his lips formed a tight line across his face.

A drink of convenience

Lizzy's urgent knocking woke me the next morning and brought me to my chamber door.

"John is gone," she said. "He has taken his horse. The commotion in the stables woke me."

I blinked away the confusion of an early morning. "You saw him leave?"

"Yes."

"Did he have any bags with him?"

Lizzy thought for a moment. "No, he did not."

"There, Lizzy." I took her hands in mine. "He means to return. Young men are prone to windswept rides when agitated. There is no harm in the news."

"But he was so changed last night, so angry. I fear he may do something impetuous, something foolish. Can you not search for him?"

"If it will reassure you." I took a deep breath. "The Society meets this afternoon, so I will spend the intervening time looking for him between here and Meryton. If he returns in my absence, send word immediately." She nodded, then turned to go, but I did not release her hands. "Lizzy, how is Miss Hayter?"

"Not yet risen. She was most distressed last night. She does not like men to behave like peacocks."

"Nor do I, but what else can they do when the room is full of peahens?"

~ ~ ~

I found no sign of John, though I was less than diligent in my efforts to search for him. When a fire rages inside a man, it is better to let it burn out in quiet isolation. News of his return to Longbourn reached me at the end of the committee meeting. Only Jackson and Fielding remained and the candles had already burned low.

Lizzy's handwriting lacked its usual precision. "Whatever is the matter, Bennet?" asked Jackson, as I finished her note.

"My friend John, who left precipitously this morning. It appears he has got himself in some trouble with that officer." My finger traced over three particular words on the paper: *please prevent this.*

"The Murden fellow from last night?" said Jackson. I nodded. "You said Mr Barton apologised."

"It seems John renewed the argument this morning at Mr Murden's quarters. They are to fight at dawn tomorrow."

"Fight? I thought your friend more sensible," said Fielding.

"Pride and love can conquer sense." I slapped the note on the table. "He likely believes himself duty bound to impress Miss Hayter with a grand gesture."

"That may be so," said Fielding. "But what use is a grand gesture if he perishes in its making? I do not know this Mr

Murden well, but his scar and manner suggest he is no stranger to such confrontations. You must stop your friend."

"I do not think that will be possible." I stood in one flowing movement, preparing to leave. "Gentlemen, I must seek out his opponent and encourage *him* to call this off. Perhaps conflict can yet be avoided."

"You will not go alone." Fielding was already rising from his seat.

"I do not intend to fight the man, Fielding, only reason with him."

"Nevertheless, the force of numbers cannot harm your cause." My old friend put on his coat. "We shall accompany you."

"I may not be the brightest fellow in England," said Jackson, pulling on his jacket. "But I know such soldiers. Mr Murden is the kind to prey on easy pickings. Let us deny him his pleasure."

~ ~ ~

As I had hoped, Mr Murden was dining below in the inn's front room. We paused at a distance to watch him laughing garrulously, clearly enjoying his meat and wine in the company of Mr Denny. His insouciance sharpened my resolve, but also sent a brief shiver coursing along my spine.

"Nervous, Bennet?" said Jackson.

"A little."

"Let me offer you a drop of fortitude." He pulled out a small bottle from his jacket and removed the cork. "To Mr Barton." Now it was his turn to shudder. "Puts fire in your loins, this. A little something I got from Sir William."

"Madmaidens, by any chance?" He nodded and held out the

bottle. My stomach tightened. "Not for a thousand pounds. Let us go to battle."

~ ~ ~

"Ah, Mr Bennet, come to dissuade me from embarrassing your young friend, Barton?"

"I worry less for his feelings and more for his life. A duel is foolhardy, Mr Murden, and you know it. Not least because your commanding officer would find it unacceptable."

"Sit down, Mr Bennet." Mr Murden motioned to some chairs. "And your friends, too. Now, who spoke of a duel? There will be no blades or pistols. Just fists." The hands he held up were bigger than I remembered. "It is merely the settlement of a dispute between two gentlemen. As long as there is no public affray, Colonel Forster will care not a jot."

"May I ask, then, as one gentleman to another, if you might go easy on the boy? Leave no lasting damage?"

"Why should I?" Mr Murden slammed his palm on the table. "*He* insulted *me. He* sought *me* out this morning. He deserves a thrashing for his insolence."

"Let us not concern ourselves with who insulted whom, Mr Murden. I would consider it a particular favour if this could all end amicably."

"Oh, go on, Murden," said Mr Denny. "No need to damage the poor man. People might think you truly are a bully."

Mr Murden tapped out an impatient rhythm on the rim of an empty wine glass. "Damned expensive business, fights. I will need new breeches afterwards." His eyes slipped down to my purse. "And if Forster does not turn a blind eye, he may fine me for breaking some army regulation or other."

"I am sure we could arrange to share some of your financial burden, Mr Murden." He sniffed and continued to drum on his glass. "All of your financial burden?"

"Most generous of you, Mr Bennet." He smiled. "I shall, perhaps, only break a bone or two."

"You will hold back?"

"I will. Spare his fingers, too, so he can keep painting. I am nothing if not a patron of the arts."

I looked at Mr Denny, who held my eye and shook his head slightly. A warning?

"Let us drink to our arrangement." Mr Murden reached over, only to find the wine bottle empty. He held it up to me. "Perhaps you might call for more, Mr Bennet?"

"No need," I said. "I have just the thing for a toast of this nature. Jackson, dear friend, be a good chap and pass me your bottle."

Into the field

Some sixth sense woke me before dawn. I would have had trouble finding my clothes had I not fallen asleep in them. Clawing my way down the stairs, I stumbled from the last steps into John. He steadied me with his free arm; the other held a candle. He was fully dressed.

"I can do this alone, sir."

"Perhaps. But *I* cannot. Help me into my boots. Let us get this dark deed over with. Try not to wake anyone."

Outside, a cloaked form waited for us, still as a grave.

"You are going to pursue this foolish undertaking?"

"Good morning, Miss Hayter," I ventured. "If you will excuse me." I propped myself up against a wall to still the effects of last night's Madmaidens.

"Mr Barton," she said. "Only fools fight over such slights, and I did not mark you for a fool. I have suffered enough of such men to know of what I speak."

"Miss Hayter—" said John.

"I do not enjoy the sight of men fighting to prove who has more strength or honour. *I* am impressed by the thrust of conversation, not of a sword, by the accuracy of a drawing, not that of a duelling pistol."

John stood motionless, perhaps caught between honour and hope.

A sliver of light cracked the horizon. "Come John, we will be late." Miss Hayter turned from us and began to walk back into the house, lifting a hand to wipe something away. A stray hair? A tear? A speck of dust?

"Fear not," I called after her. "Mr Murden is not the beast many believe. We may find him unable to live up to his reputation."

"That is beside the point," she called back, without turning.

~ ~ ~

The sun picked its way carefully through the empty branches of the beech trees surrounding the field chosen as the fighting ring. We tethered the horses, then crossed on foot, the white crust of night withering below our boots. Ahead of us were two figures. As one moved toward us, I recognised Mr Denny's gait, and raised my cane in acknowledgement.

"Gentlemen, I beseech you to abandon this folly." Mr Denny kept his voice low. "Let us apologise and recognise a misunderstanding. I would not speak ill of a fellow officer, but Murden is in an ugly mood. He has a fearsome hangover. I cannot vouch for his behaving honourably today."

"Only today?" I said.

"Mr Bennet, you know this can only end one way, whatever was said last ni…" He looked over at John. "I have no wish to witness injury to a guest of yours. Can you not convince your friend to withdraw?"

"Mr Denny," I said. "Your wish for a peaceful resolution does you credit but I fear it is too late for such sentiments." John said nothing.

~ ~ ~

Mr Murden wiped his face with a sleeve, rocking slightly. "Let us get this over with, Barton." He spat, then began to strip. Arms and shoulders bulged either side of a blacksmith's chest.

John stood there, skin pale, breath heavy, lips thin, fists held up like a parody of some London boxing pamphlet.

Mr Murden's charge came without warning, artistry or grace, but also without speed. All John had to do was wait and pick his moment. He stood his ground, then swung all too wildly at the officer's head. The punch missed and John slipped, pulling his assailant down on top of him.

To my relief, my friend squirmed out from under Mr Murden, mud and grass stuck to his back. He stood, apparently unharmed, then backed away with fists raised.

His opponent remained still a moment longer before rising to his feet. John ran at him, pulling up at the last to plant a blow on the swaying man's scarred cheek. Mr Murden's head jerked to one side, but his feet moved not one inch. John took a step back, perhaps shocked at the violence of the moment.

This was Mr Murden's cue to advance, burly arms seeking a throat. John lifted his knee and half turned, hands rising to protect his face. Whether deliberate or not, the movement had the required effect. Mr Murden clutched his midriff, curled over, rocked gently, then crumpled to the ground. John stared at him, fists balled by his sides, his face shrouded in misty breath.

Mr Denny stepped forward to shake his colleague gently. "Well, it seems Mr Murden has conceded the fight. If we can call it that. The hangover—and Mr Barton—has won."

I let out a breath before hurrying over to John as best I could. "Are you hurt?"

"Just a few scratches." He rubbed the knuckles of his right hand.

"Good, then let us put this ridiculous business behind us and return to Longbourn before anyone else is up. I have a feeling the day's battles are not over yet."

He may have been uninjured, but John's breath still came in ragged surges. All at once he leant on me for support.

Mr Murden clambered slowly to his feet, blood from a cut lip dripping down his chin. "My clothes," he mumbled.

Mr Denny held out the bundle and a handkerchief. "Use this to clean up first." Mr Murden took only his jacket, then shoved Mr Denny away.

Without a word, John ripped the cane from my grip as Mr Murden lunged forward, one arm outstretched. The cane dropped sharply. A crack, like the breaking of an oak sapling, then something fell to the ground. Mr Murden's face twisted as he dropped to his knees, but he did not cry out. Only whimpers and spittle escaped his lips as he clutched a shattered wrist.

"That was poorly done, John, poorly done indeed," I said.

He just pointed with my cane at the fallen object.

Mr Denny bent down. "Good God, Murden!" He held up a small knife, the kind used to slice an apple. "If this should get out."

"Which it will," I said, "Of that you can be sure."

Mr Denny lowered his gaze. He threw the knife down at Mr Murden's feet, then stepped back hurriedly, as if the bloodied man carried some disease. He turned to us. "My apologies."

"We should see to his wrist," said John.

"We will leave him to Mr Denny. He knows what to do with Mr Murden."

"But his arm needs proper attention."

"I was not talking of his injury. Come, John, we are finished here." I put my arm around his shoulders to draw him away, back toward our horses. We made a grim couple as we retraced our steps across the field, one lame with age and the previous night's excesses, the other bloodied and dirty.

"How did you know? About the knife?"

John laughed, a strangled sound that sent a pair of plovers screeching into the air. "I am a *painter*. Colour, movement…and *light*." I gave him a curious look. "The knife caught the sun when he took it from his jacket."

"If I know Colonel Forster, he will have Mr Murden patched up and packed off to another regiment before sunset. I do not think we will see him again."

"That is a shame." I could not tell if John was being serious.

"Let us return and get you cleaned up. Then you can enjoy some breakfast. I shall wait a little longer until my stomach settles."

"I never asked who you were drinking with last night. It must have been good company indeed to involve such copious amounts of wine."

"It was not company that might be described as good, but that is a story for another day. We must prepare for a more important task. It is time you talked with Miss Hayter."

In pursuit of the post

Three of my daughters rushed to meet us as we entered the front courtyard, Kitty red-eyed, Lydia all a-flutter with excitement, and Lizzy full of concern. Mrs Bennet hovered behind them. I noticed our carriage stood ready in front of the door.

"Is he dead? I felt sure he would die. What will we tell his poor father?" My wife held her head in her hands.

"What of Mr Murden? Did he beat John cruelly?" asked Lydia.

"Quite the reverse. And, as you can see, John is not dead or even severely injured. You will hear the story in town, but Mr Murden has disgraced himself. Do not expect to see him again at Longbourn. Or anywhere."

"I am quite well, Mrs Bennet," said John. He gazed around the yard. "I do not see Miss Hayter?"

"She has left," said Lizzy.

John smiled sadly. "Of course." He dipped his head at me. "I thank you for your help today, Mr Bennet. I believe we may have won a battle only to lose the war." He walked into the house, head down.

"Explain yourself, Elizabeth," I said. "How can Miss Hayter be gone? Her carriage is not due for another week."

"She asked Mama if she might have use of a horse." Lizzy shook slightly in the cold. "We thought she wanted to ride and distract herself. But then I found this…"

I took the note from her hand. "It is addressed to you, Lizzy."

"The contents are for everyone," she said, unfolding the paper in my palm. "Please read it, Papa."

It did not take long to do so. "Oh, dear God." I looked up. "I must go to Meryton immediately. The coach to London does not leave until eleven, so we may catch her yet. Fetch John. He must come with me."

"I have had the carriage already prepared, Papa."

"Good girl, Lizzy, good girl." I ushered my family away into the house, called for the driver and waited outside.

John reappeared a few minutes later. His face was clean, hair still dripping, fresh clothes clearly put on in haste. Lizzy followed behind him in a coat and bonnet.

"You will remain here, Lizzy. This is a business for men now." I recognised her expression. "Very well. Inside the carriage with you both. Be quick, we have little time."

John did not press me for an immediate explanation as the carriage moved off. With Miss Hayter's letter in my hand, I glanced across at my fellow passengers. John's face was unreadable, Lizzy's set in determination.

"Why are you here, Lizzy?" I said.

"I have seen the heart of a most beloved sister recently broken. I do not wish to see the same happen to a friend. To two friends." John sat upright. "John, if you were my brother, I could not wish for a better one. And I wish you were my brother so we might speak honestly with each other."

I was tired of hidden meanings. "Lizzy, if you have something to say, do so. The time for circumspection is past."

"John is in love with Miss Hayter," she said.

"Is it so obvious?" said John.

I shifted forward in my seat. "How could you know?"

"Oh, Papa." She patted my hand gently.

John stood up suddenly, banging his head on the carriage roof. "Does Miss Hayter know?"

"We talked of it. I think she did not want to accept the notion without first fully knowing her own feelings."

"And does she…" There was terrible hope in John's voice.

"A woman in her position cannot allow herself to love without giving due consideration to the matter."

"That does not sound much like love," I said.

"Do not mock, Papa. Not now. It is not a question of whether love is there but of whether it might be allowed to reveal itself. You men love easily but may love another just as swiftly." I kept my face still. "But when we place our heart in your care, we risk everything. You have our shame, our joy, our hopes, our all. We cannot give this away without surety."

"But…" John hesitated. "But she left?"

"She believed you in love with her, wanted to love you in return, but you offered no such surety. Then there was the business with Mr Murden. She could not bear to see you hurt on her account. To see you become the man you are not. In short, John, you made her love impossible. That is what her letter says."

John ran his hands though his hair. "I am such a fool. But

there must be something I can do? Elizabeth? Mr Bennet? Do not tell me I am lost to her."

"This is why we travel to Meryton. Give her *certainty*, John. Talk to her. Tell her…tell her you love her. Before it is too late. Before she accepts another and you spend the rest of your damned life drowning in regret."

We pulled in to Meryton just as the post coach moved off on its journey to the capital.

"We *are* too late!" cried John.

"They will wait at Church Street. If you run, you can cut through the alley alongside the inn and reach the post before it begins its journey proper. Go, be quick," I urged.

He burst through the carriage door and charged up the road, his coat flapping wildly behind him.

There was a tap on the other side of the carriage. "I see you received my note." Miss Hayter leaned in and looked across the square. "Should our men not run in a more heroic manner?" Lizzy embraced her friend, while I simply looked between Miss Hayter and the entrance to the alley that John had now disappeared up.

My daughter got down from the carriage in one practiced leap while I took the steps slowly, shaken from the events of the day and the indulgence of the previous night. "I told you he would come, dear Anne. The letter worked." Lizzy turned to me. "You see, Papa, we have been trying to provoke John into a declaration since Bath. We decided more drastic action was called for."

The teas, the dance card, Lizzy's headache. They had beaten us at our own game.

"And Mr Murden?" I said.

"He was definitely *not* part of the plan. But I felt sure you would never allow any harm to come to John." Lizzy patted my cheek then looked toward the alley that had offered John so much hope. "It is rather cruel of us to make him run now. He will be quite exhausted."

"And so he should be," said Miss Hayter. "They should work for our affection, Elizabeth."

"All that time in Bath…" I said.

"Yes," said Miss Hayter. "I only wish I had not been such a fool around him. Always making such a mess of conversation."

Soon I was doubled up in the pain of laughter. Both girls stood, hands on hips, disapproval etched in their tight lips. "I am sorry," I said.

"You find Miss Hayter's embarrassment amusing, Papa?"

"Not at all. I will explain another time. For now, you should know that it is John I am laughing at. But if I may ask, Miss Hayter, how long have you…"

"That day when he joined us unexpectedly for tea. He was the first man who did not try and impress me."

"Ah."

"He was honest."

"That he was."

"And completely unconcerned by what I might think of him."

"Indeed," I murmured. There was a time for truth and a time for discretion. "But how did you discern *his* affection?"

"Because I am *right*, Mr Bennet. As I said in Bath, true love cannot be so easily disguised or hidden. But a lady needs a declaration to be sure. And most men need to feel they have conquered their lady, even if quite the opposite is true."

"Well, I declare I need breakfast. Quite apart from my empty stomach, I do believe we may soon require some privacy. Let us repair to the inn. I shall ask the driver to keep an eye out for John and direct him to us."

We had no trouble getting a small room for ourselves, and I managed a rasher or three of bacon and a little cake. But as more time passed without any sign of my friend, the ladies' smug expressions faded while nervous fingers played with the cutlery.

"It has been too long," said Miss Hayter. "Where can he have got to? Was I wrong?"

A polite knock brought us all to our feet.

The door opened slowly to reveal John, hair dishevelled with sweat, his breeches and boots muddy. He stood taller than I could ever remember. Miss Hayter was free of all deception now, her high walls tumbled and broken.

"Might I have a word with…Anne?"

Lizzy and I made to leave but John held up one hand. The other remained hidden behind his back.

"Please stay." He beckoned Miss Hayter over. "I have made you something." He passed her a piece of paper.

She took it gently, and turned it over.

"Oh, John." As she threw herself into his arms, the drawing slipped from her grasp, twisting and turning, dipping and rising until it slid to a stop by my feet. I looked at Lizzy, then knelt to retrieve it.

It showed a couple standing before an altar in wedding clothes, arms linked, she with her head on his shoulder. The likeness was too perfect. I covered it with my hand, so my tears would not smear the ink.

Perhaps some things do not need to be said, after all.

Epilogue

We sat outside the church on benches, lined up like old crows basking in the bright sun. Stanhope, Elliston, and dear Fielding, our wives—and Abigail—elsewhere enjoying the festivities. As Anne Barton passed us, I called out to her.

She stopped, hands still lifting her wedding dress to keep it clear of the ground.

"May I, Mrs Barton?" I stood and stepped closer to her.

"As the cause of so much happiness, I do believe you may do almost anything, Mr Bennet."

I leaned in toward her and paused as a brief scent of lavender took me back to that first meeting in London. Then I lifted my arm to close my hand on her shoulder.

"Oh," she said, uncertainty in her eyes until my fist turned to reveal the bright wings trapped in my grasp. They fluttered once, the touch soft and delicate, like a woman's cheek. My fingers opened and we watched as the butterfly flew away, tracing waves in the sky.

"How delightful," she said.

"Exactly what I was thinking."

"Bennet," said Fielding. "Was that a Silver-washed Fritillary? And you let it go?"

"Sometimes, Fielding, things of beauty should be left free, not chased. Would you not agree, Mrs Barton?"

"I would, Mr Bennet."

"Gentlemen!" Jackson waved at us from a distance. "To arms with you. Come immediately."

"What is the matter?" I shouted back.

"Cakes, Bennet, cakes. A whole tray of them. Unattended and in danger of spoiling. We should act fast."

"Come, dear friends," I said. "We must answer a comrade's call." As I walked away, I turned back to Mrs Barton. "I did not think today could be any more enjoyable, but I had forgotten life's most important lesson."

"And that is?"

"Whatever the situation, cake will always make it better."

THE END

Acknowledgements

This book would never have happened without the support of a fair few people. My heartfelt thanks go out to…

Sarah, my editor, for her keen eye, excellent suggestions and encyclopaedic knowledge of Jane Austen's novels. Aimee for the wonderful cover design. Edwin, fellow adventurer on the publishing journey, for his advice and indefatigable support. Tom, Cheryl, Zac and Hazel at the "Albemarle Writers Retreat" for their friendship and enthusiasm (and the pulled pork). Rose for the encouragement and inspiration. The wonderful Jane Austen community on Twitter and Facebook for warming my soul with their positive responses to my Austenesque creations. Most importantly, Renate, Michael and Patrick for innumerable things, but mostly for their strength of belief in me and all my ideas, especially the stupid ones.

About the Author

Mark Brownlow is a British-born writer and humourist living in Vienna, Austria. "Cake and Courtship" is his first novel. He is perhaps best known for his reimagining of classic stories as email inboxes. When not writing or teaching, he watches costume dramas and football, depending on whether his wife or his sons are holding the TV remote.

Follow Mark on Twitter (@markbrownlow), Facebook (facebook.com/lostopinions/) or at the LostOpinions.com website.

Printed in Great Britain
by Amazon